I0713692

BEDEVILING MAJOR KENTON

Willful Winterbournes
Book Five

Sandra Sookoo

© Copyright 2023 by Sandra Sookoo
Text by Sandra Sookoo
Cover by Dar Albert

Dragonblade Publishing, Inc. is an imprint of Kathryn Le Veque Novels, Inc.
P.O. Box 23
Moreno Valley, CA 92556
ceo@dragonbladepublishing.com

Produced in the United States of America

First Edition August 2023
Trade Paperback Edition

Reproduction of any kind except where it pertains to short quotes in relation to advertising or promotion is strictly prohibited.

All Rights Reserved.

The characters and events portrayed in this book are fictitious. Any similarity to real persons, living or dead, is purely coincidental and not intended by the author.

ARE YOU SIGNED UP FOR DRAGONBLADE'S BLOG?

You'll get the latest news and information on exclusive giveaways, exclusive excerpts, coming releases, sales, free books, cover reveals and more.

Check out our complete list of authors, too!

No spam, no junk. That's a promise!

Sign Up Here

www.dragonbladepublishing.com

Dearest Reader;

Thank you for your support of a small press. At Dragonblade Publishing, we strive to bring you the highest quality Historical Romance from some of the best authors in the business. Without your support, there is no 'us', so we sincerely hope you adore these stories and find some new favorite authors along the way.

Happy Reading!

CEO, Dragonblade Publishing

Additional Dragonblade books by Author Sandra Sookoo

Willful Winterbournes Series
Romancing Miss Quill (Book 1)
Pursuing Mr. Mattingly (Book 2)
Courting Lady Yeardly (Book 3)
Guarding the Widow Pellingham (Book 4)
Bedeviling Major Kenton (Book 5)
Teasing Miss Atherby (Novella)

The Storme Brother Series
The Soul of a Storme (Book 1)
The Heart of a Storme (Book 2)
The Look of a Storme (Book 3)
A Storme's Christmas Legacy
A Storme's First Noelle
The Sting of a Storme (Book 4)
The Touch of a Storme (Book 5)
The Fury of a Storme (Book 6)
Much Ado About a Storme (in the *A Duke in Winter* anthology)

The Lyon's Den Series
The Lyon's Puzzle

CHAPTER ONE

July 20, 1820
Delacourte House
London, England

LADY BEATRICE ASHDOWNE-DELACOURTE bounced her gaze from the collection of envelopes in her lap to her younger brother Edmund. "I rather miss Graham." Her older brother had married last month and was now enjoying his honeymoon at his estate in Kent, not expected back until the autumn.

Edmund snorted. His blond hair, arranged in a devil-may-care style, shrugged. "I do not. While I don't begrudge him the wife or the wedding trip, I take exception to him telling us about Mother's scandal and then leaving Town with us holding the pieces."

"Leave him be. He deserves all good things in his life right now." She clucked at him, for Edmund had always been bitter about their older brother.

"To say nothing of Mother's infidelity, and now our new-found aunt? Stepmother?"—he shrugged, for the relation was rather complicated—"has fled to the Winterbourne property in Brighton to escape the worst of the gossip." Like her brother, she didn't mind that Graham had found the love of his life and married, especially after all the personal struggles he'd been through. But the scandal that had been unearthed inadvertently last February by what they now knew as a distant cousin couldn't be as easily celebrated.

"Yes, that was highly convenient," Beatrice mused, for she didn't know how to examine her own emotions let alone speak of them to her brother. "I would have liked to ask the dowager questions regarding her husband—I suppose our *real* father, we should refer to him as, and why he'd had an affair with our mother." As always when the conversation made its way to the subject of paternity or whether or not they were truly illegitimate Winterbournes, the muscles in her stomach clenched with worry. "God rest her soul."

"It's all such a coil." Edmund shoved a hand through his hair, upsetting the tresses into disordered waves. "Do you know that my club is buzzing about this? No matter that we have all tried to keep the secret close, it somehow got out. They are also debating whether or not to keep my membership in good standing." He shook his head. "It's not bad enough the Winterbourne family has already been hit with scandal and rumor about the antics of *those* siblings. Now our names are linked with theirs, especially if we *are* siblings."

"How can we not be?" Beatrice sighed and organized the envelopes from the post in her lap. "We resemble each other. Why, I saw the earl in passing the other day, and I nearly mistook him for Graham for a few seconds until I remembered Graham wasn't in Town." She shrugged. "Hair and eyes are the same—they call the eye color Winterbourne blue—and according to Graham, we bear strong resemblance to the current earl's father." At least there was that undeniable proof, but none of it explained why the affair had happened in the first place. "I suspect Graham has more information than he is sharing."

And what had their father, the marquess, thought of it when he'd discovered the deception of his best friend and neighbor who'd fathered children with his wife?

"It *is* a rather undeniable issue. I, too, think our darling brother has more facts than he has let on, but in his defense, he has been distracted." A frown tugged at the corners of his mouth. "Additionally, the *ton* is still abuzz about Graham's nuptials. Too many people had wagered he would never marry, let alone land a widow possessing a fortune as Mary does."

"Don't be jealous. He settled Father's debts, and I know that is a weight off his shoulders." That had been a huge undertaking. When their parents had died unexpectedly in a carriage accident a few years ago, Graham had become the Marquess of Grantley and then promptly discovered exactly how horrible their father had left the coffers. It only added to the terrible story and clues left behind.

"Yes, by selling off two properties. One of which *I'd* wanted," Edmund groused. He hadn't lost his frown. "But no. He had to be pigheaded about it. Didn't care about my wishes."

"Pish posh. Leave Graham alone. He had decisions to make that were difficult, that needed to be made with haste."

"And he got me shot in the process." He rubbed the meaty part of his left shoulder. "Of course, it's healed, but it hurts occasionally."

"At least you are alive." She sighed. The incident Edmund referred to had been frightening when they'd both had to rescue Mary from a madman. "And he did them while coming to terms with his stutter. I think that is amazing. Why should he hand you a property when you have been nothing but a wayward lord for years? How many times have your escapades made it to Graham's ears and caused him embarrassment?"

A mottled flush rose over his cravat. "I suppose, knowing what we do now, it's in my blood." Bitterness dripped from his voice. "Apparently, I can be nothing else."

"You could if you tried, but being a rogue is easier than being proper." Beatrice huffed.

"Ha! There are times when it's deuced complicated and takes planning."

For the space of a few heartbeats, she pointed her gaze to the ceiling. "Don't do something stupid merely because you want the attention back on yourself." He had recently affected an uncaring attitude ever since the family's reputation had begun falling apart. Whether that was truly how he felt, she couldn't say. Not a stranger to scandal himself, she feared he might try to be extra salacious as a way to work through his own emotions. Would that he'd mature sooner rather than later, for the Ashdowne name couldn't bear much more scandal.

I have a daughter and her future to think about.

"Give me more credit than that." He shot her an annoyed glance. "I might seek out gossip regularly, but none of it is foolish. I work hard to make certain the *beau monde* takes notice of *me*, not my circumstances." His shrug was an elegant affair. "Besides, it works well enough to bring women into my circle. Once they see me, they throw themselves at me."

Clearly, there was no hope for her younger brother. "You are too old for such nonsense. Seven and thirty should have already seen you married with a nursery. You need to take yourself in hand and move into respectability."

"A nursery. Don't make me shudder." He snorted. "That is why I take lovers, dearest sister, so I *won't* have to take myself in hand. Speaking of which, I haven't had a lover for a few weeks. Perhaps I should make inroads into finding a new mistress."

Belatedly, she realized what she'd said and how he'd twisted it. Heat slapped at her cheeks, despite her widowhood and having enjoyed the carnal side of married life. At the age of nine and thirty, she had assumed she was well past embarrassment regarding such things. "Don't be lewd, Edmund."

"You have to admit, it makes life more interesting."

"Perhaps." Beatrice smiled, for it was nice to have him drop in for a visit. Ever since her husband had died, much of her social life had revolved around her brothers, and with Graham unwilling to circulate as much as he should as a marquess, she never wanted for attention or conversation. She shuffled through the envelopes once more. "There are plenty of people remaining in Town this summer if these invitations are any indication."

"I would rather be *anywhere* than in London just now. Town has grown stale with additional scrutiny, thanks to Graham."

"Then take yourself off." She waved an invitation at him. "But if you might wish to find yourself in the same married state our brother is, perhaps you should come with me to one of these society events."

Edmund rolled his eyes, the same cornflower-blue hue as hers. "No, thank you. I am not interested in *proper* young ladies nor being leg-shackled. That is too much commitment, and at my heart, I am lazy."

Before she could reply, Beatrice's daughter came into the room, looking like the perfect picture of a young society miss. At nineteen, Eliza was already a darling. Her sandy-blonde hair was tied back with a light blue ribbon that brought out the darker blue ring around her ice blue eyes. Not quite the Winterbourne looks, but if Beatrice stood next to her daughter, the resemblance was noticeable. Willowy and tall, the girl would certainly break hearts once she was launched into society that autumn.

Dear lord, that time is rapidly approaching. So much yet to do!

It was one reason Beatrice lingered in London during the summer months. There was much to prepare for the Come Out, especially since Graham's whirlwind romance and subsequent wedding had delayed things.

"Oh, Mama!" With a letter clutched in one hand, Eliza greeted Edmund, bussed his cheek, and then flounced onto the sofa cushion next to Beatrice. "You will never guess what this is."

"Whatever it is, I can see it's made you incredibly ecstatic." Though Beatrice's daughter's looks took after her, the strong features and stronger opinions had come from her father. He'd been a third son of a viscount, and oftentimes a vocal opponent of various laws or trespasses titled men had committed against the seemingly powerless. When he'd died from a particularly bad bout of pneumonia five years prior, many people in London had felt that loss, said they'd lost a supporter for equal rights.

"As it should." Eliza pressed the letter into Beatrice's hand. "I have been invited to a summer house party at the country home of Miss Diana Cloverfield." Her eyes rounded as if Beatrice should know who that was. "The Cloverfields are in banking, Mama, and quite well-respected. That *they* should invite *me* is quite a feather in my cap."

"Well, you *are* the granddaughter of a marquess, dear. It's not as if your pedigree is anything to sneeze at. Did you meet her at finishing school?"

"I did not, but my friend Patience—from the school—is *her* close friend. She recommended me, and now we are *both* invited!" A squeal of delight issued from the girl. "How wonderful is that?"

"It is certainly interesting." Though a tad alarming. Since her daughter did enjoy elevated bloodlines, there was always that niggle of doubt as to why people wished to be connected to her. Quickly, Beatrice scanned through the letter, and it appeared quite respectable. "According to this, the house party will go on for a week in Wiltshire. And they have invited twenty young people?" Both girls and boys. Apprehension went down her spine at the prospect. "That could be quite the sticky wicket."

"Yes, and I do so want to go. Please say you will let me!" The girl fairly bounced in her seat. "I feel quite grown up and this is the first invitation of the kind." Her cheeks were flushed with excitement and her eyes sparkled with all the unrealized dreams every young lady had. "There will be young men there and many activities including an outdoor fete with dancing in the evening. Parlor games. Walking parties. Perhaps swimming—not in the boys' company, of course." Eliza glanced between her and Edmund. "All of it will end with a grand ball. Can you imagine how wonderful everyone will look in formal clothes? My first society event!"

"Oh, I very well can." Of course Beatrice had attended many a ball in her day, and she well-remembered some of her first ones. It had been a heady moment, indeed. However, she also recalled the tricky emotional waters those types of events brought with them. Throw in young men who were on the prowl and wanted nothing more than to sow wild oats, and there were problems waiting to occur that would bring potential scandal to everyone involved, and could ruin a young girl's life. "It is quite an interesting dilemma. You have never been away from home outside of finishing school. Add to that the fact I have never met the family—"

"Does that mean you *won't* let me attend?" Horror filled her daughter's voice and reflected in her eyes. "You will truly deny me this? When I have asked you for nothing over the years?"

Ah, well, that wasn't *quite* true. There had been plenty of requests for gowns and fripperies, especially the latest from French modistes. Trips to the British Museum and other sites of interest. More than a few outings to Gunter's and other such amusements. And for her birthday that followed the death of her father, there was even a pony procured... that the girl lost interest in after a few months.

"I am not certain—"

"Come off it, Bea," Edmund interrupted as he sent Beatrice a glance brimming with amusement. "You might as well let her go. It's not as if the family name is sterling any longer. And as long as people are still inviting her, you should take advantage of that. Besides, having her out of London just now might be a wise decision."

While what her brother said held merit, she still hesitated. With a frown, she rested her gaze on her daughter. "You are growing up so fast, darling," she said in a voice that wobbled. Never did she think she would need to launch the girl without her husband at her side. "When I was your age, I had just married your father. Not long afterward, you were born. I didn't have much time with him before responsibilities of a family came upon me, and while that was a wonderful part of my life, I cannot help but feel there was *more* I could do." She still felt that way now, which was unsettling in a different sort of way. She grabbed

Eliza's hand and squeezed her fingers. "I want you to do everything you wish *before* you settle down into what society demands of a woman."

It was one of the things her husband had campaigned so heavily for with the members of both the House of Lords and Commons, that giving more rights, opportunities, and privileges to women so marriage and childbearing wouldn't be their only lot in life.

"Of course I will, Mama. I am not in the habit of doing things without thought, and I certainly don't wish to do something scandalous." A bit of a haughty note entered Eliza's voice. "Everyone has instilled in me how to conduct myself as a proper miss. I won't ruin that."

"I'm glad to hear such."

Her daughter sighed. "By letting me attend this house party, it will make me not feel as awkward when the Season begins this autumn when I'm making my Come Out."

Edmund snorted with apparent laughter. "She's not stupid, Bea. That will see her go far, I think."

"Yes." Eliza nodded with enthusiasm with sparkling eyes. "Beyond that, I dream of having my first kiss…" When Beatrice glanced sharply at her, Eliza quickly added, "*Chaste* kiss, I should say. Where is the harm in that? Then I won't be such a scared little rabbit this October."

"Oh, goodness. I knew this time was approaching, but I'm simply not prepared," Beatrice whispered as she passed the letter back to her daughter. "And kisses are lovely, of course, as long as you don't get caught. That is a whole different matter entirely."

"Of course. When I was at finishing school, my friends and I talked at length about that."

I don't even want to know.

Edmund's grin was wide. "This new generation is quite clever, eh sister dearest? You should concentrate your lectures on deportment and not falling into scandal on her instead of me."

"Hush, you." Slowly, Beatrice nodded. There was no winning

on this point. "You can go, but I will accompany you as a chaperone."

Both Eliza and Edmund stared.

"What?" Her brother chuckled. "You wish to attend a house party, and as a chaperone?" He shook with laughter. "That's the most ridiculous thing I have ever heard. Why not send the governess?"

Beatrice narrowed her eyes, but Eliza was quick to respond.

"Miss Rand is too old to have fun."

"Besides," she said, taking back control of the conversation, "since Eliza had been away at finishing school, there was no need to retain Miss Rand's services."

Another hoot of laughter issued from Edmund. "Your mother is too old to have fun as well, monkey," he said to the girl, using the nickname he'd given her when she was naught but five years old.

"Uncle Edmund, I have *quite* outgrown that term of affection." A slight blush colored Eliza's cheeks. She threw a glance brimming of entreaty at Beatrice. "You won't change your mind?"

"I'm afraid not." On this she was adamant. "If you wish to attend that house party in Wiltshire, you will do so with me trailing behind you, but I promise not to interfere in your day-to-day activities." When the girl would have spoken, Beatrice held up a forefinger. "Unless, of course, you put yourself into situations that have the potential to grow scandalous."

"It truly is your best chance of escaping London just now," Edmund said to the girl with a grin. "Don't look a gift horse in the mouth."

"Fine. You can come." Eliza impetuously gave Beatrice a hug. "Thank you, Mama! I need to consider my wardrobe!" Then she sprang up from the sofa and pelted from the room.

"Well, that is that, I suppose," Beatrice said with a sigh as she looked at her brother with doubt building in her chest. "I'll be spending next week in Wiltshire."

"Better you than me." But Edmund leaned over and took her hand, squeezing her fingers. "It will do you good to be away from Town for a bit. Give you something else to think about besides Mother's infidelity."

"Perhaps you're right." For long moments, she stared at the envelopes in her lap. None of those invitations held appeal any longer. "Don't you wish life were as simple as it was when we were children? We had such fun on Father's country estate in the summers."

Those days seemed so far away now.

"Ah." Edmund snickered. "Where you had your first kiss, if I remember right. And what was more, you were much younger than Eliza."

"Oh, drat. I had forgotten." The heat of embarrassment went through her cheeks. "Yes, with Graham's best friend back then— Owen Kenton. His family moved away once his father died. I wonder what happened to him." She had been a young girl of fourteen when she'd experienced that kiss, and if she recalled correctly, Owen had been only a year older—a young man with messy chestnut hair and dreamy brown eyes who had a love of Shakespeare, which he would quote, and was one of the reasons she'd let him kiss her while they'd been lying in a meadow full of summertime flowers.

"Believe it or not, I did enjoy those summer and winter stints in the country." Edmund cleared his throat. "It was the only place I felt I could truly be myself without censure or disappointment."

"Yet we were forced to grow and mature, and now that we are adults, we are still forced to puzzle through life. It's as confusing as it was back then."

"Indeed."

They were both lost in thought for a bit. Then the long-case clock struck the two o'clock hour, and Beatrice shook herself from her musings of days gone by.

"I'd best call in a modiste for new clothes for both me and Eliza." But her thoughts once more drifted to her mother and why she'd broken her marriage vows to conduct an affair with her father's best friend and neighbor in London. Regardless of the fact that she had difficulties conceiving—which was what Graham had mentioned in passing—what her mother had done still felt dirty and exponentially wrong.

And it had left her doubting her own identity even if she and her brothers were a direct result of said infidelity. Were not the marriage bonds sacred? She'd certainly thought that of her own union.

It was all too murky to ponder.

"I hope you'll return to London refreshed, Bea." Edmund stood and helped her into a standing position. "What is in the past should probably be left there, for we have too much living to do, and remember, whatever sins our mother committed are her own—not ours."

"Thank you for that." She bussed Edmund's cheek. "Perhaps this house party might be just the thing to banish my ennui and the discontent I have carried since the distasteful news broke."

If it didn't, she feared for her sanity.

CHAPTER TWO

July 21, 1820
Brown Wren Cottage
Kent, England

MAJOR OWEN KENTON was slowly going insane.

The bucolic peace of his afternoon was ruined when his children—dear miracles that they were, he had to remind himself—had intruded into his calm in the drawing room where he'd been reading one of Shakespeare's comedies. Since the summer day was all too lovely, the windows had been thrown open to catch the breeze that brought with it the scents of grasses, flowers, and if one could discern it, the sea, even though that was a bit farther off than where the property lay. Their constant bickering could not be borne for much longer.

Why the devil were they arguing again? They hadn't done this when they'd been younger, but now that his son was twenty and his daughter eighteen, it seemed they were constantly at each other's throats.

God, I wish they were small again.

Though, to be fair, since he'd been on the march in those days, he'd missed much of his children's early lives, but when he'd been injured eight years ago—which put a permanent end to his military career—he'd come home and had begun making inroads into spending as much time as he could with them both. It was something he truly enjoyed, except for when they fell to arguing.

Which felt like all the time these days.

"Enough!" Carefully, Owen set aside the book with its crumbling leather cover then he took up his cane with the ivory head that had been carved into an elephant. Fitting, that, for much of his military career, he'd been stationed in India as part of the East India Company. "Can you not pass one day in peace together?"

When his career had come to an abrupt end with the injury, he'd eventually made his way back to England, and since living in London was a rather expensive prospect with only a pension, he and his wife had decided to relocate to Kent, which was where his parents had resided when they'd been alive. He'd inherited the property once his father passed long ago, but had not made use of it since he'd been in the military. Of course his mother had stayed there until her death, but that had no bearing on his decision.

The fact of the matter remained that in Kent he'd found some of the quiet and rest he'd craved from being away in the military, and it was where he remembered his wife the best, was where he'd finally been able to bond with his children, where he assumed he would pass the remainder of his days on this earth.

And yet, the constant bickering was making him rethink everything.

"What the deuce has brought on the spat this time?"

His son Perceval—Percy to most everyone who knew him— heaved a long-suffering sigh. A much creased and crumpled letter was clutched in his hand. "Mary is bedeviling me about attending a house party in Wiltshire and I don't wish to go."

"Because he is a great nodcock! The connections alone would be priceless for his future," his daughter—Mary—said as she punctuated her statement by lunging for the letter, but Percy held it away, for he was taller than her by several inches. "See how he is?" Her chest heaved and a blush her cheeks. Pieces of her chestnut hair had escaped their braid, but annoyance flashed in her brown eyes.

"The letter was addressed to *me*, so *I* can respond how *I* wish," Percy reminded her with a flush on his face. How his dark brown hair had become rumpled, Owen would never know but he suspected the two had been scuffling for some time before the argument spilled over into the drawing room.

As per usual.

"Good God." Owen ran his free hand over the side of his face—the unscarred right side, that was—and wished he were anywhere but here. He heaved himself off the sofa where he'd been lounging. "Let me see the letter." When he held out his hand and wriggled his fingers, Percy had no choice but to comply, for both his children knew he had been provoked to his limit.

"You must understand, Papa, I have other things with which I wish to fill my time," his son said in an attempt to explain as he handed over the missive. "Soon enough I'll report for duty and begin my commission."

Owen gestured with the tip of his cane. "Sit. Both of you."

With another sigh, Percy dropped into a chair with delicate legs, while Mary flounced onto a sofa in a flurry of pale-yellow skirting.

"Ever since we moved here, I have only wanted twenty-four hours of uninterrupted quiet so that I might attempt to hear my own thoughts for the first time in my life." His parents had bickered quite a bit, and then when he'd gone away at the age of seventeen to honor his first commission, the general chaos and noise connected to the military had stolen that solitude. Then, after he'd been wounded and had returned home, the children were young and would fuss and argue as children do. Once the wasting disease had got hold of his wife four years prior, both children had been away at school, and at the time, his thoughts weren't pleasant or restorative.

Now, with Percy home until he went into the military and his daughter having one year more of finishing school, it seemed he would still need to wait until he had that much-needed silence.

With a huff of annoyance, Owen skimmed through the letter, which was indeed an invitation to a house party in the Wiltshire countryside sponsored by the Cloverfield family. The name wasn't familiar to him, so he frowned as he read the remainder of the letter. It appeared the week-long event would host a variety of games, activities, social events, and other things appropriate to that sort of endeavor, all ending with what they called a grand ball.

Finally, he glanced at his son. "Who is Alfie Cloverfield?"

"A friend from Oxford. He is going into the family business soon, but wants me to come to London instead and celebrate his twenty-first birthday. Neither of us wish to attend the house party."

As if that location and two spirited young bucks would be any better. "And what does Mr. Cloverfield do?"

"He is a jeweler of some acclaim," Mary responded as if Owen hadn't a brain in his head. "Mr. Cloverfield has made jewelry for some of London's most elite clients, including dukes, duchesses, and even one of the Regent's paramours."

I don't even want to know how she came by that knowledge.

"In any event, Papa, I would rather go to London and stay with Alfie's aunt. That way I can finish shopping for the things I need to take with me when I go away."

"Ah." Owen had purchased the commission for his son, and since England currently wasn't in a war with anyone, he didn't see the harm in sending Percy away to learn discipline and a good work ethic. It might tame him and curb the chances that he'd become a scandalous young man about Town. Which might happen anyway if he didn't attend the house party.

On the other hand, if Percy *did* go to Wiltshire, it might be good for him to start making connections, especially throughout the *ton*. Those would be important once he was finished with the military.

"I am old enough to know my own mind, Papa." Percy was quite adamant in his argument. "I would rather go to London with Alfie than tarry in the country with his annoying and clinging sister. And I certainly do not wish to dance with her."

"That is too bad, for dancing is quite a refreshing and invigorating form of exercise. Additionally, you'll need those skills, for when you are home on leave, you will no doubt be invited to routs in London to make up numbers. Especially if you move up the ranks."

As he had.

But then, those promotions had been given on the battlefields and for acts of extraordinary courage or valor.

"Bah." Percy shook his head. "I would rather visit clubs and the like." He set a hopeful gaze on Owen. "Shouldn't I spend this time with my friends before I'm sent abroad? Perhaps they might give me a post in India, like you. That would be jolly fun."

Which was what Owen wanted to keep him from, at least at this age. "Ah, yes, jolly fun indeed when I was nearly sliced open by a saber during an uprising that cost me the eye," he said dryly, and in a soft voice, with a gesture to the black leather eyepatch covering his left eye socket.

His son's confidence wavered slightly. "I'm certain nothing like that will happen to me."

Mmm, because an untried twenty-year-old man couldn't fall into the same misfortune as Owen himself had at two and thirty.

Right.

The arrogance and seemingly invincibility of youth was inconvenient at times.

Mary cleared her throat. "I think Percy is wrong. Attending the house party is a great opportunity for him socially. If he doesn't go, not only will he be snubbing the Cloverfield connection, but it might damage his future chances in society." She huffed and pinned her brother with a searing glance. "You know how Mama wished for you to find a lovely girl of good pedigree to wed. That is something you won't have a chance for if you don't cultivate connections now."

Ah, good. Owen had wondered when guilt would be applied

in the argument. It would seem his daughter was not without societal weaponry. Wherever had she learned it, he couldn't say, for her mother hadn't been that sort. Linette had been everything good and sweet and docile. She had been the daughter of a vicar and *her* mother had been the sixth child of a baron, which meant she'd received training on manners and deportment.

Mary must have learned assertion and manipulation at the damned finishing school with her classmates. But that was a worry for another day.

"Do I not have a choice?" Percy raised an eyebrow as he stared at Owen.

"Tell him he does not and that his future is more important than finding trouble in Town," Mary insisted with clasped hands and flushed cheeks.

A pox on all young adults who thought they knew best.

With a sigh, Owen handed the letter back to his son. "Against my better judgment, I will allow you to go to London and stay with your friend. Town bronze is just as valuable as connections, which you can cultivate while on your first leave." While his children exchanged bitter and victorious words, he held up his hand. "However, if even a hint of scandal comes back to my ears, I will come down and fetch you myself." Then he slid his gaze to Mary. "That being said, I think Mary should go to the house party in Percy's stead. She is to make her Come Out next year, and having this bit of experience will be a good thing for her."

And perhaps she could make other friends that would help guide her away from the cattiness of the *ton*. No matter which decision he made, Owen felt he was failing as a father at raising these two.

Finally, he would be alone for the first time in his life since he'd been a young man of his children's ages. A whole glorious week spent by himself with nothing pressing upon him, no arguments to attend, no loud noises to shy away from, and nothing except time.

"Oh!" Apparently, his daughter hadn't thought of that solution, for she'd been rendered apparently speechless for the space of a few heartbeats. "Why, do you think they would accept me in his place?"

Percy shrugged. "I don't see why not. As I said, Alfie won't even be there, so this is more for his sister's benefit before she has her Come Out his autumn." He glanced at Owen, who frowned. "Besides, there will be many other people in attendance, so what does it matter which one of us goes?"

"Will you go with me, Papa? Be my chaperone?"

"I beg your pardon?" Owen stared at his daughter as if she'd suddenly announced her intentions of jumping off the Dover cliffs. "Why the devil should *I* have to attend a house party? I was looking forward to finally having solitude here."

"Pish posh, dearest of all papas." Mary sprang off the sofa. She fairly skipped over the floor to slide her arm around his and then stare soulfully up at him with eyes so much like her mother's it almost hurt to look at her. "You should come with me as my chaperone. I'm a little frightened but excited all the same."

"Yes, Papa, that sounds like a capital idea," Percy said with a nod as he, too, stood. "Then you won't worry about me while keeping an eye on Mary."

His daughter nodded. "Besides, *you* could possibly meet someone at the ending ball. No doubt there will be women there from the neighboring villages. Gentry, and such."

"I…" He gawked at his son, who shrugged. "Well, I do miss dancing. Don't know how I'd manage on a ballroom floor with the limp." Though it was slight, exercise did tend to aggravate it at times. All because of the saber wounds that had sliced through muscles and tendons.

Hell, he missed much about having a woman by his side, but after the death of his wife, he didn't wish to find and go through another love or what inevitably followed again. It tore a man up too much.

"You do well enough here," Mary said with a grin.

Percy's grin was the one he didn't quite trust, though. "Perhaps *you* can get up to a bit of scandal yourself. Don't the ladies think a man with scars is mysterious?"

"I wouldn't know." His wife had certainly clucked over him when he'd come home looking like a dog's breakfast. "I rather think I might frighten women now."

"Do hush." Mary stepped in front of him. "Look at me." She frowned as he trained his right eye upon her. "You are a fine man, regardless of your scars. Any woman worth her salt will look past your injuries and your missing eye to peer into your lovely soul."

Ah, *there* were the vestiges of his wife in Mary he'd hoped she had. With a sigh, he patted her cheek. "Thank you for those words, but if I go to this house party, it will be as your chaperone only. I am not in the market for a second wife, and perhaps I'm too old, besides, for another romance."

It hadn't been something he'd actively pursued once his wife had expired four years before, and frankly, it had only been until recently that he'd stopped looking for Lynette everywhere he turned. Yes, he had accepted her death and had properly mourned her, but that didn't mean her absence didn't hurt any less.

Percy chuckled. "Well, now that I don't need to go, I'll write to Alfie and tell him I'm coming to London in a few days." He gave Owen's shoulder a good-natured jostling. "Good luck with the rest of your conversation with Mary. She is both a killjoy and a managing baggage by turns." Before Mary could respond, he quit the drawing room.

The boy was growing up too quickly, and that was something he couldn't square with.

"Oh, he is quite annoying," Mary said from beneath her breath. Then she put on a bright smile and once more encompassed Owen in her gaze. "Please say you will give *thought* to a romance, Papa. I want you to have fun at this house party." She patted his arm. "Surely you remember what is like to love? Don't you want that again?"

"Honestly, poppet, I am not sure." Loving someone in any

capacity meant that sooner or later, the price would come due. Mourning and grief were the payments exacted for letting oneself close to another person, and he'd barely survived losing Lynette. "I have only loved your mother, you see."

Except, that wasn't quite true. While a frown tugged at the corners of his lips, the years fell away as he flew through memories, all the way back to his youth when he'd been a boy of fifteen. At the time, he'd quite fancied a neighbor girl who was his junior by only a year. In fact, her father's country estate neighbored this property. They had been in each other's pockets in those days. She'd had two brothers, and they were all a rough and tumble set who'd explored the property and took him with them on their adventures.

One day, her brothers had gotten themselves into some sort of mischief that had involved a beehive and many stings, so while they were properly looked over and bandaged up at the manor, Owen had been left to his own devices with Beatrice Ashdowne. They'd had a good ramble in the woods then cooled off that afternoon by lying in a wildflower meadow while watching the clouds. The first kiss he'd ever given a girl had been with that blonde angel.

I wonder whatever happened to her.

Hell, as far as he knew, Ashdowne Hall had sat empty for many years, but rumor had it there was someone in residence now. Perhaps the marquess had died and now his son held the title and had come for the summer. Owen had been rather busy with his own life and hadn't seen fit to make a social call.

"That doesn't matter," Mary said, and the sound of her voice yanked him from those musings. "If the right woman comes along and plucks at your heartstrings, fate will take it from there."

"I'm not sure it works in such a serendipitous way." He chuckled, for his daughter was a darling when she wished it. "Besides, I will no doubt be ignored when area ladies are given the choice of handsome young bucks at this house party. Though I am not keen to marry again, I can't help but feel... hopeful in the fact there might come a time when I will want that again."

Mary nodded. "Fair enough. Does that mean you will come with me?"

"Of course. As if I could ever deny you anything." Perhaps that was part of the problem with her petulant and outspoken attitude. Had he gone wrong in her upbringing after his wife had died? But he remained adamant. If for some reason he did indeed meet a woman with whom he shared a few points, he wasn't going to rush to give away his heart again. That remained retired behind a wall of stone.

"Oh, thank you!" She threw herself into his arms and hugged him close. "You won't regret this. I promise."

"Hmph." While he did occasionally miss the excitement life had when he was in the military, he wasn't quite ready to find himself within mixed company that had gathered together to be social. "What matters is that you have a lovely time, and perhaps I'll gain advice from some of the other chaperones or parents on giving you a *possible* Season next year." Nothing had been decided in that direction either, and such endeavors were rather expensive, but if he wanted a better life for Mary than what he'd had, it was necessary, and she could fall back on the rather thin *ton* connections of his mother if needed.

"You are the most lovely father ever." She bussed his cheek. "I need to pack! And order a few gowns!"

Hell's bells. What had happened to his life.

It was certainly easier when the children were younger.

Too bad the hands of the clock couldn't reverse, for a variety of reasons.

CHAPTER THREE

July 25, 1820
Cloverfield Trace
A few miles east of Chippenham
Wiltshire, England

BEATRICE ATTEMPTED TO stifle a yawn behind her hand but failed miserably. It had been a long day of travel, but they'd arrived for the house party about an hour ago. Sunset would occur in another hour, wherein a dinner reception would be served to give other stragglers time to arrive. Honestly, the last thing she wished to do was wait in her room, so in an effort to stretch her legs and banish the feeling of restlessness, once she changed into the gown she would wear for dinner, she sought out Eliza, who had the bedchamber across the corridor from hers that she would share with two other girls.

"Darling, I am in need of a walk. Would you like to come with me?"

"No thank you, Mama." A giggle escaped her daughter when a brunette young lady came into the room. They clasped hands, clearly knowing each other. Then Eliza remembered Beatrice was there. "You go ahead. I wish to discover which of my friends have already arrived at the house party and to catch up on the gossip." She gestured at the other girl. "This is Patience."

"How lovely to finally meet you."

"Hullo, Lady Beatrice." The girl executed a tiny curtsy. "I am so happy you let Eliza come to this house party."

Then the two of them giggled and put their heads together, whispering.

Feeling particularly unwanted and unneeded, Beatrice had no choice except to leave the house. She went outside to walk the back lawn.

And was immediately out of her element, for she had always favored life in bustling, busy London over quiet, bucolic country living.

As the world hovered on the cusp of the golden hour, the low buzz of nighttime insects reached her ears with every step she took. Though the day had been rather on the warm side, now that the evening had arrived, there was an ever-so-slight thread of chill in the air. Glad for the cashmere wrap, she tucked it about her shoulders and continued on.

It was an odd feeling, to be sure, to discover one isn't particularly needed any longer by her only child. Once the girl had found others her own age, there wasn't space for her in that life. There was no denying that time marched onward, but she wasn't ready to let go. After losing her husband, she'd clung all the more tightly to Eliza, and simply wasn't in the correct moment to let her daughter live her own life, make her own mistakes. There was still the urge to protect the girl as if she were still a little child, and just now, she had no inclination to do the pretty with the other adult people there—would there even be people her own age that weren't attending as companions?

Regardless of the state of her thoughts, the property was well-manicured, and when she reached an impressive hedge maze, Beatrice paused at the entrance. The dinner reception would happen in under an hour. Did she have time to explore? For that matter, would she be able to escape once engaged? The fact of the matter was that she'd never been good at directions.

Yet Mr. Cloverfield was rumored to be talented at horticulture. He allegedly paid his gardeners handsomely to maintain the grounds and flower beds. In the summers, he entered roses into fairs and his blooms were much sought out for gifting. Perhaps she would see some of those prize-winning roses.

I'll just take a quick peek.

The moment she entered the maze, the pungent scents of evergreen assailed her nose. The crunch of gravel and shells beneath the thin soles of her slippers accompanied every step, but it was fun and exciting making a few turns and running into dead ends a couple of times. The paths and decisions engaged her mind and made her forget about the house party, as well as how she'd keep her daughter out of trouble if she wasn't with her every second of the day.

All too soon, Beatrice was so turned about and discombobulated that she couldn't remember the steps to find her way back to the entrance. Not yet concerned, she continued to follow the path, for the evening was lovely and the chance to breathe in the fresh, clean air was quite a boon.

You can do this, Bea. Make better decisions.

How could she make a good decision, though, when she had no idea of what was coming up beyond the next turn? Perhaps it didn't matter. Sooner or later, she would either reach the heart of the maze or she would locate an exit point. And if neither occurred, surely someone would come looking for her when she failed to make an appearance at dinner.

Not overly bothered by any of the options, when Beatrice rounded another corner in the hopes it would soon lead to the heart, she collided with a man coming from the opposite direction. "Oomph!" The force of the impact sent her scrabbling for purchase.

"How clumsy of me," he murmured, and to prevent her from falling, his arms came around her and he held her close to the hard wall of his chest. In the process, he dropped the cane he'd been carrying. "Are you all right?"

"I think so." She peered slightly up at him, for he stood several inches taller than her shorter height. "And you?" There was no denying the man was interesting and slightly mysterious, with an eye patch over his left eye and a scar down the length of his cheek on that same side.

"No harm done." He held her gaze with his, and the longer they stared at each other, the more tiny flecks of gold appeared in his brown iris. "I didn't know anyone else was out here, but I am certainly glad for it."

"Oh? Why is that?" There was something slightly familiar about the man she couldn't immediately place. Had she met him in London? An errant summer breeze ruffled the waves of his chestnut hair, and she knew a powerful urge to finger comb those tresses back into some semblance of a style.

"I have been endeavoring to locate the heart of this maze for almost an hour and still haven't done so. I keep going around in circles." Amusement twinkled in his eye. "Perhaps now I shall have help."

A chuckle escaped Beatrice. "I don't know how much assistance I can render, for I am just as lost as you, and I'm directionally challenged."

"Ah. That is too bad." The man had yet to release her, and his grin was particularly pleasant, and he was entirely too close for her peace of mind.

"I don't mind attempting to find our way out of the maze together." Oh, his arms around her were strong and firm, and his body pressed far too close to hers was warm and quite beguiling. It had been all too long since she had enjoyed the company of a man who wasn't one of her brothers. Resting a gloved palm on his chest, she returned his smile. "Unless you have another engagement?"

"Thankfully, I do not." The baritone rumble of his voice tickled through her chest. "We might as well muddle through together, if you are of a mind."

Something about the set of his mouth niggled at the back of her memory, but she still couldn't identify him. "I am." Lost in a maze seemingly so far removed from the manor house, there was an air that anything could happen, that magic was simply waiting. Perhaps it wouldn't be remiss if she wished to do a bit of light flirtation. Who would ever know? And he was quite a handsome man with a bevy of secrets. She gave his lapel a gentle tug. "One never knows what one will find within a maze."

"Indeed." Finally, he released her from the impromptu embrace, and she immediately missed that intimate connection. When he bent to retrieve his cane, she took the opportunity to rake her gaze over his lean form. Whoever he was, he kept himself fit, and his tailor had enough expertise to enhance that body with the dark clothing requisite for a dinner engagement.

By the time he'd straightened, Beatrice had stepped back to allow him privacy. Perhaps he'd received his injuries in the war, but she was too well-bred to ask. When their gazes connected once more, she offered him a smile, which he immediately returned. Tingles scudded through her belly, a reaction she'd assumed was very much dead. "Are you from this area?"

"I am not." He didn't offer more, and she didn't pry. In the end, it didn't matter. Temporarily removed from the polite world, there was a certain expectation that allowed for less restrictions than normal. Then came around to her other side and offered her his left arm, bent at the elbow. "Shall we discover what there is to see on this journey? We can't both remain lost, now can we?"

"I don't suppose we can." As she slipped her hand through his elbow and wrapped her fingers about his upper arm, she was once more captivated by the solid feel of him. "What brought you here in the first place?"

"Boredom? The need to have a moment to myself." The limp was hardly noticeable. Did he keep the cane with him more for an emotional support than physical? "Life, just now, has been... aggravating."

"I can well understand that sentiment." Strolling beside this stranger both shocked and intrigued her. When was the last time she'd let herself do anything that bordered even slightly on the edge of scandal? "In recent months, I have very much needed an escape of my own."

"Ah, then it's fortunate we are both in this maze. Being lost isn't such a large burden if one isn't in immediate need of being found." He grinned again, and it was so pleasant that she couldn't help but do it as well. The subtle citrus and sage scent of him added another layer of intrigue to him.

Drat it all, but she couldn't stop staring at his mouth. What would a kiss from him feel like? "That is a lovely way of thinking." Daring much, she nudged his side. "But then, you are a lovely man." What had come over her? A woman simply didn't think these things about a man she'd only just met.

Did they?

He snorted. "I have a looking glass in my possession, and I am well aware of my appearance." They took a left turn and then followed it with a right. "Men with my injuries and scarring are never lauded as lovely." A slight note of resignation clung to the statement.

"Then you should replace your looking glass. You are quite mysterious and all too dashing with the scars and eyepatch." Though she desperately wished to hear his history, she didn't want to disturb the feeling of make believe that wrapped around them.

"I, think, perhaps, I stumbled upon a fairy in this maze instead of a human woman, for you are trying to bewitch me." Something in his glance—admiration, honesty, or perhaps a tiny bit of heat—sent delicious awareness dancing over her skin. "For who else could wear such a delightful gown of pale green and blue and pair it with come-hither eyes of that hue without being a fairy?"

Ah, it was wonderful having her flirting returned. Even still, heat jumped into her cheeks. "While I appreciate those words, somehow I think I am too advanced in age to have them ring true." A woman of nine and thirty shouldn't inspire such talk, should she?

"There is no such thing when it comes to a woman's beauty." He tugged her around another left turn on the path. The high hedges blocked out the sun's descent, and in the shaded areas, the slight chill in in the air provided more mystery. "It matters not if a woman is eighteen or eighty, what makes her beautiful comes from within. There is a glow there that cannot be achieved with a finely crafted gown or expertly coiffed hair."

A collection of flutters moved through her lower belly at his flattery. "How bold you are to say such things."

"I have learned long ago that to give compliments is the highest form of flattery, and that oftentimes they are needed most." When he shrugged, his arm brushed the side of her breast, and the unexpected contact pulled a tiny gasp from her. "Besides, a man who has seen war appreciates beauty all the more when he finds it."

Ah, then he *had* been in the military, which explained the injuries. Still, something about the set of his mouth, the tiny bit of irreverence in those brandy-colored eyes seemed familiar. Why couldn't she remember?

"Another wonderful perspective on life." When they made yet another left turn, suddenly they were spilled out into the heart of the maze, and it was every bit as magical as she had hoped. "What a wonderful garden!"

Mr. Cloverfield had apparently taken the description literally, for his well-kept rose garden at the center was in the shape of a large heart or valentine. Within the beds were countless rose bushes full of red, pink, and yellow blooms with a bevy of others waiting for their buds to open. The heavy scent of the flowers filled the air the closer she came to them.

"He truly does have a gift for gardening." Though there weren't many different shades in the garden, Mr. Cloverfield had managed to incorporate several different varietals, and that interested her the most. A marble statue of Aphrodite on a clamshell was nestled within the rose bushes, with the gentle tinkle of water dripping from a small fountain hidden within.

"Oh, goodness, look here. A China rose. Ooh, and a musk rose. I wonder how long it took to grow these to such splendor." Truly, she adored flowers, but roses were her especial favorite. Perhaps because her mother had enjoyed growing them at their country estate in Kent. "My mother used to keep roses, and I sat with her for hours in her gardens, watching her tend to the flowers."

Lord, but it had been an age since she'd visited that property. She made a mental note to write to Graham there and ask him to look over their mother's roses...if any of them had remained.

"Ah, what a pleasant memory to have." The man drifted close to her, bent to touch a gloved fingertip to a pink rose that was already fading. No doubt a gardener would come tomorrow morning and remove the head. "I hold never-ending admiration for people who can cultivate flowers. They are one of the more lovely things in life, and if I could, I would have freshly cut blooms in every room of my home."

"It isn't often that a man expresses fondness for flowers." Who was he? Not knowing, she traced a fingertip over a damask rose and then a Provence bloom. "Simply gorgeous." The petals proclaimed a softness she would very much like to feel, but she refused to remove her gloves in front of this as yet unnamed person.

"Yes, well, I fear I am not like many men."

"That isn't such a terrible thing, for there are many men whose behavior, opinions, and manners leave much to be desired."

"Mmm, this is so, and I certainly don't wish for my son to become one of the more scandalous types."

Her eyebrows lifted. He was a father! Did that mean he was married or had he been widowed? But again, she held her tongue, much preferring the anonymity of their meeting.

"I am also fascinated with the different meanings of flowers. It is a subtle language all of its own, and unless I miss my guess, it will gain popularity as the years progress." He looked at her before transferring his regard back to the roses. "I am well-read, in the event you wondered, and flowers play important parts in some of Shakespeare's plays."

"Indeed, they do." Though, when was the last time she'd read any of the Bard's works? The fact he was intelligent impressed her, and only added to his mystery.

"Ah, here is the perfect bloom." Seconds later, he'd snapped off a rose that hadn't fully opened in a deep burgundy color, not quite red but not quite pink, as if it couldn't make up its mind what hue it wished to settle upon. "This color represents simplicity and beauty." So saying, he closed the distance between them and dared to tuck the flower behind her right ear. "I believe it is quite fitting for you."

Oh, dear.

The fleeting touch of his fingers as he brushed her cheek while coming away sent a tremble cartwheeling down her spine. The scent of roses competed with his own delicious smell. Since he hadn't introduced himself, Beatrice assumed he wasn't a part of the *ton*, for those titled men were quite arrogant regarding their standing. In most cases, they wished for everyone to know just who they were and what their position was in society.

"I don't know what to say." This man was different. He had the manners and breeding, and since he'd been in the military, he might be a second, third, or even fourth son. Or perhaps he was a gentleman and had felt the urge to defend his country against Napoleon. His knowledge regarding the language of flowers perplexed her, for he'd mentioned having a son instead of a daughter. And he enjoyed reading, to boot. Since he'd given her that bloom, was he attached or merely being polite?

How would he know that she was not?

"Why say anything?" His voice had dropped to a rather seductive level, and it felt entirely too scandalous to stand so close to him within a veritable bower of blooms—alone. "Why cannot two people enjoy each other's company without superfluous words to fill what is quite a perfect silence?"

Suddenly, it was all very confusing and something she'd not

had cause to give thought to before. "There is a certain truth to what you've said." But it didn't answer the questions that kept multiplying in her brain.

Perhaps it didn't matter. The urge to do something reckless on this magical night took hold and wouldn't let go. "Forgive the trespass if it is not wanted or you have other obligations, but there is something about you that I simply cannot resist." Then, because Beatrice had apparently lost her ability to think clearly, she came a step closer to him, rested a palm on the hard wall of his chest, lifted onto her toes, and then pressed her lips to his. Oh, yes, the feel of that mouth against hers was every bit as lovely as she had imagined, and oh, how she had missed doing such a thing with a man.

You are being a complete ninny, Bea! Stop it this instant!

But she shoved the voice of her conscience to the back of her mind while sliding her hand up his chest to glide over his shoulder. As he searched her gaze, his eye widened, and slowly, ever so slowly, his arms came around her and he once more dropped his cane.

CHAPTER FOUR

*H*ELL'S BELLS!

Once Owen got over his initial shock that this strange woman had kissed him, he slid his arms around her form. No, he didn't know who she was, but there was a vague familiarity about her, something about her eyes, and they'd already had an interesting conversation. He wouldn't be a living, breathing man if he didn't kiss her back.

With a slight groan, he settled her into a more comfortable embrace, then proceeded to introduce himself to her by way of moving over her lips that were as soft as the rose petals looked. One of her hands stole behind his nape, and it might have been his overactive imagination, but it certainly felt as if she encouraged him closer. He took the hint, nibbling at her lush bottom lip, that wonderous piece of flesh that was as plush as the upper one. They cradled his with a perfection that had interest shivering through his shaft. Daring much, he explored the seam of her mouth with the tip of his tongue.

A soft squeak mixed with a moan left her throat, and the sensual sound of it heightened the awareness that had fallen over him since she'd crashed into him in the maze. The palm resting on his chest flexed, her fingers curling into his lapel, and all the while, the woman in his arms who smelled like lilies of the valley pressed her body against his, as she matched him kiss for kiss.

With every meeting of their lips, he couldn't help but let the fairytale feeling of the moment creep into his bones.

The fact that neither of them had introduced themselves fed the anonymous, fleeting, almost scandalous meeting. Not since his wife had been in full health had he felt this sort of frantic passion, and that he did for this stranger left him wanting to berate himself, but he couldn't help it. Sliding a hand down her back, he dragged his lips along the column of her throat. What he would give to explore the secrets those curves were hiding. For all her earlier flirting and his responses, she wasn't a young woman any longer, but that didn't mean her figure still wasn't impressive.

"Should we move this surprising tryst into the shadows for more privacy?" Was he seriously considering taking this series of kisses deeper? But then, how often did a woman find him attractive enough to kiss him?

Her eyes fluttered open, and she stared at him with that cornflower blue gaze. "That largely depends on what else you would like to share." The throaty whisper shivered across his consciousness with alarming accuracy.

"What wouldn't I like to give...or receive...from such a storybook creature?" What had happened to him to make him fall into her pattern of flirting? Suddenly, he wanted the few shared kisses they'd just had to become something more entirely, regardless of the potential scandal. The image of this woman laid out on the soft, cool grass popped into his mind, with her pale skin on display as he teased various sensitive parts of her with a blooming rose.

Get off it, man! You have only just met this woman and now you want to see her naked? What the devil is wrong with you?

"What a deliciously wicked answer." Her kiss-swollen lips formed a perfect *o* of surprise, and just as she nodded her consent, the sound of someone else intruding into their hideaway broke the spell.

"Mama? The dinner reception will begin shortly and I don't

wish to go in without you."

Dinner reception? Did that mean they both belonged to the house party? His interest had already been piqued, but now it strengthened in a different way.

The woman in his arms sprang away as if he'd suddenly turned into fire and had burned her. "I should go." A blush stained her cheeks as she cast about the grass for the shawl that had slipped from her shoulders. "It won't do for my daughter to see me locked in a stranger's embrace. Especially after all the lectures I've given her on her own deportment," she said in a whisper.

"Mama? Are you here?" The sound of the young lady's voice was stronger now. She would be upon them any minute if she made the correct turns.

Amusement circled through his chest, but he also didn't wish to quit her company so soon. "I understand completely," he said in an equally low voice.

"Oh?" She retrieved her shawl and wrapped it about her shoulders and upper chest.

Damn, but it was a crime to hide that delicious décolletage. Too bad he'd not been able to explore those particular charms. "I have a daughter. No doubt she's around the same age as yours. She had been sullen with me for most of the trip to Wiltshire."

"Whyever for?"

The camaraderie between them, as well as the puzzling attraction, did much to restore his good humor. "One of the gowns she ordered wasn't finished in time for the trip. It apparently ruined her life, and the world is now a horrid place."

A delighted chuckle issued from her. "Oh, heavens. How well I know the petulance. Mine was annoyed at first because I didn't wish for her to come at all."

Owen snorted. "Needless to say, it was a quiet ride."

"Mama? Where *are* you?" Aggravation was evident in the young lady's voice.

"Truly, I must go, but this interlude has been most pleasant."

She gave him one last lingering look and then sighed. "Perhaps I will see you during the house party?"

"I am counting on it. Do you attend as a guest, then?"

She pointed her gaze heavenward for a moment. "In a roundabout way. I am playing the role of chaperone to my daughter." Then, with a wave, she fled down the path that had brought them both to the heart of the maze to begin with.

Somewhat bemused and particularly aroused, Owen stared after her as if he couldn't quite believe what had just occurred. For a man who'd adamantly told his children he wasn't interested in finding a romance during this house party, he'd certainly rendered that a lie with his actions here in the rose garden. Also, his admonitions to both children not to fall into scandal seemed blatantly hypocritical since, if someone had come upon him and the unidentified woman before they'd broken apart, that would have been quite the scandal in itself.

Then he couldn't help but smile. The good thing? His children need not know about this one-off indiscretion. No, he wasn't in search of a romance that might lead into a marriage, but he wasn't averse to a week-long tryst if a particular lady was willing.

That wasn't a crime…as long as his children never found out.

Later that evening

THE RECEPTION DINNER came and went, and though he'd spotted the lady at the table, he'd been seated too far down to strike up any sort of meaningful conversation. An introduction would need to wait until later. To say nothing of the fact that his daughter chattered nonstop at his right side, and it was all he could do to keep up with that stream.

Afterward, everyone was invited into the drawing room. For this first night, the habit of men lingering over the table for drinks and cigars had been suspended. The hosts of the house party wished for everyone to make inroads into socializing—through games and conversation—instead, so Owen was obliged to escort Mary into that room while anticipation and worry twisted down his spine. Would the mysterious lady attend the gathering with her daughter?

He rather hoped that she did, for she'd been uppermost in his mind ever since that brief flirtation in the maze. And if he were honest with himself, he wanted to know what she'd thought of their shared kisses. As he made his way about the room, he introduced himself to a handful of people, for it wouldn't hurt to form a few lasting connections, if only for his daughter's future.

"Papa, should I join the group organizing for charades?" A trace of uncertainty threaded through his daughter's voice.

"I don't see why not. After all, you were the one who wished to attend this house party in an effort to make you less ill at ease when you enter society." He patted her hand that rested on his arm. "Remember, I will be here if you stumble."

She nodded and her gaze darted across the large room where a group of young people around her age had gathered. "Do you promise you won't leave?"

"I promise." Perhaps she wasn't as grown as he'd feared. "Go make friends. If you find this sort of event isn't for you, we will make our excuses and go home. No harm done."

Relief etched over her face. "You would do that for me?"

"Of course, poppet. There will be other times to dip your toes into society."

"Thank you." Though she smiled, a hint of apprehension lingered in her eyes. "I suppose I won't know until I try."

"Indeed."

"You will do the same? Enter into a conversation with someone?"

"I will try my best." Then he gave her a gentle push toward the knot of young people. "Go on. Dazzle them with your wit and charm."

As she left his side, a feeling of loss came over him. There was no doubt his children were coming into their own and growing into adulthood. Soon, they wouldn't need him any longer, and then what would he do with the remainder of his life?

Not in the mood to suffer through shallow conversations, Owen moved to the well-stocked sideboard. A few other men were already there. One of them asked for his drink preference, and when he handed over a snifter of brandy, he offered his thanks.

The man, perhaps several years his junior, roved his gaze throughout the room. "There are enough fillies of all ages at this party to warrant enjoyment for the week. A pleasant mix of *beau monde* and gentry, it would seem."

So this is how it would start? Protective instinct surged through his chest. He certainly didn't want Mary to fall victim to the charms of such a man. She was *not* a "filly." "Careful, my good man. One of them is my daughter." Owen frowned at him from over the rim of his glass. "And she is only here to be amongst her friends."

"I understand your sentiment; I've a niece her age." The other man gave him a knowing glance. "However, I am not interested in debutantes or those who will soon have their Come Outs. Luring innocents to my bed is not my game."

Another man joined them, and this one was as short and dumpy as the first one was tall and thin. Standing so close together, they resembled the number ten. "I agree there are some choice pieces in attendance." He raised his own glass in a salute to the room at large, apparently. "While there are a few thoroughbreds, there are quite a few long-in-the-tooth entries."

Owen bounced his gaze between the men and out at the room where guests had broken off into separate groups. The largest of which was the knot of young people who'd finally organized their game of charades. Why did men refer to women with equine terminology? He'd never understood that, even during his days in the military.

The first man chuckled. "Indeed, though one in particular has caught my eye."

"Oh? Who? Perhaps we will be rivals."

He paid little mind to the banter, until a name in particular tripped across his consciousness and flooded his mind with memories from the past.

"Lady Beatrice Ashdowne-Delacorte. Daughter of a marquess. Widowed these past four years. Playing chaperone to her daughter."

Bloody hell.

He hadn't heard that name bandied about in polite circles for years, but then, he wasn't one to linger in drawing rooms or society in general. And how odd that he'd only a couple of days before remembered that fleeting kiss in the meadow they'd shared as children.

Yet he'd kissed the hell out of that same woman in the heart of the maze not a few hours past. No wonder her eyes had seemed familiar. *Why the devil didn't I recognize her straightaway?* It seemed all too obvious now. Perhaps he was becoming a doddering old fool.

"Indeed." The second man nodded while Owen stared with shock at that same woman who stood across the room, enduring the conversation of what appeared to be a couple of other chaperones, governesses and the like. Lively conversation buzzed through the air, punctuated by nervous laughter, but he'd recognize hers anywhere now that he'd been apprised of her identity. "Family coin makes the age more palatable, but if you wish to pursue her, perhaps I'll go after the daughter."

"Eh, I remain undecided. There has been much gossip regarding the Ashdownes recently. Something about mismatched paternity."

"That matters not," said the second man. "I'm not looking to advance in society, just gain funding to modernize my property."

The conversation would turn Owen's stomach before too long. Just as he'd felt a rush of protection toward his own daughter, another wave moved through him for Beatrice's girl. It was definitely out of respect for the friendship they'd shared as children. "Whatever you do, make certain you have the correct mindset about you before you pursue any woman here." With a bad taste in his mouth, he deposited his brandy glass on a nearby table. "Otherwise, it's simply cruel, and at the very least, every woman here deserves respect."

They both stared at him with mixtures of amusement and pity. "With that attitude, you'll need to join the thicket of prudes huddling together in that corner, my friend," the squatter man said with a chuckle.

Then the two returned to their interrupted discussion.

"Regardless, you'll no doubt be grateful to have a woman to warm your lonely bed, eh Bertram?" The first man chuckled. "At least she's not horse-faced."

"There is that." Then the two men moved off to latch onto a smaller group of men.

"Bah." *Idiots*. Men who chased skirts merely for the hell of it wasted everyone's time. Which meant he would need to keep a more diligent eye on not only his daughter, but every young woman at the house party. For the moment, he would let Mary remain, but if he saw even an ounce of impropriety regarding her, he would toss her into a coach himself and return quickly home. Yes, the girl needed to grow into a young lady, but not at preventable risk.

As he wandered through the drawing room, once more he was compelled to glance in Lady Beatrice's direction only to find her gaze resting upon him. A shiver went down his spine, for even at that short distance, the shock in her cornflower blue eyes was evident. Had someone told her who he was? That rather stole the element of surprise, and he somewhat missed the mystery they'd had between them.

Regardless, he remained curious about her. Did she remember their connection to the past? Owen gave her a tight grin and a tiny shrug. She barely nodded and then said something to the woman standing beside her. Was that a cut direct? Since he had little experience with the ways of the *ton*, he truly had no idea. Had he offended her? That was entirely possible. After all, a man doesn't kiss a woman nearly senseless in someone else's hedge maze without at least asking her name. A bit of heat climbed the back of his neck. Of course, she had been the one who'd initiated the embrace, but did that matter?

Probably not. Women acted offended by all sorts of things, related or unrelated to an inciting incident.

Perhaps, then, she was embarrassed by her behavior. That made more sense. She was the daughter of a marquess and a lady besides. To say nothing of wishing to provide a proper role model for her daughter.

If that wasn't the reason for her snub, it could very well be she was disgusted by his looks. The eyepatch did tend to catch people off-guard, and once the insanity of kissing an anonymous man in the heart of a maze wore off, perhaps she'd been aghast when she'd truly looked at him.

There were too many questions, and answers to all of them put a bit of disgruntlement in his craw. Somehow, he expected more of a friend from childhood.

"Why are you overthinking? It is the first evening of a house party, Major Kenton. Not a question for the ages."

The sound of her voice behind him sent a shockwave through him. Slowly, he turned about and gripped the head of his cane. "Who told you my name?"

Her shrug was an elegant affair. "It was bandied about amongst some of the ladies. One of them said in passing you were a lovely dinner conversationalist despite your less than savory looks."

"Ah." Well, that was rather deflating for one's ego. "At least I know the general consensus now instead of laboring under false pretenses."

A trace of amusement lurked in her eyes. "Do not listen to the words of shallow women. Half of them are only interested in a man's financial worth, while the other half want a man to look like a god."

That struck him as funny. A chuckle escaped. With a wink, he whispered, "A rather hasty judgment, for none of these women have seen me *sans* clothing. What makes you think I *don't* look like a god?"

The faintest hint of a blush stained her cheeks. "That is beside the point."

"Perhaps, but to put you at the same rocky footing as you did me, rumor through the bachelor set holds your family name is under a bit of besmirchment, but in the event you wondered, they won't hold that—or your age—against you." It wasn't well done of him to mention that, but he wanted to see if she would still respond to teasing as she did when he'd known her as a young girl.

"How uncouth of you to mention that, Major." She shook her head, but a tiny smile curved those delectable lips he'd kissed several hours ago. "However, I am *quite* past the age when I matter to anyone, so I don't take offense. Much." Then she lowered her voice. "I was shocked to discover who you were."

"As was I." Owen readjusted his hold on the head of his cane. "I hope that, uh, interlude in the maze didn't prematurely color your opinion of me."

"It did not. Neither of us are the young people we were all those years ago."

Then a new thought occurred to him. "Incidentally, the last time we parted was after a kiss. Though that first one hadn't the heat or passion to it as the one today did." Knowing who she was, the passion between them made absolutely no sense.

"Ha." She laughed, and the delightful sound seemed to wrap itself around him. "Speak for yourself. I was quite enamored of you at fourteen."

"Ah." Inordinately pleased with the admission, Owen grinned. "We have both lived a few lifetimes since that day, eh, Lady Beatrice?"

"Of course." She briefly laid a hand on his arm, and the touch sent awareness dancing over his skin. "Since we are already acquainted, you might drop the title in private. After a few kisses, one doesn't stand on ceremony."

"No, I don't suppose one does." Warmth went through his chest, for it seemed they might resume their friendship. "Please, refer to me as Owen, if the use of 'Major' wears thin."

"Thank you." She nodded but darted a worried gaze to the knot of young people, who were continually growing louder with each phase of the game. "I should encourage the game to come to an end. Nothing good will come of the children becoming wild so close to the time they should retire."

"I am surprised at you."

"Why?" She frowned, but there were questions in her eyes.

"When you were a girl younger than them, I seem to recall you running all about the countryside after dark with your brothers… and me, more than a time or two."

The blush reappeared. "That was different, and I'm afraid Eliza is too much a novice in rebuffing the attentions of young men."

"I worry about that as well."

Beatrice nodded. "Well then. We have unpacking to do, besides. Perhaps I will see you tomorrow?"

"There is a high probability if our respective children choose the same activities to attend." Though loath to lose her companionship, he couldn't offer a protest while there were so many people about. "I would enjoy another conversation, to catch up on what has occurred in the years that have separated us."

Her grin faded as quickly as it came. "I would enjoy that as well." Then, with a mumbled good night, she moved across the drawing room to speak with her daughter.

Owen eyed her with a hearty dose of speculation. Perhaps the house party wouldn't be as dull as he'd assumed.

CHAPTER FIVE

July 26, 1820

AFTER A LATE breakfast, a walking party was formed, and since her daughter wished to attend, Beatrice consented to join.

"If you are not interested, you don't need to come with me," Eliza said as she tied the ribbons of her bonnet beneath her chin.

"I'm not going to let you go off alone." Yet it was a difficult endeavor to concentrate on the mundane task of walking through the corridors when her mind stubbornly refused to fixate on anything other than Major Owen Kenton.

At some point after he'd moved away from the property in Kent, he'd gone into military service, and he'd done it with enough bravery and aplomb that he'd climbed the ranks to end at a major. And that was no doubt where he'd been injured so dramatically that he'd lost an eye. Oh, there were so many questions she wished to ask him, but she still hadn't overcome the shock of discovering who he was last night.

No wonder he'd seemed so familiar!

"Mama." Eliza scoffed as they descended the grand staircase and then followed yet another corridor toward the rear of the manor. "I won't be alone. The walking party consists of at least fifteen people."

"Then all the more reason for me to come and keep an eye on the young men who might be prowling on innocent girls."

And if there was a god in heaven, Eliza wouldn't act as forward as her mother had done when presented with a mysterious man at the heart of a maze. Her cheeks still burned when she remembered the kiss she'd initiated that had led to an even more heated embrace. A day later, she still marveled over the flash of attraction between her and Owen. Was it possible that fate had brought them together for a second time?

How silly to think such, Bea.

There was no way of his knowing she would be there or even who she was in that maze. And why would fate throw them together now? They had nothing in common, over and above being parents.

Yet…

It had felt so lovely being held in a man's arms again. The strength and safety found there, coupled with the unexpected attraction, as well as being wanted for no other reason than she was a woman and he'd been a man. For those few moments, the world had ceased to exist. Heady stuff indeed, but unfortunately, it couldn't last beyond those stolen seconds.

Could it? Yes, it was true she wouldn't mind being married again. But it was folly to think shared kisses in a hedge maze might lead to that eventually, and with a man she knew nothing about, other than they'd grown up together.

On the other hand, she simply couldn't merely have a tryst, not after the horrid shock of discovering her mother's affair that had rocked both her family and that of the Winterbourne connection. No matter the fact that if her mother hadn't been unfaithful to her father, she wouldn't exist, it was the thought behind the act that left her confused and suddenly without identity. Truly, she needed to talk about that to someone, and it couldn't be her daughter for obvious reasons.

Would the major want a return of the friendship they'd enjoyed so long ago, and perhaps help her to find her place in this ever-changing world?

"Mama, are you even listening to me?" A trace of annoyance went through her daughter's voice.

With a start, Beatrice realized they'd exited the house and had gained the back lawn. Ahead, the walking party had assembled and was already moving off. "Uh, honestly, no. I was woolgathering. I'm sorry. What were you saying?"

Eliza huffed in apparent frustration. "I was asking your opinion between two different boys. Which do you like—Mr. Atkinson or Mr. Featherington?"

Oh, dear.

Considering that she didn't really know which young man was which, Beatrice shrugged. "I think it's entirely too early for you to be vying for men's attentions."

"They are hardly men. Both are a handful of years older than me."

She tamped down on the urge to sigh. "Basically, they are still men, and at that age, men who are most certainly on the prowl. I would ask that you mind yourself while in their company, and absolutely under no circumstances are you to be alone with either."

"Yes, yes, I understand the rules, but conversation will be rather difficult under the circumstances. Once I am introduced to them properly, that is."

Well, her daughter was certainly making the best use of her time, since this was only the first morning at the house party. "That is one of the pitfalls of being of courting age." The realization sent tickles of cold panic down Beatrice's spine. Where had the time gone since Eliza was a little girl with her hair down and running amok during outings in Hyde Park? Of course every child grew into adulthood, but surely it wasn't time for her baby to be interested in having men court her, set her mind to marriage?

Another huff—harder this time—recalled Beatrice's mind to the present. "Isn't this why you let me attend the house party to begin with?"

Give me patience. "No, I let you attend so you would be more comfortable in society so that by the time your Come Out arrives, you won't be a nervous, retiring miss."

"Ah." Eliza rolled her eyes heavenward. "I am hardly that. It is more what you are, slinking off to the sides of the room and avoiding conversations."

As if her ego needed any more bruises than it was already suffering. "I don't avoid conversation. I merely selectively choose which I participate in." Beatrice shrugged. "There are a few interesting people I might enjoy speaking with."

As they walked over the grass to catch up with the walking party, Eliza shot her a glance brimming with shock. "You aren't thinking of finding a man for yourself while you're here, are you Mama?" She gasped, as if the very thought of it would send her into a faint. "That would be too awkward. You are entirely too old for that, don't you think?"

"I'm not exactly doddering." Nothing kept a woman humble like hearing how her grown daughter thought of her and any potential romantic prospects. "It isn't entirely out of the realm of possibility that I might marry again. In fact, it seems a lovely thought, for I enjoyed such a state with your father immensely."

"Oh, Mama." Eliza shook her head. "Do you wish to find yourself matched *here?*" Her tone of voice suggested she—and everyone else her age—would be scandalized by the mere thought.

"Not at his house party, exactly…" She chose to ignore the heat in her cheeks. "But sometime, perhaps. Since you will soon step into your own life, I'm feeling a tad lonely. Having a man by my side will give me someone to talk to besides your uncles."

Her daughter paused and laid a hand on Beatrice's arm. "While I can understand that—you haven't been yourself since Papa died this is true—*please* don't encourage a romance right now. I don't want the other girls to make jest of me, and I don't wish for anything to call the attention to you."

At least Eliza was truthful. Beatrice heaved a sigh and told herself that thinking about possibilities in general—and Owen in particular—should be saved for another day. "Fear not." She patted her daughter's cheek. "I am only a chaperone. I know my place for this week."

"Good." Relief lined the girl's face. Then she leaned in and bussed Beatrice's cheek. "I appreciate the discretion." A speculative light lit her eyes. "That man I saw you talking briefly to last night in the drawing room. Is he an acquaintance?"

This time the heat in her cheeks was stronger. "Uh, it turns out, his family and mine were neighbors in Kent. It was a surprise to see him here of all places. He escorted his daughter."

"How lovely. At least you have someone to talk with while the rest of us engage in various activities."

"Yes. I'm glad I won't need to linger with other governesses and companions," she said, in a dry voice brimming with sarcasm that completely sailed right by her daughter.

"I should catch up to the party. Patience said she would introduce me to a girl named Mary. The Cloverfields invited her brother, but since he didn't want to come, she arrived in his stead. She's a year younger than me, but she's clever and pretty."

"One can never have too many friends."

"Oh, and then she'll introduce me to Mr. Atkinson or Mr. Featherington. They arrived too late last night to attend dinner. She said Mr. Featherington is knowledgeable about trees and birds and the like. If that proves true, she is going to convince him we should look at the native foliage and animals this afternoon."

That didn't sound so bad. "Make sure you stay on the paths. It's muddy. And stay within eyesight the whole time."

"Stop worrying, Mama. I promise not to fall into scandal so early in the game." Then she ran off and soon caught up to the knot of young people that formed the walking party. Her friend Patience greeted her and clutched at Eliza's hand. Seconds later, both girls were chatting merrily with another girl in a jonquil walking dress with matching ribbons on her bonnet and chestnut hair.

A familiar chuckle behind her sent awareness shivering over her skin as the major caught up with Beatrice. When his arm accidentally brushed hers, delicious tingles danced down her spine. "Good morning, Beatrice. It seems your daughter and mine have formed a friendship of sorts."

"Until they both end up fancying the same boy, then it will be war." She resisted the urge to glance at him, but her spirits had improved exponentially to see him.

"Surely that won't happen during this party. A week isn't long enough to find oneself enamored of anyone."

"Stranger things have happened, and at that age, any sort of attention or touch of a hand is tantamount to love." At the last second, she managed to keep most of the sarcasm from her tones. "Regardless, I hope the girls are content enough with stretching their wings. I am simply not ready to usher in that part of my life where I need to watch Eliza's heart be buoyed and broken."

"Neither am I, yet here we are. Relegated to the roles of silent companions. Chaperones who can condemn with our eyes while our charges are with their contemporaries, but will lecture with words when we have a spare moment." His grin was evident in his tones, and when she turned her head to catch the gesture, it only enhanced that lingering attraction. "And, in the event you wondered, you are *not* old."

"Ha." A trace of heat went into her cheeks. "I am not young either."

"Experience gives a woman a greater attraction than an innocent young debutante. If men were wise, they would chase older women instead of innocents."

"Oh." She couldn't help a smile as she glanced at the walking party. "Thank you for that." The continuing heat in cheeks was silly. *I'm a widow and a mother for goodness' sake!*

"As long as we don't fall victim to accident or disease, we should be able to see another twenty years perhaps. And if we don't, we will join those who went before us." A sigh escaped him. "Morose thought, hmm?"

The thread of sadness and grief in his voice played upon her own. She glanced at him with a frown. "I suppose that depends on your definition of morose. No doubt our loved ones have gone on to more joyful places." At least she liked to hope that was true, for perhaps then her parents would have stopped fighting, stopped their intent to seek a divorce, but on the other hand, her mother might be finally happy to be reunited with her lover—the real father of her children.

My brothers and me.

"Mmm, indeed, but that would only lead to more questions, I think."

"It would." Was she comfortable enough in his presence to talk about the scandal sitting on her doorstep and how to make sense of it?

They continued on in silence for a bit. When the walking party stalled at a hedgerow to examine spring leaves and sprouting flowers, the major led her over to a nearby fallen log. "It would appear we shall be here for some time. When young people chatter about, they have no concept of time passing." He removed his tweed jacket, draped it over the log, then invited her to sit. "We might as well be comfortable."

She stared at him even as her soul rejoiced at the chivalry. "No doubt you are, but appearing in your shirtsleeves is the first step to walking into scandal. And in front of impressionable young men and women." But she perched on the log, grateful for the covering of his jacket, for there was damp and moss clinging to the fallen tree.

"Considering the fact I'm well past the age of caring and you are a widow, and the fact we are both a decent distance away from our charges, anyone with half an eye can see I offered a service with the removal of my jacket." He bestowed a grin upon her. "No one is paying us the slightest mind."

"What of the other companions?" There was a small group of women who stood on the other side of the young people. They were of various ages and dressed in varying degrees of somber colors.

"None of them care about us. They are all too busy talking about their own miserable lives to notice what we are doing. And even if they weren't, you are a marquess's daughter. They wouldn't dare to speak out of turn about you."

"Ah, yes, a benefit of privilege." Beatrice shook her head. "Since we're out of earshot what do you suppose they're talking about? Our children, I mean. Flora? Fauna? Their hopes and dreams for the future?" It seemed an age since she'd been in her daughter's footsteps doing exactly that.

"Perhaps." The major trained his gaze on the group. Soft laughter drifted to their location. "No doubt much of the talk is gossip and flirting. They are sizing each other up, pondering the possibilities of pushing boundaries, wondering how to escape their chaperones."

A giggle escaped her throat. "I don't think the hedge maze has occurred to them yet as an option."

"Good, for I wanted another look at it myself." When he glanced back at her, he winked. "If you consent to accompany me, we can amuse ourselves with years' worth of conversation."

Was he flirting with her? A hint of warmth filled her cheeks. She looked at the walking party. What the devil was so fascinating about leaves and summer berries? "Somehow I think my daughter is going to be a handful."

He snorted with apparent amusement. "Weren't you the same when you were younger than she?" Then his grin widened. "I seem to recall the time when you stripped down to your petticoat and chemise merely to put your feet in a cool stream one summer."

"You have to admit, it was quite hot that year." Even though she returned his smile, Beatrice shook her head. "And that wasn't well done of you to bring such a thing up."

"Perhaps not." The rumble of his laughter tickled through her chest. "I'm sorry I didn't introduce myself to you before last night, but I didn't wish to break the magic we'd temporarily found."

Magic was a good word for what had sprung between them, what was—even now—wrapping about her and urging her closer to him in spirit. "I could have done the same, but I liked the anonymity of being in the maze with a stranger."

"As did I. There is precious little excitement of the sort in life these days." Shadows flitted through his eye, gone with his next blink. "However, that doesn't mean the fun of knowing each other from before needs to put a damper on our relationship now."

"Agreed."

"That is to say if you wish to engage in a friendship? After all, we have known each other from childhood and have much to talk about since then." The slight wistful tone in his voice mirrored what she'd felt.

"I would enjoy that." Then, not knowing what to do, Beatrice trained her eyes on the walking party. Thus far, nothing had occurred that needed broken up. Perhaps it was time to open the dialogue. "How long have you been a widower?"

"A bit over four years. Lynette perished from a wasting disease of the lungs." He glanced away, but a muscle in his jaw twitched. "It was one of the most horrid things I have ever borne witness to. Watching her slip further away, labor to breathe while her strength ebbed from her body, knowing there was nothing I could do to alleviate her suffering."

"I'm sorry for your loss." This was a man who understood what it meant to love and lose someone. That gave them something else in common. "We never expect grief to be as deep as it is at times."

"Indeed, but why should we not? We felt love as deep."

"Yes." Her heart squeezed when she remembered life as it had been with her husband. "Did you enjoy being married?"

"I did." The major glanced at her once more, and there was a warm glow in his eye, brandy-hued in the sunlight like it had been so long ago. "There was something easy and familiar about it. Being a family. Knowing I had a purpose outside the military. That someone cared I was alive and adored having me home."

"Yes, there is a certain sense of belonging when a match is true." She swallowed around a lump in her throat. "Do you miss your wife?"

"Of course. Some days are easier than others." He tightened his hand on the head of his cane. "My children say I should marry again."

"Oh?" Her heartbeat accelerated. "Why?"

He shrugged. "They say I'm the type of man who needs a woman in order to be happy."

"Are you?"

"I don't know yet. Haven't found one I have felt anything like that for since my wife died, but if I had to answer you right now? I don't wish to marry. However, I am not adverse to a liaison of some sort." His eyebrow arched in challenge. For long moments, they stared at each other. "How long have you been a widow?"

"Five years. I lost my husband to pneumonia one winter."

"I can hear the waver in your voice. You loved him very much." It wasn't a question.

"I did. We enjoyed a long union." She uttered a soft chuckle. "I married him when I was around Eliza's age. Young, stupid, but with stars in my eyes and dreams in my heart."

"There is nothing wrong with that." When he grinned, she couldn't help resting her gaze on his mouth. "Would you marry again?"

"I would like to. I adore being married, having a man by my side. However, certain… things have come to light regarding my family that make me sick to my stomach regarding the married state and why people do it at all." She glanced away with burning cheeks. How would he react to such scandalous news? "Knowing what I do now, I wonder if I could remain faithful should a second husband not perish of health problems."

"You wish to pursue an affair, perhaps?" A hint of interest

wove through the inquiry.

Heat slapped at her cheeks. "That would largely depend on the man, wouldn't it?" It was such fun to flirt and tease with him.

Shock rounded his eye. "Somehow, I can't picture you as consenting to be someone's mistress."

"I never said mistress." Such a line of questioning had lifted her temporarily flagging spirits. "That means being *kept* by a man and used for *his* pleasures and whims. I would be more receptive to a quick, illicit, torrid affair, because that means equal of everything, and I would have my freedom shortly following, unless feeling crept in that might transfer into love and marriage." She gasped. Had she revealed too much about herself?

A slow grin curved Owen's mouth. "You have obviously given this thought."

"There is reason for it."

"That sounds mysterious. Will you share with me why you feel that way?"

"Yes, but not just yet." For long moments, she held his gaze. If they were alone, would he have taken her into his arms again? "It is… awkward feeling lonely. I wasn't prepared for this part of life. This learning how to live without my husband, learning how to come to terms with my daughter growing into adulthood." With a sigh, she gave her head a little shake. "Everything is confusing."

"It can be." He moved a step closer, put a hand on her shoulder in a fleeting show of support. "But you aren't alone. In any of it, Beatrice."

"Thank you." Emotion rose in her throat, but she wasn't comfortable enough to show it in his presence. "Perhaps during this week, I'll want to tell you all my secrets, even though I fear you'll think I come from tainted stock and won't talk to me for the remainder of the party." There. At least one of her fears was out in the open.

The sound of laughter reached her ears, and she again glanced toward the walking party. It seemed as if the young people were preparing to depart.

"I can't fathom that will happen, since I don't put much stock into rumors or gossip."

"Oh?" That was lovely to hear. As she watched, the party moved around the hedgerow and were temporarily blocked from their view. "We should go. While it's darling our children seem to believe we aren't as clever as them, I don't trust them by half."

"Neither do I." Owen looked over his shoulder. "Never fear. The other group of companions has gone after them, so you and I are given a temporary reprieve of a handful of seconds."

"What difference does that make?"

"Enough to do this." Quickly, Owen closed the distance. He put a gloved finger beneath her chin, raised her head, and then lowered his until their lips touched. Gently, and with exquisite care, he kissed her, and this meeting was much different from what they'd shared in the maze. This time he leisurely introduced himself with a surety that impressed her, and left her a bit breathless in a way the prior heated passion couldn't.

When she reached to put a hand to his shoulder, he broke the embrace, put a few feet of space between them. "Why did you do that?" Not that she minded. A lovely heat sailed through her blood, but it left behind a certain longing.

"Why not?" He shrugged, but there was a cheekiness to his grin. "We both needed it after what happened between us yesterday. Also, I want you to know I appreciate rediscovering a friend. Might we talk again? Perhaps when we don't have chaperoning to do?"

"I would like that." Beatrice let him pull her upright. The lingering heat of his fingers on hers was all too delicious. She turned slightly away while he retrieved his coat, for that all-too-brief kiss had hardened her nipples. It wouldn't do to show such a reaction. "I believe the children have decided on parlor games again tonight. We might have an opportunity to talk afterward."

"Mmm, somewhere private? Perhaps a portrait gallery or even the library after the house retires?" When she nodded, he grinned. "I look forward to it." Quickly, he shrugged into his jacket and manipulated the silver buttons. "For now, let's make sure they haven't gotten into scandal. While I enjoy being a father, I'm *not* ready to be a grandfather quite yet."

"On that, I quite agree."

CHAPTER SIX

July 26, 1820

OWEN GLANCED OUT his bedchamber window as he sipped a cup of strongly brewed coffee. He'd fallen into the habit of drinking the beverage while in India, even though most of his fellows preferred tea as well as the Indian style of serving it. Something about the bitter liquid helped to keep him alert and awake, and after one and a half days at this house party, he sorely needed the additional alertness.

Today, a group of young people had decided it would be just the thing to go boating on one of the ponds around the property. He wasn't particularly thrilled with the idea, for being on the water wasn't something that agreed with his stomach, but if that was what his daughter wished to do, he would accompany her. There was another faction of people who wished to go berry picking, so it would all come down to which young man Mary wished to follow.

As of yet, she hadn't made an appearance, so that afforded him the quiet time to himself he'd been craving for far too long. While he enjoyed the coffee, his thoughts went back to the kiss he'd shared with Beatrice yesterday. Though it had been much tamer than the ones exchanged in the hedge maze, it had been no less interesting. The fact he'd caught her by surprise had amused him, but it had been a sweet gesture that he hoped had given her a bit of comfort and a promise for a return of the energy their first meeting had.

What had prompted the kiss? They'd both spoken of their deceased spouses, and in that quick moment, they had been united in grief but hadn't gone too deeply into their feelings. It had been enough to know they'd each understood. Added to that was the need for acceptance from someone on a different level than mere friendship. Thoughts from that kiss they'd had years ago had distracted him, and seeing her amidst the backdrop of the sunlit countryside had affected him more than he'd anticipated. Needing a return of those halcyon days when he'd not been responsible, where he could do what he'd wished without censure, had caught him up in their pull, and he'd kissed her.

If he wasn't careful, one of them would make a misstep and cause a mild sensation, which would end with them being asked to leave the house party, and quite frankly, he didn't want to risk his daughter's wrath if that occurred. Mary was particularly moody just now, and he didn't know why, but every time he tried to ask, she huffed and said she had other things to attend.

Did Beatrice encounter the same problem with her daughter?

It was something he wished to discuss with her. Being a father to nearly grown children was a somewhat tiring business. The boy he understood much better, since he'd been that age before, but Mary would drive him to drink soon.

With another sip of coffee, he allowed a small smile as a summer breeze riffled through his hair and the folds of his cravat. It was proving to be a glorious day. The one fly in the ointment this morning was his inability to remain alert, for sleep had eluded him for the most part last night. Between thoughts of Beatrice and an unexpected nightmare from the war, he'd spent far too much time tossing and turning. That, in turn, had made the muscles on his left side ache, and that made him remember the day when the steel of that saber had sliced through his body and left searing pain and permanent injury behind.

Did Beatrice think him less-than because of it? There was no way of knowing, for they hadn't been afforded the chance to properly talk.

What I wouldn't do for a nap beneath the shade of an oak tree.

A soft knock on his door had him turning and bidding the caller entry. A quick acceleration of his pulse hoped that it was a certain lady defying convention in order to visit him before most of the household had risen for the day, but when Mary came into the room, he tamped down his disappointment as best he could.

"Good morning, poppet."

"Hullo, Papa." The girl was the perfect personification of a summer day in a light blue dress of what she'd called sprigged muslin when they had ordered clothing before coming here. "Are you excited for today's offerings?"

"That remains to be seen." He sat in a comfortable wingback chair of navy and gold brocade, then settled in to finish his coffee. "Where will you spend your day? I'm told there will be picnic baskets given out to the parties."

"I haven't decided yet, but I am leaning toward berry picking. Since the weather has been rather lovely, there are still strawberries about the brambles. Gooseberries will be ready for a second harvest now too."

"Ah, those are a particular favorite of mine."

"I remember." The girl smiled. "I shall gather some for you."

"What a lovely gesture, but if you do go foraging, if you find raspberries and black currants, I would adore some of those as well." It had been an age since he'd had sun-warmed berries or stained fingers from the gathering of such.

"Will you come with me? It might be fun to gather berries with my papa," she said in a soft voice with a frown. "As much as I am enjoying being here and talking with the other girls and boys, I am a bit ill at ease."

"Why?" That was a surprise to learn. Setting his empty cup on a nearby table, he offered a hand, and when she took it, he brought Mary close, encouraged her to sit upon his knee like she had when she'd been a little girl. "Tell me what has you bothered. I noticed you were in a mood last night."

The opportunity to connect with his daughter on an emotional level took precedence over everything else. The time for that would become even more scarce as the years went by.

"Honestly?"

He nodded. "That is preferrable."

A sigh escaped her. "I miss Mama." Her brown eyes welled with tears while his heart squeezed. "I think she would have adored being here with me, while you would have had much more fun if Percy had come."

Grief unexpectedly smacked him in the chest, and it was all he could do to keep his breathing even. Yes, he'd mentioned losing his wife to Beatrice yesterday, but seeing his daughter struggle with the same, remembering she'd been fourteen when her mother had died, left him low. "Why would you say that?"

"You aren't one to sit about drawing rooms and making desultory talk with strangers." She peered into his eye. A soft smile curved her lips. Gingerly, she traced the left side of his face with her fingertips then the top of his eyepatch. "And when you do, you are certain to put them on your right side, so your injuries aren't immediately noticeable."

"I do?" He'd not noticed that about himself before.

"Yes." Mary nodded. "You sometimes do it with us." She brushed away a tear that had fallen to her cheek. "Even though Mama has been gone a number of years, I still turn about and almost ask her a question… but she's never there." Her chin quivered as she stared at her hands that were now clasped in her lap. "Being with boys confuses me. I am both excited and frightened when they talk to me. While I understand such things are vital to my future, I don't know if I want to be an adult just yet."

"Oh, poppet." The poor thing. "You don't need to do anything at all right now if you don't wish it."

"I know I will need to make these decisions. Next year isn't so far away and—"

"Hush." Owen gathered his daughter into his arms and held her. "You are far too young to let the pressures of life press down on you. Everything you encounter at this age should be gay and fun and lighthearted. Without worries."

She put her arms about his neck like she'd done when she was small and bussed his cheek. "But I'm to marry, and in order to do that, I have to talk with boys." Then she sucked in a breath. "There is a rout coming soon and there will be dancing. What if I don't remember the steps and make a fool of myself?"

"Then you just laugh and make those missteps a part of the bigger picture." He patted her back then set her a bit away. "Your mama would be proud of the woman you're becoming." With a tug to the tail of the ribbon that went about her waist, he smiled. "So am I. You needn't do anything you don't wish, and if you have dreams in your heart that do not include marriage this early, that is perfectly acceptable. Explore them. Explore who you wish to be before doing anything else. There is plenty of time for marriage."

"Truly?" Her eyes rounded in surprise.

"Truly." Damn but he felt older than he should. "Both you and your brother shouldn't fall victim to society's dictates when it comes to expectations on your lives."

"Would Mama feel the same? She used to tell me all the time that when I found the man I would marry, everything would change."

He grunted. "That's true enough, but it needn't change so soon. Discover who you are first. Gain confidence in that woman. Then you can search after that man, hmm?"

A shuddering sigh left her throat, and Mary looked much more relaxed than she had when she'd arrived. "Did the war make you wise?" She perched on the foot of his bed, then promptly tucked her legs beneath her.

"I rather think it has been life experience." His grin felt all too sad. "For what it's worth, I miss your mother too."

For long moments, Mary regarded him with that brown gaze which seemed to see deep down into his soul. "You talked to Lady Beatrice again yesterday." It wasn't a question.

"I did." Oh, God, did his daughter happen to see that impromptu kiss?

"Were you talking about your earlier friendship?"

"Among other things." Heat crept up the back of his neck. "We share an interest since you and her daughter are of an age."

"Mmmhmm." Again, that far too speculative gaze rested on his face. "Are you enjoying the house party thus far?"

"As well as I can, I suppose." Made much better in the moments he was in Beatrice's company. "Why? Did you wish for me to leave the chaperoning to the others?"

"Those old crows in black?" With a snort, Mary shook her head. At least part of her old spirit had returned. "I think not. They are all bitter about being old maids. Resent us for being young and hopeful." She smiled at him. "With you keeping watch, I know you aren't plotting for me to twist an ankle in a rabbit hole."

An unexpected chuckle sailed from his throat. "I doubt they are thinking that."

"I rather think they are. They certainly look it." Then her expression turned shrewd. "However, I would suffer through them if you wished to have the freedom to find a lady to court. There will be plenty at the upcoming rout, if you didn't like any of the women already attending the party."

"That is something you sanction?" Curiosity prompted the inquiry.

"You were honest with me just now, so I will return the favor." A dreamy sort of expression crossed her face. "If it would make you happy, it would be a good idea. It has been a long time indeed since you were truly that."

"Now who is the wise one?"

She giggled, and it did his heart good to hear the lighthearted sound. "You and I are the same, Papa. Bored but confused, curious but frightened. While we want life to change, we really don't want to explore such a thing."

"Perhaps." God, his daughter was a marvel. There was certainly more to her than he'd assumed. "I suppose we shall have to muddle through together." And he would ponder those words that had hit too close to home.

"Promise me you will chase fun while we are here, Papa, and I will do the same. We both won't worry about the future the whole of this week."

"Done." He stuck out his hand and laughed when she shook it. "Now, shouldn't we go down to breakfast? I'm looking forward to some berry picking afterward, and perhaps a nap."

Her tinkling laughter took some of the tension from his shoulders. "I might take a dip in the lake after berry picking."

"As long as there are no boys present. On that, I am adamant you follow society's rules."

"Yes, Papa." But she said it with a smile as she slid from the bed.

Perhaps everyone needed a bit of understanding, a listening ear, and the confirmation that being themselves was acceptable.

"I THINK IF I see another berry it will be too soon," Owen said around a groan as he followed his daughter to yet another set of brambles. The particular area they foraged through was at the far edge of the property. Already, he carried two baskets that brimmed of raspberries, strawberries and blackcurrants, and he'd eaten more than his fair share.

Mary giggled. Even though the party that had gone berry picking had contained ten people, they'd broken off into small groups of twos and threes. He hadn't minded, for that meant he was able to spend time with his daughter, and over the hours in which they'd picked berries, they'd talked of many things that had nothing to do with marriage, matches, or society. "Dear Papa, as soon as we find gooseberries, we will return to the manor."

When he glanced up and down the thicket of brambles, he frowned. "Where is the rest of the party?" For that matter, what time was it?

"They are apparently not built of the stern stuff as we two." She nodded at him with an expression of pride. "Haven't you always told me that when I start a job, I should follow it through until it's done and I'm proud?"

"I have indeed." It was something that had been instilled within him during his cavalry days, and quite frankly, the message applied to every aspect of life. After setting the baskets on the grass while Mary foraged, Owen tugged his battered brass watch from his waistcoat pocket. On its lid, a lead ball lay imbedded in the brass, for that watch had saved his life the first time during the war. Now, he carried it as a remembrance, as a reminder that life was short and that he should strive to fill each moment with something good. "I'd hoped your brother would have learned that lesson, but he soon will." Flipping open the lid, the watch face told him it was nearly two o'clock. "Didn't you wish to go wading?"

"I did and still will. Just let me finish this task."

Before he could respond, a cry of dismay filled the air. "Oh, drat." The sound of fabric ripping met his ears. "I am properly stuck." He recognized the voice as Eliza's.

"Then stop moving, dear. Each time you do, the briars become more wedged into your dress." Though there was patience in Beatrice's voice, it was rapidly nearing the breaking point. "Too much more of this, and I'll have to cut you out."

In silence, Mary nudged him and gestured toward the area with her head. She widened her eyes. "Go render assistance," she mouthed to him.

Had they been nearby this whole time? Well, damn. "I will return as soon as I can."

She softly snorted. "No doubt I'll be done before you will."

Then she winked. "Go play the hero. Both of them could use one, and I have been all too selfish of your time today."

What the hell did that mean?

He frowned. "Did you know they were out here the whole time?"

"Possibly." Then she popped a berry into her mouth and chewed.

"Minx."

She giggled. "I'm making my way up to reckless."

"I don't mind if you continue to have slow progress." As he approached the area where he'd heard the voices, Owen replaced his pocket watch. Then he carefully pulled aside some of the bramble vines and his gaze met the cornflower blue of Beatrice's. "Good afternoon, ladies. Can I be of assistance?"

"Why didn't you join us before?" A basket of raspberries and gooseberries lay at her feet, and when she lifted a hand to her neck, her fingertips were stained pink from berry juice. As were her lips, and damn if that wasn't the most tempting thing.

"I didn't know you were here, so since the party went their own ways, Mary and I had a perfectly lovely afternoon together." Would she think him weak from the admission?

A soft expression crossed her face. "I'm certain you both needed that." Then she stood aside. "Unfortunately, my daughter couldn't resist the lure of gooseberries, went too far into the brambles, and now the thorns have her stuck."

He peered into the bush. "Hallo, Miss Delacorte." The poor girl's skirting had been snagged in more than a few places, and there were thorns pulling at her hair, for her bonnet as well as her mother's lay on the grass nearby. "I, too, have fallen victim to the late summer gooseberry. No need to wait for cooking them." The berries at this time of year were soft and sweet.

She glanced at him an expression of relief mixed with embar-rassment. "It makes me a glutton, I know, but it's a fleeting season."

"That it is." Gently, he nudged Beatrice out of the way. "Let me help." He glanced at her. "I'm going to hold back the brambles the best I can while you work at freeing her skirting." Then he looked at Eliza. "The key is to go slowly. Once you are freed, come forward, and we'll keep doing that until you are away from the bushes."

The ladies exchanged glances. Finally, Beatrice nodded. "Do have a care, Major Kenton. The thorns aren't playing nice today."

"I suspect they have good reason, for their job is to protect those berries." Then he used both hands and gingerly pulled back the branches. "All right. Easy now. It's a game of patience."

Beatrice snorted. "I'm afraid that is not my strong suit." But she kneeled before her daughter and began the arduous task of unhooking the small thorns from the fabric.

"It's never too late to learn." As the lady worked, he addressed Eliza, to keep her calm. "Your mother and I grew up as neighbors in the Kent countryside."

The young lady gasped. "He is the one you were talking about last night?"

"Yes." Was the color in Beatrice's cheeks due to the sun or the realization?

Owen chuckled. "In any event, if there was anything your mother liked doing above all others once July and August came upon us, it was berry picking. She was always partial to raspberries, and we used to eat our fill for as many days that we could." As he talked, he kept his tone soothing in the hopes she wouldn't try to panic and run. The more he pulled back the brambles, the more those tricky stickers tugged at his hair, his jacket, his cravat. "So many days we returned home with stained fingers and ruined clothing. It's a wonder our parents didn't forbid us to berry pick."

"I never knew that." Eliza bounced her gaze from her mother to him. "What a lovely memory, and how wonderful a friend from your past is here at this very house party."

"It was rather serendipitous, and a bit of a shock," Beatrice said as her nimble fingers moved over the ivory skirting. Inch by inch, her daughter came toward her. "I look forward to talking with him further."

"My daughter intends to go wading later this afternoon. You are more than welcome to join her," Owen said, for that meant he could spend time with Beatrice. "No doubt you are quite heated stuck in that bush."

"Actually, wading sounds lovely," Beatrice said before her daughter could respond.

He couldn't help laughing again. "That was another one of your mother's favorite things when we were children," he told Eliza. "Always wading until her toes were wrinkled from being in the water and her hems hopelessly wet."

"My mother despised me returning to the house looking bedraggled," the lady said, and then with a triumphant smile, she pulled on Eliza's skirt. "You're free."

"One second." The girl put her fingers into her hair in an effort to untangle the worst of the brambles from the tresses. With a cry of pain, she wrenched from the bushes and left more than a few strands of hair behind. "Remind me never to follow the leadings of my stomach again." But she hugged her mother as soon as Beatrice stood. "I'm sorry I damaged the dress."

"It is nothing a few hours with a needle cannot fix." Beatrice dusted her hands together and glanced at him. "Thank you, Major."

Eliza gathered her hat and basket. "Might I go back to the house to change clothes and have some lemonade?"

"Of course."

The girl nodded. She looked at him. "I appreciate your help. Otherwise I'd either be embarrassed deeply or forever stuck in the brambles." Then she scampered down the hedge row, pausing only to speak with Mary.

When Owen released the branches, thorns pulled at his sleeves. One of the more mature thorns stuck to the leather strap of his eyepatch, and when the branches sprang back into place, they took the patch with them. "Bloody hell."

"What…?" Beatrice took one glance at him, her gaze swiftly

taking in the empty eye socket that had been stitched permanent-ly closed, then she looked into the bramble bush. "Dear heavens, I'm so sorry."

For seeing him thusly or the removal of the patch because of his rescue?

Horror rushed through his chest and up his throat. He turned quickly away. "No one of genteel breeding should ever need to see that." Risking having the sleeve further snagged, he reached into the bush, grasped the strap of the eye patch, and then yanked the piece out with more haste than finesse. "It can be quite shocking."

"I'll admit, it took me by surprise," she admitted in a soft voice, but before he could replace the eyepatch, she laid a gentle hand on his shoulder, turned him about to face her. "Does it still pain you?"

"No." He could barely force the word from his tight throat as she continued to stare at him, at the wreck of his eye, his face. "At times, there is phantom pain, but not as much as what I had directly following the injury."

"May I..." The delicate tendons in her throat worked with a hard swallow. "May I touch it?" Already, she had a hand raised, paused it in midair as he held his gaze.

"Only if you wish to out of curiosity and caring instead of pity." He'd had enough of all of that over the years.

"I am not one of those shallow *ton* women, Owen." Then she traced his eyebrow, danced her fingertips with the veriest of touches over the scar that ran the length of the side of his face. Finally, she caressed his cheek, the corner of his eye, the empty socket and the scars from the myriad of stitches it had taken to seal the gaping hole shut in the battlefield makeshift hospital. "I had no idea..." She swallowed hard again. "What you must have suffered..."

"What can I say?" He shrugged, and though uncomfortable with her scrutiny and touch, he let her continue. "War is hell, and no one comes home unscathed."

Tears pooled in her eyes. "I am sorry you had to go away and meet this sort of violence all the same." The way she stared at him, with her tempting lips slightly parted and those eyes inviting him closer would quickly see him undone. "Will you tell me about how this came about?"

"Papa? Do you accompany us back to the house? I'm famished and thought to take a picnic out to the lake."

The sound of his daughter's voice snapped him out of the spell that was becoming all too familiar when around Beatrice. "Not today." Already, her attention was too much, too unexpected, and various parts of his anatomy were becoming all too interested in her compassion. Stepping away, Owen replaced the eyepatch and fit the leather strap about his head. "Coming, poppet. Just had to free myself from the damned thorns."

She snickered. "Language, Papa."

Heat crept up the back of his neck as he looked at Beatrice. "I apologize."

"Think nothing of it." When she bent to retrieve her bonnet and basket, he took full advantage and snuck a peek down the front of her dress. Lace-trimmed undergarments framed perfect, full breasts.

Bloody hell, but the rest of the week was going to prove a challenge.

Then Beatrice stood and sent him a smile, and his shaft continued to twitch to life. "Lunch sounds lovely. I'd forgotten how hungry country air makes me."

Because he was in a mood and wished for a continuance of their flirting, he asked, "For food or something else entirely, my lady?"

He was rewarded by a chuckle. "That depends entirely on the man, doesn't it, Major?" But she smiled as she walked beside him, easily matching his slower pace due to the limp.

Once they reached the girls, he gratefully took his cane from Mary's hand and followed his daughter over the grass. "Indeed, it does."

Now what to do about that obvious invitation? For by her own admission, the lady wasn't looking for a tryst, and if she was, it would certainly need to lead to a proposal. And he was adamant he wouldn't marry again.

Bloody, bloody hell.

CHAPTER SEVEN

THE DAY HAD certainly bemused Beatrice. Between the antics of her daughter and the major's, the berry picking, as well as Owen himself, her mind was constantly spinning.

Once Eliza had changed her clothes, she rejoined Mary and a few other girls in their age group. Owen had come along for the outing. He'd taken it upon himself to gather the picnic baskets for everyone and carry them outside. It certainly looked as if he would try for a nap once they were settled. Now everyone had removed to a jaunty little stream that fed off the river and went through the area. The sunlight on the constantly moving water sparkled like diamonds. While she and the major sat beneath a stand of oak trees in the shade, the girls removed their stockings and shoes in order to wade in the inviting water.

Beatrice removed a glass bottle of lemonade from her basket, uncorked it, and then took a couple of sips. "I didn't realize how warm it had grown today until we stopped moving."

Owen glanced at her with a lazy grin. "It is definitely a feature of an English summer." He leaned back on his elbows with his legs stretched in front of him, the perfect picture of a gentleman at leisure. "So many times I longed for just such a day while suffering through the outrageously stifling heat of India. There, it was so humid that one's clothing stuck to one as soon as the day began."

"It must have been a time fraught with excitement and danger." She'd not heard anyone speak of India before, but she yearned to ask him many questions regarding his time there.

"Indeed, it was that, but there were also lovely moments as well." His brow creased with worry as he watched the antics from the young ladies. Giggles and teasing calls rang from their location. "Of course, there were things I would rather forget, but instead, they haunt my nightmares."

"How often do you battle with such?" No wonder lines of tiredness framed his eye and mouth.

"A few times a week. Oddly enough, they come to me when I'm not tired and when nothing extraordinary has occurred during the day." A ghost of a grin curved his sensuous mouth when one of the girls splashed water onto his daughter. "No matter how hard I have tried to forget, no matter how much I shove those unsavory times to the back of my mind, they insist on popping up. When that happens, I am rendered helpless."

"That sounds horrible." Compassion for him welled, and while she wanted to touch his arm in support, she didn't dare. Not while the girls would shoot them glances upon occasion. "How do you manage it?"

"I don't know I do all that well." A soft self-depreciating laugh escaped him. "Right now, I'm suffering from exhaustion. I had hoped Mary would keep herself occupied today so I could steal away for a nap."

"What happened to thwart that?"

"Her fledgling confidence flagged. All of a sudden, she became unsure of herself and the thought of mixing with young gentlemen left her ill at ease." His gaze reflected a bit of that same uncertainty. "I am both relieved but concerned."

"She is young yet. Don't fret." Beatrice glanced at her own daughter. "Eliza seems to be doing well, except for her getting stuck in the brambles." She snickered. "However, she is still discovering who she is in this whole new world opening in front of her."

"You certainly are taking it all in stride better than I am." He struggled into a sitting position. "In many ways, I fear launching my daughter into society will prove more difficult than serving in the cavalry in India." A long-suffering sigh left his throat. "Since her mother was loosely connected to the *ton*, we'll use that to our advantage, of course, but I fear needing to go through this on my own." His voice wavered. "My wife was much looking forward to Mary's Come Out, but I am not. I don't want her to enter into adulthood quite so soon."

The raw emotion of his admission caught in her chest, and she nodded. "I feel much the same with Eliza. She's a year ahead of your daughter, and even though I was married at her age, I'm not certain I want that for her. Times have changed, and I want her to explore her interests as much as she can before entering into marriage."

"The fact of the matter is there are few opportunities and avenues for women in our world, but I don't want that to hold our girls back." He gently tugged the bottle of lemonade from her lax fingers. "While there is nothing wrong with marriage, surely there is more they can do to find fulfillment than fall into the expected patterns of wives or mothers."

"Yes. That is exactly what I told my daughter." How lovely to find he held much the same mindset. When he brought the bottle to his lips and took a deep swig, she couldn't help but stare at his mouth. What she wouldn't give to feel those lips pressed against hers again.

Stop it, Bea. Such thoughts aren't becoming.

"I hope each generation that comes after ours continues to push for reform and change." He offered the bottle to her, but Beatrice shook her head in decline. "There are far too many clever women in the world who deserve a chance to change that world, but the fight for that right will be a long one, I'm afraid."

"This is true, but nothing worth having was ever given to us for free." With a sigh of her own, she once more glanced at the girls, who were now sitting on the stream bank with their feet in the water. From the animated way their heads and hands were moving, the conversation was most intense. "It is often in the struggle we discover who we truly are."

"Wise words." He again took another sip of the lemonade. "I hope both of my children learn that." Though he watched the girls, his eye held a faraway look. No longer was he beneath that oak tree with her. "Did you know I cheated death twice while in India?"

"I knew of one of the times due to your injuries, of course." Would he tell her of his time in the military, then?

"Yes, well, that was the second time." For long moments, he stared into the middle space, clearly lost to memories. "There was an uprising. Some of the Indian soldiers whose factions had promised to side with the British over the current ruler of the region decided we had lied about our reasons for the occupation." He shrugged with a grunt. "Oh, I don't doubt there were lies going on, but I wasn't high enough on the ladder to be privy to that information."

"What happened?" Already caught up in his tale, Beatrice leaned slightly toward him, stuck in the web his words had woven around her.

"The attack came in the dead of night. It had been raining, which was a blessed event in the area and didn't happen often unless during monsoon season." He tapped a finger against the side of the lemonade bottle. "The men in my barracks closest to the door had no chance at survival, for they were the first to be slaughtered."

"Oh, no." As much as she dreaded the outcome of the tale, she was enthralled, nonetheless. "How did you escape?"

"My bunk was toward the rear entrance. When I heard the commotion, I took up my pistol and my saber, vanished outside with a handful of my men. All of us in stages of half-dress." His Adam's apple bobbed with a hard swallow. "The intruders followed, engaged us in hand-to-hand combat."

Beatrice sat quietly, fearful that if she said anything, it would break him from his story. Sharing would hopefully do him some good.

"The dark and rain showed us to a disadvantage. There was mud everywhere. Torrents of rain made it difficult to see. Chaos reigned throughout the area." He took a sip of the lemonade. A sheen of sweat broke out on his brow and upper lip while he groped about the ground with his free hand for his cane. Perhaps it provided a bit of security for him. "I'd gotten off a shot with my pistol, but of course had no time to reload, so it was rendered basically useless." His breathing shallowed and shadows filled his eye. "The attackers closed in. A few of my men fell until there were only a knot of us left, all fighting back-to-back with our sabers."

She could almost put herself in the scene. "How did you survive?"

"I don't know that I did." When she assumed he'd stopped talking, Owen resumed his account. "Eventually, reinforcements came down from the fort. Quickly, the uprising was subdued, but not before my weapon was knocked from my hand and I was thrown into the mud." His swallow was audible, his fear almost palpable, which was an odd juxtaposition to the gay chatter and laughter from their charges. "My attacker, knowing help bore down on us, was almost zealous in his attitude. Despite my trying to deflect and defend, the mud fought against me, and when the man thrust downward with his blade, the tip caught me in the eye. The downward trajectory continued until he'd sliced my whole left side. Without the benefit of being fully dressed, the cuts went deep."

"Oh, Owen, I'm so sorry." Closer still she leaned toward him, instinctively knowing she should comfort him but not sure how, since they weren't alone.

"I can still smell the metallic scent of blood in my nose." A choking sound came from him. "Still hear the commotion around us, the squelch of the mud, the tearing as the blade sliced up the side of my body." Shivers racked his form as if he'd been transported back to that time. "I laid in agony in that damned mud until a couple of soldiers dragged me to safety." Finally, he turned his gaze to her, blinked as if seeing her for the first time. "I nearly died from blood loss; the pain was excruciating."

"I cannot imagine how you lived through that, how you didn't suffer from infection in such a place." Nothing her mind could conjure could ever compare to what his reality had been. "How did you manage to pull through?"

"Sheer willpower? Stubbornness?" He shrugged, but he clenched his fingers around the lemonade bottle so tightly his knuckles stood out beneath his gloves. "I battled fever during those early days, and lived within a laudanum haze. The loss of the eye nearly broke me. I didn't know how I would overcome the pain or the learning to live without it, to say nothing of the stigma or needing to wear a patch to hide the socket. Vanity, of course, but any man would have the same thoughts."

A shudder went down Beatrice's spine, for she had only just examined that socket where his eyeball had once been, and although the lids had been stitched together, there had been no denying the fact that not seeing an eye was odd and traumatic. "I fear I don't have words appropriate to the discussion."

"Then don't say anything. I don't want pity or misplaced sympathy." A note of bitterness had crept into his voice, and when he attempted to look away from her, she moved back into his line of sight. "What?"

"You won't have pity from me, Owen, only support and anger that such a thing had to happen at all." Briefly, she touched his hand, not daring to hold it when the girls were not twenty-five yards away.

He grunted. "Some of my muscles don't work as they should even now. I am not a whole man in any sense, not even in my mind." The major transferred his focus to the girls, who'd decided to wade in the stream once more. "I will always need the assistance of a cane; my ability to dance is questionable at best, my appearance off-putting when I am in public." Slowly, he shook his head, but he clutched one of her fingers with one of his. "What haunts me at night besides the memories and occasional bouts with phantom pain? It's the fact that the attack was carried out by men who had pledged their friendship to me, who I'd had multiple conversations with, shared meals with and stories. I thought we were loyal to each other."

That was rather the worst sort of betrayal. "No doubt emotions ran high that night. Confusion abounded. Loyalties were probably tested. Generational traditions had to have played a part in the attack." Beatrice sighed. "It was a difficult thing all the way 'round, but you survived, and I am glad."

A shuddering sigh issued from him. Finally, he nodded. "Perhaps I have purpose on this earth still." He chuckled, but it was a shaky affair. "And I pray it is for more than chaperoning my daughter to various events ahead of her official Come Out next year."

"I'm certain you do." But she understood the sentiment. "Thank you for telling me the story. That couldn't have been easy."

He shrugged. "Nothing has been simple since that day, quite honestly."

"For what it's worth, I'll wager you will be quite popular at the upcoming rout. Everyone adores a mysterious man, and you do look rather dashing in evening dress." When he snorted with apparent amusement, she offered a small smile. "If you enjoy dancing, you should indulge in it unashamedly regardless of your cane."

Squeals from the girls carried through the air as they splashed each other.

"I appreciate that, and just the fact I am here to witness my daughter having fun with other girls her age makes me all the more grateful to have survived and come home." Owen grinned. "By the by, you haven't changed all that much from the young girl I used to know back in our Kent days."

"Oh?" Mild surprise went through her. "What makes you say

that?"

"You were always kind and compassionate, and those eyes of yours always showed your emotions before you ever spoke a word." He finished the lemonade then recorked the bottle. "It set you apart from your brothers. Edmund was the reckless one."

She snorted. "He still is. If there is a hint of scandal, you can be sure he's a part of it." Except, her whole life had been founded in scandal, so what did that say about her?

"Graham was a quiet thinker, if I remember correctly. He was more difficult to read. Not quite shy, but reserved. Wanted to be included, but forever worried what your father would think of him."

Ah, dear Graham. "He is much that same type of man, only at some point during his youth, he developed a stutter, and I never quite knew why." Did it have something to do with their mother's indiscretion? She should have questioned him more heavily before he departed for his honeymoon. "In later years, he became a recluse because of it. Something sent him deep into himself, and when our parents died in a carriage accident, and then he took up the marquess title, life was even more difficult for him."

"Which is why it is easy for you to extend compassion to others."

"Perhaps." She'd never thought of it that way before. "Graham did manage to marry recently, which shocked us all. He is taking his honeymoon on the Kent property."

"Ah! I thought someone was in residence of late. I should try to pay him a call once back home." When he regarded her, nothing in his expression gave away his thoughts. "Will you tell me why there are shadows in your eyes? Why you hesitate to speak of your family even though you and I share a prior history threaded around those same people?"

Knots of worry tightened her stomach muscles, and it was her turn to look away. "Not at this time." A sudden ball of emotion lodged in her throat. "I fear that if I tell you the truth, share with you the story on which the horrible rumors currently circulating are based, you might think differently of me. That it might color the memories we share of those long-ago days."

She hadn't meant to let that admission bubble up into words, but it had simply slipped out. Something about the major invited confidences, and she hadn't experienced that since she'd been with her husband.

"I can respect that, but I will tell you now, nothing will change those memories." As he shifted position, he brushed her fingers with his. Tremors of sensation danced up her arm. "As for whatever it is you struggle with? You will find no judgment from me. Neither should you let it affect the woman you are. Oftentimes sins of the past have no bearing on the future."

"Oh." How did a woman respond to that? Heat stung her cheeks as they stared at each other, and suddenly, she wanted to tell him everything that bothered her, that confused her, that made her feel frightened or insecure. "Thank you. Perhaps I will share that during the week. When we're alone."

And I'm stronger.

"Too bad we cannot just go off and find a wildflower meadow, hmm?"

Oh, dear. But she nodded like the ninny she was. "Life was so much simpler in those days."

Owen snorted. "The problems we had were as weighty. We just weren't immersed as deeply, I think." Then he struggled to his feet and offered her a hand. "Shall we check in on the girls? I'm afraid their hems are well and truly watermarked by now."

"I don't mind telling you I envy those girls the simple freedoms of putting their feet into the stream." A sigh escaped her. "Chaperones cannot do that without someone calling it scandal or improper behavior."

"It's a shame society has so much hold over our lives so that we oftentimes can't actually live them." He emerged from the sanctuary beneath the trees a few steps ahead of her and reached the stream before her. "You lot look like a chapter pulled from the Greek pantheon merely to tease mortals."

Delighted laughter issued from the young ladies, and Beatrice couldn't help a grin. "At least they know how to enjoy a summer's day. The water must be so inviting."

Eliza extended a hand. "Come in and experience it for yourself, Mama."

"Would that I could, darling." She stood at the very edge of the stream bed with the toes of her slippers hanging off the grass. "But this week isn't for my entertainment. It is for yours." Such carefree days were long past for her.

Weren't they?

"Oh, Mama, where is the harm this one time?" Her daughter scooped water into her palm and flung it in Beatrice's direction. When a cry of surprise left her throat, Eliza laughed. "If Major Kenton would be a gentleman, you could indeed wade with us."

Six pairs of eyes flew to Owen.

He executed a half bow from the waist. "It would seem my time has come to leave you in the more than capable hands of Lady Beatrice." When he winked, a couple of the young ladies tittered, for he was quite charming when he wanted to be. "And that means I finally have time to nap as I'd hoped." With a wave at his daughter, he said, "Make certain you do justice to the picnic lunches the Cloverfield cook has made for you, and I look forward to hearing about your adventures at dinner."

Then he took himself off, his back ramrod straight, his bearing as proud as if he were still in the military as he walked with a slow gait away from the stream.

Beatrice watched his retreat until she could no longer see him, and then, stifling a sigh, she gave the whole of her attention to her daughter. "Shall I join you?"

"Yes, please do, Mama!"

"You know, now that there isn't a man about, I don't see the harm of tucking our skirting into our waists to truly enjoy the water on our lower limbs," she said, as she sat on the bank to remove her slippers and stockings.

"What a marvelous idea," Eliza said with a wide smile. "What other tips can you teach us, I wonder?"

Oh, my girl, you have no idea. For the moment, she would enjoy this precious time with her daughter, but she meant to spend another afternoon with Owen at the first opportunity.

CHAPTER EIGHT

July 27, 1820

G OOD LORD, THE *rout is tonight.*

He wasn't ready. As Owen sat in the drawing room, he frowned at the gathering in general and his daughter in particular as they talked in small knots while they attempted to make plans for the afternoon. It was brilliantly sunny, and he hoped they didn't waste such a boon by staying inside. Once they sorted themselves, he would take himself off to indulge in a nap.

But that didn't soothe the mild panic setting into his veins for the very fact his daughter was here, and the fact that she would cavort about in mixed company, partnered with young men in dance sets tonight, as the young lady she was coming to be.

"I know what you're thinking," Beatrice whispered from his right side as she, too, kept an eye on the various conversations. Currently, she was the only other chaperone in the room, for there were other young people elsewhere in the manor that apparently needed supervision.

"And that is?"

"You are struggling against wanting to keep Mary young, but hoping she grows into an adult who will make an impact on the world." One of her eyebrows lifted in question.

"Yes." He gave a shallow nod and then finally rested the

whole of his attention on her. "Being a parent is difficult." Damn, but he was certainly glad fate put her at the house party with him. Too often he sought out her counsel.

"It is, and this week is making that even more so." She sighed. "Look at Eliza. When did she grow so poised and ladylike?"

While it was comforting to have someone just as startled and confused as he when it came to parenting, it was also slightly amusing. "I think, perhaps, we have no choice but to go along with it, smile, and let life happen as it will."

"You might be correct." When she gave him a grin, awareness shivered over his skin. "Too much more of such fretting and I will need to find a pianoforte and play until I have come to terms with it."

He frowned. "I didn't know you played."

"I do." A self-depreciating laugh escaped her throat. "Well, let me preface that by saying I teach young ladies how to play. It had been a very long time indeed since I've played for myself and enjoyment."

Now that *was* interesting. "How did that come about?"

Her shrug was elegance personified. "I have always adored music, and in the past, it has always soothed my soul. Why I haven't sat and let the music flow through me in recent months with all the turmoil, I cannot fathom." A faraway look came into Beatrice's eyes. "From a young age, I felt an affinity with music and had an aptitude with the pianoforte. I love the way the notes feel as they flow through me, the way my fingers fly over the keys, the coolness of the ivory, the way playing a piece has the power to transport me elsewhere."

What a lovely description. "Then how did that become teaching?"

"Out of boredom, I suppose." She sighed. "When my husband died, I was left without purpose for a bit. So I turned to music as I've done my whole life. Eliza wasn't interested in learning, but some of her friends were, and such things are valued skills for young ladies in society. I have continued with the lessons a couple times a week."

"Do you ever play for yourself any longer?" It seemed a shame if she hadn't.

"Every once in a while." When she focused her gaze on him once more, her grin was wry. "Music is something one never forgets, and I do miss it." She leaned closer to him, and even though she sat on a sofa and he a matching chair, the heat of her called out to him. "Truth be told, I have harbored a tiny dream in my heart all my life."

"Oh? Will you tell me?"

The lady nodded. "There was a time when I wished to nurture my talent and play on stage. I thought it sounded so elegant and grand to share my passion with London, in various drawing rooms if doing so on a concert level wasn't possible."

What a lovely sentiment. "What stopped you?"

"Life?" Again, she shrugged. "Raising my family. Supporting my husband. Being the daughter of a marquess, but still, even to this day, that silly dream persists, and my fingers itch to return to the keys to see if I remember the pieces I memorized so long ago."

"It is not silly, and if you wish for it, then take the steps to move you closer to such a thing." Suddenly, the urge to listen to her perform took hold. "Or at least promise you will play sometime during this house party…or merely for me," he added in a soft voice meant for her ears alone.

"Oh!" Her eyes rounded with surprise. "Perhaps I could arrange that."

Before he could answer, the sound of Mary's voice ripped through the spell that always wove around him whenever Beatrice spoke.

"My father was in the military. He served in a cavalry unit in India." The pride in her tone was unmistakable, and caught him in the chest, for he'd never heard her brag of his career before. Whatever had brought on the subject, he couldn't say, but the air of the room had shifted.

Seconds later, he was descended upon by the various young people. They draped themselves over the back of the sofa, sat on pieces of furniture nearby, all with expressions of eager curiosity.

"Do tell us some of your stories, Major Kenton," one of the young men implored with the same vigor that he'd felt at that age when he couldn't wait to join.

"Well, I…" In some confusion, he glanced at Beatrice, who shrugged with an amused grin. "All right, but I shall need to keep the content without gore since there are ladies present."

A few groans went up from the young men gathered about.

"I'll be certain to include a few thrills all the same."

For the next half hour, Owen entertained the gathering with stories from his military career, how much work it entailed, how much discipline, and honestly, how fun it had been…until it hadn't. He detailed the scenery in India and what his duties had been, how the relationship between him and his mount was vital to success, how diplomacy and manners were critical when in a foreign country, and then he'd ended his stories with how he'd come by the injuries, how much it hurt, how difficult it had been coming home and acclimating to civilian life as well as facing the remainder as an injured veteran.

Throughout the stories, the young men hung on his every word. Some of the young ladies regarded him with awe and stars in their eyes, which made him exceedingly uncomfortable. But it was the admiration and respect on Beatrice's face that made him the most proud. Being able to tell his stories in front of her seemed the most natural thing in the world.

"Since the major has knowledge and experience with horse-flesh, we should get up a horse race toward the end of the house party," one of the young men suggested. "Right before the ball."

"That sounds like just the thing we need!" another boy agreed with shining eyes. "We can all ride and the major can give up pointers on how to gain speed around the turns."

One of the young ladies—Mary's friend Patience, in fact—nodded. "We can have a small celebration of sorts for the victor, and he can choose who to lead out in the first waltz at the ball!"

"Most excellent!" One of the young men who Mary favored, Owen couldn't remember his name, nodded with enthusiasm. "We'll make it into a derby, and Major Kenton can be a judge."

"Right!" Patience grinned. "There are plenty of horses in the Cloverfield stables. Anyone participating can practice riding throughout the rest of the week. We ladies can go out and assess the property for the best racecourse."

Suddenly, the room erupted into excited chatter and exclamations.

Well, damn. He sent a helpless glance to Beatrice, who looked about her with surprise and a bit of amusement in those cornflower blue eyes. "The other chaperones will have my head." Yet the idea held merit, and despite his misgivings and the knowledge that he was here to prevent such things from happening, excitement buzzed at the base of his spine. Life had been entirely too dull of late.

"Oh, I don't doubt that," she whispered back to him. "However, I don't see the harm as long as everyone is careful. I rather think the Cloverfields won't be pleased if this impromptu derby interferes with the ball that is their centerpiece of this party."

All eyes were on him. Finally, he sighed and nodded. "I agree with the idea. We'll do exercises for the next few mornings."

A cheer went up about the room.

Then Mary frowned from her vantage point across a low table. "Why do the boys have all the fun of riding? Some of us girls would enjoy participating."

Hell's bells. What to say to that?

It was one thing to put the boys in a semi-reckless state, but quite another to allow the girls the same. "We are already walking on the edge of misbehavior by even having the derby at all. I would rather not incur our hosts' wrath by allowing girls as riders." He gave her a grin that he hoped would disarm her. "Besides, our riders will need spectators, and what better incentive than seeing ladies in colorful dresses ready to welcome them at the finish line?"

"Oh, Papa, really?" So much annoyance wove through his daughter's voice it gave him pause. "As if we are only good for that? To be dangled out in front of a man?" Then she stood up and flounced from the room, clearly in high dudgeon.

Owen frowned. "I didn't think I'd said anything wrong."

"Which is exactly why you said it." Beatrice shook her head, but amusement still danced in her eyes. "I'll go talk to her. Your daughter has a stubborn streak to be sure and it chafes against the rigorous rules of society. I understand that all too well." As she stood, she gestured to her daughter. "Have fun handling this scandal in the making."

Then she and Eliza left the room, but he wasn't given time to think about the ramifications, for the young men descended upon him like locusts, all talking at once.

Later that afternoon

BEATRICE FINALLY TRACKED the major down when she went looking for her daughter. Luncheon had been a sparsely attended affair, since most of the party had gone off to attend their own pursuits or were pouting, so she'd packed a basket of food and then gone looking for either Eliza or Owen.

Eventually, she found the major lounging beneath a willow tree on a hill that overlooked a wildflower meadow. A queer tremor went through her heart, for he'd removed his tweed jacket and lay propped on an elbow while reading a book. His shirtsleeves and been rolled up to reveal his forearms, and as she quietly approached, she couldn't stop staring. They were arms, for goodness' sake, and everyone had them, but seeing him in that manner of undress increased her pulse and made her long for another kiss from the man. If she were honest with herself, not just any kiss would do. Oh, no. She wanted to experience the return of the passion that had sparked between them in the hedge maze that first day.

Get hold of yourself, Bea. You are not a wanton, desperate woman.

Yet, she could be if the timing was right. Couldn't she?

"Ah, I have tracked you to earth," she said by way of greeting. "Do you mind terribly if I interrupt your solitude?" Beneath the sweeping branches of the tree, he wasn't readily seen.

When he glanced up, welcome sprang into his eye, and he closed his book with a snap. "You are the only one who I'd grant that privilege to."

"How lovely." She held the basket aloft as she moved beneath the willow tree. The coolness of the shade gave her immediate relief from the summer's heat. "I have brought lemonade and some cold cuts if you're hungry. I promised myself that I would offer them to either you or Eliza, whomever I located first, since you both missed luncheon."

"I appreciate that." Owen gestured to the mossy grass beside him. "Please sit and keep me company. Truth be told, I'm hiding."

"Oh? Why?" After she handed him the basket, Beatrice settled next to him and folded her legs beneath her, smoothing her skirting over them as she went. The rose-colored muslin made a pretty contrast against the greens of the ground and the smoky blue of his waistcoat.

"The boys are especially—"

"—enthusiastic?" she provided with a grin.

"I was going to say bothersome to the point of annoying with their questions regarding horse racing—which I have very little knowledge about—and military endeavors—which I don't wish to talk at length about. War is not the glamourous, romantic notion they assume."

"What you told them earlier was enough, I think." Beatrice sighed and rested her back against the tree trunk. "Have you seen Eliza while you've been up here hiding? I rather suspect she's let one of the young men turn her head."

"Oh, that is probably true enough, for she is down in the meadow strolling with one of them right now." He held up a hand when she would have scrambled to her feet. "Hold, Bea. Mary is also down there with a walking companion, as are two other couples, and we can see them all from our vantage point if we creep to the edge of the hill."

Relief shuddered down her spine. "At least you are keeping an eye on them."

"Indeed. There is method to my particular form of madness." A chuckle escaped him. "Add to that is the benefit that from the meadow, they cannot see us."

"Even better, for I did desire a few moments to myself."

"Yet you are here bedeviling me." His eyebrow rose.

Heat went through her cheeks. "Would you prefer I leave?"

"No." When he laid a hand on her knee to stay her flight, tingles went through her lower belly. "I will always prefer your company." The major tapped his book. "I could read to you from Shakespeare. 'Shall I compare thee to a summer's day?'"

"Ah, Sonnet 18, hmm?" Belatedly, she recalled he'd had a fascination with the Bard's writing. "Perhaps later. For the moment, I'd rather talk."

Unless you are of a mind for kissing…

"Fair enough." Owen set the book aside in favor of rooting through the basket. "While I'd hoped my presence alone was enough to soothe your worries, I can see that it is not. You are all too tense."

There are ways to relieve that, Major.

Aloud, she said, "I worry that being around young gentlemen will distract Eliza from the things she should explore about life before marriage eventually catches her up."

"God love the Cloverfield cook; there is a slice of sponge cake in here," he said, with so much enthusiasm that she couldn't help but chuckle.

"Well, you wouldn't be a typical man if you weren't concerned about your stomach first, I suppose." Wasn't that always the way? "My husband was rather fond of sweets too."

"It is one of the things that makes life enjoyable." Then he set the basket aside and focused the whole of his concentration on her. "I can give you this comfort. Your daughter is clever and intelligent. While she wishes to fit in with girls her own age, I have seen a spark in her eyes that reminds me of the one in yours when you talk about music."

"Oh?" He'd noticed that about her?

"Indeed. Yes, Eliza is enjoying herself at this house party and stretching her wings to enter society, but she is also thinking of other, perhaps grander, things. I hope she will tell you where her passion lies soon, for it is always uppermost in her mind right now."

"Thank you. I appreciate the insight." She glanced away from him and blinked in the attempt to keep the quick tears at bay. "What of Mary? Does she have a passion as well?"

He snorted. "Mary is rather a handful at the moment. And she's not best pleased with me besides." An expression of bafflement came over him as he shook his head. "It's not that I don't feel her capable enough to ride in the race the boys have got up, it is the fact it's not safe, and I don't wish for her to be hurt."

"Yes, but you should say that in a way where she doesn't feel slighted." It was difficult navigating the path they both walked. "I understand the frustration. I oftentimes wanted to do the same things my brothers did, but to do so would cause scandal and label me a hoyden." With a laugh, she gave him a smile. "As if that is the most terrible thing."

"True, and I seem to recall you were quite wild during those days." He returned her grin, and again, flutters went through her belly. "I just want her to have the best chances for her future. Why must she prove so obstinate?"

"Because she is of that age and doesn't know what she wants just yet. She only knows that she chafes against rules." Beatrice touched a hand to his arm. "Give her time. Mary will soon return to the sweet girl you knew before."

"In some ways, raising my son is much easier."

"Men always have a better time of it simply because they are male." There was no bitterness in her tone, for it was merely a fact.

"It shouldn't be that way."

"No, it shouldn't, but here we are." A sigh escaped her. "My husband spent much of his life fighting—hoping—for reform and change. There is still an enormous amount of work to be done before women are considered more than chattel in the eyes of the law or the minds of men."

"Some men," Owen amended softly. "The intelligent ones already know what a good woman is worth and will take measures to treat her as the treasure she is."

"This is so." Another round of heat went through her cheeks. "Mary is fortunate that you are an intelligent one."

"Ha. I fear that I am merely marking the time until I muck it all up."

"We all feel the same at one point or another." She resisted the urge to creep out from beneath the tree to peer into the meadow below. Another part of letting her daughter grow into the woman she would become was trusting her to do the right thing.

"Yes, there is that, but do you want to know why I know everything will eventually work out?"

"Of course." Curiosity to learn more about him fell over her in a wave. "*How* can you know anything of the sort?"

"This." While still lounging on his elbow, Owen tugged a brass pocket watch from his waistcoat. Stuck within the tarnished lid was a lead ball. He handed it to her. "This pocket watch saved my life two years into my commission. It was the first time I survived death in India, and the first time I realized there was something else on my path for me."

She traced a finger over the ball that would have taken him if not for the fortunate placement of a watch. "Then you think that because your life was saved in such a serendipitous manner, everything else in life will fall into place as easy?"

"No. I believe that there is no point in worrying over the things we can't possibly control. It only sours our own existence and steals the joy from the present day." He glanced from the watch in her hand to her face, and she hoped he found whatever it was he sought. "It still keeps time, which is remarkable for all it's been through." With a shrug, he took the watch back and deposited it into his waistcoat pocket. "Belonged to my father. He gifted it to me on my departure day to India."

"I hope you wrote to him and told him that he essentially saved your life."

"Of course I'd intended to do so, but by the time I had the time and the words, he had already passed. Bad heart, apparently."

Life was a series of losing and loving. No one could escape it.

He continued in the same soft tone. "Death has a way of tempering the lovely memories, and though some people say that time heals all wounds, that is only half true."

"Why is that?" Beatrice shifted position, which put her a bit closer to him. The subtle sandalwood and citrus scent of him wafted to her nose.

"Time distances us from those deaths, but it doesn't take the pain from them. Instead, they are tempered with the remembrances of the love we had for the ones we lost."

"That's what I feel too," she said in a soft voice. "Sometimes it seems like forever since I lost my husband, but then there are other times when my heart hurts as fiercely as if it just happened." A trace of tears lingered in her eyes. "To say nothing of my parents. Now more than ever, I miss them both."

His stare was intense, his brown eye as dark as melted chocolate. "They left you with many unanswered questions."

"Yes." She nodded. "It is one reason life is difficult right now."

"I'm sorry." Then he rested his free hand on her knee, and the heat of it quickened her pulse. "Will you tell me what weighs down your heart but makes you fearful all the same?"

"Perhaps." Beatrice met his gaze, dipped hers slightly to his mouth and then back upward again. "For the moment, I would rather enjoy the afternoon. We will be distracted enough tonight with the rout."

Interest flickered over his face. "What sort of distraction, hmm?" Slowly, he slid his hand up her leg to rest it at her hip. Shivers of awareness tingled over her skin. "I could surely use one, for knowing I must attend the rout and do the pretty will drive me insane if I'd let it."

"You poor man." As giggles and the murmur of conversation drifted to her ears from the meadow, Beatrice threw a bit of caution to the wind and shifted position until she was lying on her side next to him with only a hand's width of space separating them. "I promise if you stay close, I won't let you falter."

"Much appreciated." He glided his hand up her arm to eventually cup her cheek. "You are quite something, did you know that, Beatrice?" he murmured, seconds before he claimed her lips with his.

With a sigh, she kissed him back, and then when she laid a hand on his shoulder, he groaned, slipped his hand to her nape, pulled her into his embrace, and then apparently set out to kiss her senseless. And she adored every moment of it. This kiss was much like the ones they'd shared in the hedge maze, and she reveled in the soft but firm feel of his lips on hers, how they cradled hers, how the lean, hard length of him fit against the plusher curves of her body.

They fought for dominance with tongues, but then that intensity eased a bit, and when he pressed a line of nips and kisses beneath her jaw, peppered them along the column of her throat, she explored his back, danced her fingers along his spine. At the curve of his buttock, she gave it an experimental squeeze. He groaned into the curve of her shoulder but then retaliated by brushing the pad of his thumb over her nipple.

Pleasure streaked through her chest, set fire to her blood, but oh, how she wanted him to continue that sweet torture! "Owen,

I—"

A squeal of surprise went up from the direction of the meadow and broke the fragile shell of desire that had fallen over them.

He immediately released her and cocked his head, listening. "Was that… Mary?"

"It might have been." Beatrice flopped over onto her back as she willed her body to settle from his abbreviated explorations.

"One moment." He crept from beneath the privacy of the willow tree, but not before she spied the evidence of his arousal at the front of his tan-colored breeches.

"Why won't it stop looking at me?" Yes, definitely Mary's voice.

Seconds later, Owen returned with a chuckle and mirth in his eye. "It would seem my daughter has come face-to-face with a wandering cow, and she doesn't quite know what to do."

Beatrice snorted her amusement, but she sighed, for the major didn't join her. "Are you going down there?" Would they ever be afforded privacy to recapture what they'd shared at the heart of the maze?

"I'm afraid I should." His expression was too difficult to read, but she hoped he was as peeved as she. "However, I intend to take the picnic you've so generously offered, and once I escort our lovely wayward daughters back to the house, I will find place to hide, eat, and then nap. I'll need to save my strength for the rout."

"Coward," she whispered with a grin.

"Indeed, I am, for if I don't retreat now, I will most likely ravage you, and if that were to happen, I surely don't want an accidental audience."

"Owen?"

"Hmm?"

"Why do you still carry the pocket watch? Surely you can keep it somewhere safe and purchase a new one."

"Seeing this one," he patted his waistcoat, "reminds me that every day forward is a gift and I shouldn't waste it." Then he winked. "Until tonight, my lady."

She watched him depart with heated cheeks, but she smiled and propped herself up against the tree trunk. If only there was more than polite conversation and dancing waiting for them both tonight.

CHAPTER NINE

Cloverfield rout

BLOODY HELL.

The heat from the day lingered in the air by the time the rout began, and just as the sun began to set, everyone gathered in the drawing room. There were so many guests, in fact, that panels of the wall between said room and another smaller room on the other side had been removed to give the party more space.

It hadn't taken long for an hour to pass, and already the volume of noise in the room seemed like a cacophony to his ears. Everywhere he looked, young ladies dressed in pastel-colored gowns festooned with flounces clustered in small groups. Between attempting to keep an eye on his daughter and watching Beatrice flit through the room while the furniture was being moved to the sides, easily talking to men and women alike, his nerves felt strung too tight. Indulging in two tumblers of brandy had done nothing to soothe his anxiety, and neither did the few women who'd attempted to engage him in conversation. While he appreciated the initiative on their parts, two out of the three kept staring at his eye patch, and the third had a laugh that sounded much like a donkey's bray.

Obviously, he steered well clear of her and though it wasn't the gentlemanly thing to do, he introduced her to one of the other men there, then fled as fast as his feet would carry him across the room. In moments, dancing would begin. Even now, a young lady sat at a pianoforte while an older gentleman drifted to stand by the instrument with a violin in hand.

Dancing. Bah. As much as he might wish to indulge, the insecurities he battled with suddenly reared their ugly heads and all he wanted to do was shrink away, vanish from the curious, pitying stares.

Simply put, he wasn't in the mood to do the pretty, for the only thing he could think about was those kisses beneath the willow tree earlier that afternoon, and what would have happened between Beatrice and him if his daughter hadn't been spooked by the wandering cow. Damn but he'd meant what he'd said to her parting, and once the idea of ravishing her fully had entered into his consciousness, it wouldn't leave.

So, he remained near the open double doors that led to an outdoor terrace. The relatively cool breeze made him not quite as feral as he might have been otherwise, and the proximity to the outside world gave him a modicum of peace, for it meant a quick escape was nearby. Other chaperones stood at the opposite wall, overlooking the proceedings with expressions of longing mixed with distaste. It seemed no one enjoyed their duties fully. When his gaze fell on Beatrice, his chest tightened and a shiver of need twisted down his spine.

Dear God, she is beautiful.

Clad in a gown of robin's egg blue, she laughed and talked to a few gentlemen. The candlelight glimmered off her upswept blonde hair, and her cornflower blue eyes held amusement. Each time she smiled, jealousy stabbed through Owen's chest, for it seemed she was well within her element during society events. One of the men took her hand, and she nodded as he led her onto the impromptu dance floor.

Well damn.

That should have been him leading her out for a country reel, but with the muscles in his leg being what they were, it simply wasn't possible. That set was more lively than what a waltz would demand from him, and though he knew how much she adored the exercise, he simply couldn't manage it. He nodded to Mary when she took the floor on the arm of a young gentleman, but he took heart in the fact that she didn't seem happy about it.

Yet something still niggled at him, like an itch he couldn't quite scratch. What the devil was the matter with him? Surely it wasn't the event itself. He'd been at the house party for a few days now and had become accustomed to the antics therein. As the music started and the couples moved about the dance floor in time to the reel, he frowned. Perhaps it was this form of socializing he took exception to.

"Major Kenton?"

He jerked his gaze to an unremarkable woman who'd approached him in a gown of brown taffeta. "Yes?"

"I am Miss Steiner. One of the other chaperones here."

"Yes?" From the tip of her brown hair to the toes of her serviceable brown slippers, there was nothing about her that a man would remember, except perhaps for her intense green eyes.

"I had hoped… Er, that is I would very much enjoy…" She shook her head as a blush raged in her pale cheeks. "Would you like to partner me in the next set?"

Well, that took a fair amount of courage to come up and ask. She had his respect there, but she wasn't the woman he wanted in his arms this night. Yes, *that* was it entirely. It was ridiculous to waste time here when all he wished was to have Beatrice to himself to do wicked things with. And since she was likely to remain ensconced at the rout, he would make an exit, for he wasn't of a mind to make inane small talk with strangers. "I do apologize, Miss Steiner. My presence is needed elsewhere just now, but I wish you good fortune in obtaining a partner. Perhaps Lord Linton? He looks exceedingly out of sorts."

Then he turned tail, slipped through the open doors to the terrace, and then fled into the night as quickly as his limp would let him. *God, I am such a coward.* There was nothing inherently wrong with Miss Steiner, but until he managed to evict Beatrice from his mind, he wouldn't be able to think about anyone else.

Buzzing nighttime insects and the scurrying of nocturnal animals provided an accompaniment as he crossed the back lawn. Though he had no destination in mind, the damned hedge maze called to him. It was the first place he'd met the elusive and intriguing widow; perhaps he could banish the urge to claim her from his mind there.

At the very least, he'd have the long-coveted peace and quiet there and could perhaps sleep until the dawn. A night beneath the stars would do him good, and he hadn't experienced that since he'd left the military.

Navigating the twists and turns of the maze with a brain slightly fuzzy from the brandy he'd imbibed on an empty stomach proved a bit of a challenge. After many false turns and dead ends, he reached the heart and immediately, the cloying scent of roses met his nose, and damn if those flowers didn't remind him of Beatrice.

Never had he been bedeviled by a woman so badly before.

Needing something to take his mind off Beatrice, Owen wandered to the rose garden and inspected the blooms. It was truly amazing that some had closed for nightfall while others remained open. After resting his cane on one of the stronger branches and removing his kid gloves, he tucked the edges of them into a waistcoat pocket and then gently stroked a fingertip along one of the open blooms. The silky softness of the petals was remarkable. Truly, the Cloverfields' gardener had a gift.

What would Beatrice do if he were to gather an armful of these flowers and drop them into her bedchamber? He snorted in derision. She might enjoy them, but Cloverfield wouldn't be best pleased to find his rose bushes fall victim to a thief.

"How dare you, Major Kenton."

At the sound of *her* voice, he jerked around. "Lady Beatrice." How could she have guessed the direction of his thoughts? For that matter, what the devil was she doing out here? It bore repeating aloud. "What are you doing out here? I thought you had a room of adoring admirers that you would be busy for hours."

"That was lovely, of course, and I adore dancing." When she made her way toward him, her steps were slightly unstable.

"Are you well?"

She waved off the comment. "A few flutes of champagne have gone straight to my head. Thought you might meet me at the refreshments table." A sheepish smile curved her highly kissable lips. "It has made everything feel so bubbly and bouncy, but I can never resist it."

It was all too endearing and a tad arousing, for she wouldn't be as guarded as usual. "You should go back to the house." After all, he was a gentleman even if the thoughts he wrestled with said otherwise, and that gown with its damned low neckline that showed enough of her décolletage to tempt any man who saw her, kept drawing too much of his notice.

"*You* should go back."

"No."

"Why?"

"I am decidedly out of place in such an environment." He returned his attention to the roses, but damn if the warmth of her called out to him. She was so close it would take very little effort on his part to tug her into his arms. "And I didn't feel like mingling, besides. It is, uh, not as easy for me as it appears for you or even Mary."

"Ah, so you came here to pout." She waggled her eyebrows at him. "Or to hide. I'm beginning to know you better."

"Ha." Owen shook his head. "Since I arrived at this property, the one thing I have ever chased after is a place to be undisturbed so that I might nap." But he grinned. "Not hide. There is a difference."

"You planned to do that during a rout." It wasn't a question.

"Why not? Seemed as good a time as any." Every strum of his heart called out to her, and the more he tried to ignore it, the greater the need grew. What they'd barely started beneath the willow tree that afternoon wasn't nearly finished.

"That is a poor excuse, and you well know it." Beatrice leaned over one bush and put her face close to one of the blooms. "They smell so good."

"Mmm, perhaps." As if he wasn't bothered at all, Owen moved to a bush that contained the most splendid, plump blooms. He selected one that was half-closed for the night, snapped it off, and then turned to her. "None of that means you needed to leave the rout. Someone should keep an eye on our daughters."

"There are plenty of chaperones who are nothing more than successful wallflowers. There is no chance our young ladies will find themselves in trouble."

"Except both you and I have managed to slip away unheeded." That was concerning enough, but he trusted his daughter and hoped she knew better than he. Daring much, he closed the distance between them, for after everything he was naught but a nodcock, and then he tucked the rose behind her right ear. "Red roses mean passion," he said in a low voice, even if no one was there to overhear.

A slight sharp inhalation of breath was the only betrayal of her reaction. "Why did you really leave the rout, Major?"

Perhaps she *was* owed an explanation. He shrugged, brushed his knuckles along the side of her cheek. "No one wished to dance with me." With a laugh, he peered into her face. "Let me rephrase that. One of our fellow companions wished to, but I turned her down."

A huff escaped her. Whether he exasperated her, or the thought of someone else with him did, he didn't know. "I did."

"Oh?" Apparently unable to put distance between them, Owen let his fingers drift along the side of her neck. "Why didn't you?"

She tugged lightly on the edge of his cravat. "Quite simply, you didn't ask." When he remained quiet, her fingers drifted to the top button of his tailcoat, and his stomach muscles clenched with anticipation. "I waited and waited. Finally, I decided you were either shy or stubborn, and since I adore dancing, I took in the exercise with others."

"So I saw." Damn him for not being able to keep the bitterness from his voice.

"Jealousy? I must say I didn't expect that from you, but how wonderful to know." One of the buttons released from its hold. "Dancing with other men is not a crime, Owen. That is how people come to know each other if they weren't given the opportunity to talk during dinner."

"Perhaps." Annoyed with himself for letting his physical appearance and limitations defeat him, he snaked a hand to her hip. "I *will* dance with you, though."

"Once we return to the house?"

"No. We will dance here."

"Here?" Surprise ran through her voice as she worked a second pearl-and-silver button from its hold. "Seems unlikely."

"Why not? It is a perfect venue, and no need for flowers in vases since there are so many roses already here." It was rather nice keeping her at sixes and sevens.

"Mmm, perhaps, but there is no music." The urge to have her closer slammed into him, and with a grin he already knew was this side of cheeky, Owen let his other hand drift to her shoulder and down her arm. He couldn't be certain he was completely distracting her, but he felt the gooseflesh that trailed in his wake.

She gave into a slight shiver. "We don't need music. Dancing isn't about that."

"What *is* it about, then?" The only reason he asked was to keep her talking, for the dulcet sound of her voice was both comforting and arousing.

"It's about movement and feeling and heat." When she finished with the final button, Beatrice slipped a hand up his chest to rest at his nape. It would be all too easy to kiss her now, for she was very nearly in his arms, and with her head tilted and her lips slightly parted, she was the perfect picture of a woman waiting for exactly that. But he was all too intrigued to discover if they would, indeed, dance. "Besides, I could hum. After all, I teach the pianoforte. It is no hardship."

"Hmm, quite a tempting proposition." It was only right that he tease her a bit, but he slipped his hand to the small of her back and urged her closer to his body. "Dancing *is* a lovely way to converse without words."

"I agree, and this way, we won't be hampered by the parameters of a crowded drawing room." Her voice was practically a purr, but she rested her other hand on his shoulder, and her faint floral scent wafted to his nose in competition with the roses.

"Indeed. Shall we begin?" When she nodded, Owen guided them into the first steps of a waltz, modified for their circumstances and his limp.

Beatrice watched his face the whole time, and as she did, she hummed the melody of a popular song in three-quarter time. Then the music got the better of her, and her eyes shuddered closed as she lost herself to the music. There was no doubt in his mind that she was amazing and talented, and his length twitched in both approval and need. His feet didn't feel as if they even touched the ground as he led her in circles that went about the rose garden at the center of the maze. If he thought her beautiful in the drawing room, that was nothing compared to how she appeared while ensconced in the music and dance. And with each turn about the garden, she slipped her arms more firmly about his shoulders until their bodies moved against each other, various parts of her brushing over various parts of him that only added a sensual friction to what was rapidly becoming an incredibly scandalous waltz.

Eventually, he drifted to a halt and brought her with him. When her eyes popped open and she met his gaze, even a blind man could see the need glittering in those blue depths in the faint moonlight.

"Owen…"

"I know." Because he felt that same desperate longing and desire. It burned through his veins, thrummed to each nerve ending until he might burst from it. Then, he gently gathered her into his arms and slowly lowered his head and claimed her lips in a kiss that left him thirsting for much more.

That was when the simple embrace went all to hell, and like setting a match to a pile of dry tinder, heat caught between them until it was an all-consuming entity.

"Ah, Beatrice, what are you doing to me?" he whispered as he dragged his lips along the side of her neck. The satiny skin left him drunk on her; his fingers itched to explore more of that expanse. The tinkling of the water in the fountain of Aphrodite on a clamshell nestled within the rose bushes filtered to his ears, but he didn't stop to wonder about it, for the woman in his arms took his full attention.

"Hopefully, the same thing you are doing to me." She shoved the tailcoat from his shoulders and then assisted him out of the garment. "Please say you want to continue what we started earlier today."

"What do you think?" Again, he pulled her into his arms, and this time when he kissed her, he wasn't subtle about it. Immediately, he bossed her lips apart and chased her tongue with his. Oh, he wanted to devour her, explore every centimeter of her body with his fingers and lips, but first he would show her exactly how he would claim her, how much he desired her.

To the lady's credit, she didn't stand idly by and let life happen to her. Oh, no. Beatrice gave as good as she got, chased his tongue, even went so far as to lightly bite his bottom lip before wrenching away to loosen the knot of his cravat. The bit of skin she covered at the base of his throat apparently pleased her, for she made a sound of approval before pressing her lips to that spot.

It was both heaven and hell, as well as the beginning of a trip that had no return. Owen held her a bit away from him so he could look into her eyes. "Are you certain you wish to do this?"

"Didn't you promise to ravish me earlier today, Major?"

There was a definite challenge in her voice.

"Yes, but—"

She leaned into him, put her lips to his ear, lightly bit his lobe, and then whispered, "I don't believe I told you no."

Well, damn.

In her, there was no censure or pity, only respect and the same need that quickened his pulse. "No, you did not." Then he kissed her once more, and happily lost himself in the glory that was this woman.

Oh, he might regret this decision tomorrow, but for tonight, lying with her would be everything he'd ever wanted since losing his wife.

CHAPTER TEN

Beatrice shoved every thought from her mind except Owen. Once more she was in his arms and kissing him with abandon. The champagne she'd ingested from earlier worked with the sensations rushing through her body to make her head even more fuzzy than it already was.

And she didn't mind in the least.

As much as she wished to explore his body, she contented herself with getting her fill of kissing him, for his mouth created magic everywhere he put it. Fires started in her blood; passion made her senses sing, and she was once more transported to the first time they met where desire ruled over caution. It had been years since she'd felt needed or even wanted by a man, and with every kiss and caress, he made her feel alive again.

With a grunt, Owen gripped her hips and lifted her up. "Come with me." Then he carried her into the rear of the garden, deep into the shadows. "In the event someone else has snuck away from the rout and finds themselves here, they won't immediately be able to see us." As soon as he moved into the more pronounced darkness and tree leaves blocked out the twinkling stars, the major released her. When she lost her footing, he was there, toppling to the cool grass with her, taking the brunt of the fall, shielding her body from harm.

Her delighted laughter echoed in the night. The pungent

scent of evergreens from the hedges and grass from where their bodies crushed it when they landed, she on her back and him on his side with one arm cradling her neck and head. "This is quite the most exciting thing I've done for far too long." Her whisper sounded overly loud in the hush of the night.

"Once we're finished, I hope this episode will be your new benchmark." He followed the comment by nuzzling the crook of her shoulder, and the faint rasp of his stubble added heightened awareness to the sensations already zipping through her body.

"That largely depends on your performance, hmm?" It was such fun teasing him!

"Oh, I'll give you a performance, my lady." Pulling her closer to his body, he fit his lips to hers and once more her world tumbled and spun about her.

As it was between them, the attraction spiked into an inferno, and she couldn't keep her hands off him. Thank goodness she'd already encouraged his jacket off, for it gave her better access to his form that she continually thought about. Did that mean she was desperate or was there truly a deeper connection there? It was difficult to say, but she wanted to find out.

She promised herself to do just that, but in the meantime, she couldn't wait to discover how they fit together during inter-course. "Owen..." Pleasure pinwheeled through her when he cupped her breast, gave it a firm squeeze as he peppered the underside of her jaw with nips and kisses. The second he worried the hardening nipple with the pad of his thumb through the fabric of her gown, she moaned her approval. "Oh, yes, just there." It was lovely knowing he had experienced and apparently knew what women enjoyed. Heated need zipped between her breasts to between her thighs, and it was heady stuff indeed.

"It's good to learn I haven't lost my ability to bring a woman pleasure." Amusement threaded through his tone seconds before he dragged his lips down to follow the edge of her bodice.

"Mmm." Beatrice was nearly lost. She floated along on a sea of lovely feeling, but she slid a hand up his chest to his shoulder, and as she looped it behind his nape, her fingers furrowed through his hair. The soft crispness of it spurred her onward, made her want to know all his secrets. "Who would have thought that chaste kiss from years ago would have led to this?" Needing so much more, she nipped her teeth beneath his jaw and chuckled when he gasped, then groaned. The raw, rugged, maleness of him infiltrated her brain, and she explored his jawline, his cheek, his earlobe with nips and licks and kisses.

Oh, he was everything she wanted in this moment, but she couldn't help wondering if he was marriage minded.

Then her thoughts flew away like butterflies. He shifted and resettled her head in the crook of his elbow while kissing and licking the hollow of her throat. Then he did the same to the tops of her breasts over the edge of the gown. It was highly intoxicating. "You may beg off at any time."

"Stop with such talk, Major. I want you in every way afforded to me tonight." There was something to be said for being a widow after all.

"I am coming to adore your progressive attitude." Seconds later, as if he were far too familiar with how women's clothing worked, Owen tugged down her bodice as well as the fabric beneath, and as her breasts were bared for his inspection, a gasp shuddered from her. "So damned beautiful, and I wish we were in the full sunlight."

Inordinately pleased with his praise, she urged him closer with the veriest of pressure to his nape. "The trick is how you use them." It was perhaps the dullest thing she'd ever said, but being with him in this capacity was slowly stealing her ability to think.

"I don't know what I like more: your wit, your charms, or the fact you aren't like typical women of the *ton*." Then he took one of those erect and pebbled tips into the warm cavern of his mouth, and she was immediately lost on a wave of stark need.

The way he worked that nipple had her nearly flying. Then he released it and blew his warm breath over the damp flesh. The effect was amazing and heightened the desire boiling through her blood. As her back arched, he worried the nipple with his fingers and friction, but the second he rolled the bud from the root to its tip, pleasure shivered into every nerve ending, and she very nearly fell over the edge into bliss merely from this play.

"It's only you and me here, Beatrice. Let yourself fall." His whisper was quite wicked in the dark, and then he shifted position once more to better press his body along hers.

"Touch me. Let me feel all of it." Her back arched, which put her breasts more firmly into his care. The major followed orders wonderfully well, and as he settled between her splayed legs, he fondled both breasts, took them into his hands, massaged them, tormented the nipples with such care and intensity. Moans escaped her throat and she writhed against him.

Lost and falling through layers of sensation, when Owen delved a hand between her thighs beneath her skirting, trembles of anticipation danced down her spine. The moment he found her sensitive folds, she held him closer, urged him onward with kisses and nips to the side of his neck. And the lovely man didn't disappoint, for he parted that flesh, opened her up to his exploration, brought the nubbin at her center and then strummed his fingers over that swelling bud.

"Oh, yes." Beatrice could hardly utter those two tiny words, for her throat was all too dry. She pressed a hand over his, guiding him to where she needed him the most, and once more he took instruction well. Again and again, he worked that button with his fingers, changing the friction and the way he touched her so that she was always guessing, straining for the moment he would send her flying.

"If we were elsewhere, perhaps in a bed, I would devour you with my mouth," he whispered as he licked and sucked her nipples while keeping constant pressure on that all-important button. "It was something my wife enjoyed."

Throbbing need pulsed in her core, for she had always wondered what being pleasured thusly might feel like. "My husband was never one for such intimacy, but that didn't mean he wasn't spectacular in other delicious ways."

"Then perhaps this shouldn't be our only time together." And he renewed his efforts with increased friction and speed.

All too soon, the pressure building within her broke apart. The need to shatter became too much, and merely talking about another time with such a wicked act in the offing sent her over the edge. With a surprised cry, Beatrice gave herself over to the sensation of falling, of pinwheeling, of floating, and still he worked that nubbin as if his life depended upon it.

"Come again. Give yourself over to it and let your worries go, if only for a moment." The encouragement and urgency in his low voice crashed into the utter bliss of what he still did to her, urged her to follow his command.

With a hand to her breast, she pinched a nipple, and when he did the same to that bundle of nerves, her whole body shuddered as she tumbled again into that void where light and sound and being evaporated.

How was it possible that her first time with a man since her husband died could make her feel such intense things? She didn't know, but she surrendered to the bliss as her limbs shook from the paces he'd put her through. Vaguely was she aware that his hands had left her person, that he fumbled at the buttons of his frontfalls, and just as she came back to herself, he fit the wide tip of his length to her opening, and she gasped anew, for this was, again, both familiar and new. Truly, they would couple together, and it was what she'd wanted since their first meeting in this very maze.

"I cannot wait to feel you inside me." One of the things she adored about intercourse was talking intimately with a partner, in both inspiration and teasing. While looping her arms about his shoulders, she tugged him closer and wriggled into a more comfortable position. "And I—oh!" The ability to form words fell right out of her brain, for he flexed his hips and speared into her, penetrating her as deep as he could go.

"Damn but you're so tight, so wet," he whispered, and there

was both admiration and smugness in his voice. "And this is so improper that perhaps we might need a chaperone afterward."

Beatrice snickered as she bumped her hips with his. Shivers of enjoyment went through her lower belly, for the movement only served to send him deeper. "No one ever thinks the older people will get up to scandal at a house party." Would that they'd had the time for her to fully explore his shaft and body, but if they came together like this again, she absolutely would.

"Ha. Their mistake is our marvel." Holding the bulk of his weight on his forearm, Owen put his other hand beneath her thigh, urged her leg up to curl about his waist, and then he slowly, oh so slowly, stroked in and out of her body.

Teasing, always teasing, and it was the most glorious thing she'd experienced in far too many years. It took next to no time to find a rhythm, for neither of them was inexperienced, and soon soft gasps and moans filled the air around them. The scrape of his clothing over her sensitized nipples added sweet friction to the act, and with each new thrust, her world trembled and rocked on its foundation.

"I won't last," he said against the crook of her shoulder. "Been too long…"

"Shh. It is wonderful regardless."

His strokes grew faster, harder, went deeper, made more of a connection, and while he moved, she took his hand and put it between their heaving bodies, for she needed additional stimulation to fall over that edge once more. Owen took the hint. He worried that nubbin for all he was worth, and when she gasped and her body stiffened, he claimed her lips, took her scream into himself as she shattered once more and let the act hurtle her into the bliss-filled void.

Twice more, the major thrust into her body, then he too went over the edge to join her in that sweet release. "Dear God." A grunt followed as he ground his hips into hers while his shaft pulsed. "That was all too satisfying." Then he collapsed onto her form, trapping her between the hard wall of his body and the soft, fragrant grass at her back.

"Indeed, it was." For long moments, while their breathing returned to normal, Beatrice held him close. His citrus and sage scent teased her nose, and lying there with him while still so intimately joined left her reeling in a way she'd never thought possible after the death of her husband. "I have missed this."

Owen lifted his head, and though she couldn't see his face well in the darkness, she assumed that he grinned. "Why, Lady Beatrice, does that mean you fantasized about me in the years we have been apart?" Yes, there was definite amusement in his voice.

"No! Of course not." Though she didn't wish to tell him that she'd not given him more than a fleeting thought since that long ago day in the wildflower meadow, she smiled and pressed a line of whisper-soft kisses beneath his jaw. "I was quite happy with my husband, and never thought that kiss with you in our childhood would ever lead to anything."

"Well, that is certainly a blow to the ego." The major rolled onto his side and took her with him. "Might I tell you a secret?"

"Of course." With a tiny sigh, she rested her head on his chest as he slung his arm about her hip.

"I had developed a small tendre for you back then."

"Oh?" Her heartbeat accelerated slightly. "I never knew that. Why didn't you make your interest known?"

Would it have made any difference to the course of her life?

"Those were the addlepated thoughts of a fifteen-year-old young man who'd shared his first kiss with a girl." While he spoke, he drew idle patterns on her hip with a fingertip, and every pass over her skin sent frissons of renewed need through her insides. "I had the notion that pursuing my neighbor was an idyllic story and that marrying the daughter of a marquess would have finally made my father take notice of me."

"I never knew that."

"It was true. At that point in my life, I wanted away from my bickering, noisy parents, had this nodcock idea that I'd marry you and we would live in bliss on my father's Kent property." His chuckle tickled through her chest. "However, the error of my ways was quickly pointed out to me when I told my idea to your older brother."

"You'd talked to Graham about such things?" She had known nothing about any of that.

"I did, and those words were naught but the rambling, erroneous dreams of a young man infatuated with his first crush." When he slipped his hand to her bottom and gave that cheek a squeeze, Beatrice squealed in surprise. "Besides, Graham promptly told me I wasn't good enough for his sister and to gain some life experience before trying something of the sort again."

"He didn't mention that conversation to me." But it was no less flattering.

"Yes, well, I asked him not to. After a few days of rational thinking, I realized I had nothing to my name and less than nothing to offer you. When my parents returned to London, I went with them, finished my schooling."

"And then you took a commission in the military. I never saw you again until this week." It was interesting how life moved. "When I turned eighteen, I met then subsequently married my husband."

"Yes, this is so." A sigh escaped him, rife with nostalgia. "We were, perhaps, star-crossed from the beginning, but I won't retract my earlier statement that this coupling was more than satisfying." With another sigh, he flopped onto his back to lie next to her. "On my first leave, I met the woman I would marry by the end of that trip home. Life in the military meant decisions needed to be made quickly in the event time wasn't afforded us..."

"Understandable." In the darkness, Beatrice touched a hand to his. There was something so risqué, yet right, about laying on the grass with midnight approaching while talking so intimately to this man. "She went to India with you?"

"Yes. I couldn't bear to be parted from her, not knowing if I would come back to England, so she lived at the fort, and later, once I gained my first promotion, we moved into a tiny little house nearby." There was a definite grin in his voice as he put his trousers to rights. "That's where we started our family."

"It's an exciting history for your children."

"Yes, it is. When tensions grew high in the region, I sent my family home. Two years later, I followed them, since I was no more use in the field." A trace of bitterness went through his tones. "It was on that passage back to England my wife contracted her illness. We thought she'd been healed from it, but by the time I returned to Kent, she was still battling it in some form or another. My mother perished of natural causes shortly afterward."

"You have survived more death than you should have since surviving the war." She curled her fingers around his. "We all have."

"Indeed."

"Sickness took my husband from me, and honestly, I thought my world had ended at the time, for my whole life had been wrapped up in him and my daughter."

"I know what that feels like. And at times, it almost doesn't feel as if you've had a chance to breathe, to grieve, because there were the children and being strong for them was an overruling factor."

"Yes." Unexpected tears filled her eyes, and she let them spill onto her cheeks. "I miss him. Some days are easier than others." When he squeezed her fingers, a few more tears fell. "Eliza was just fourteen when she lost her father. Mourning seemed to go by in a flash, and I'm afraid I lingered there for longer than a year, but then, just when I felt well enough to reenter society, my parents died in a carriage accident."

"Which made you remember losing your husband all over again." He turned his head to regard her, and when she did the same, the heat of his breath skated across her cheek. "You don't need to carry your worries alone. Talk to me. Let me help with the load for a bit."

"How sweet." A queer little ache went through her heart as

she tugged her bodice back into place. "I thought that if I let Eliza attend the house party, it might take her mind off everything we've been through, but then I remembered she doesn't know about the scandal that has taken hold of my family name since it came out around Valentine's Day."

"I have heard snippets bandied about." Another squeeze on her fingers gave her a tiny shot of courage. "But I wish to hear it in your own words."

"Of course." Beatrice nodded and took comfort in the fact he was here and wouldn't judge her on the sins of her parents. "It seems that my mother not only had an affair with our London neighbor—and my father's best friend—but they also shared a deep and devoted love together that resulted in… three children," she finished in a barely audible whisper.

"Ah." Owen struggled into a seated position. "The marquess truly wasn't your sire."

"No, and I haven't been able to come to terms with that knowledge." She sat as well and hoped there weren't too many grass stains on her gown. "How do I find my identity in this mess, Owen? I'm the daughter of the Earl of Ettesmere, which makes me half a Winterbourne instead of a full Ashdowne."

"While I'll admit that knowledge is a large mouthful to swallow, it isn't the end of the world." Leaning over, he traced his fingertips along the side of her face. "The earl, from all accounts, was a decent man, and while I have never met any of the Winterbourne family, I can only assume they have followed in those footsteps."

"Perhaps. I have heard the same. And those Winterbournes have children, which means my daughter has cousins. Perhaps she should meet them." With a sigh, she took his hand in hers and held it. "Shoving all of that aside, I am frightened."

"Of what? The lady I have witnessed this week has been nothing except brave."

"I appreciate that." Warmth went through her chest. "However, my mother violated her marriage vows. She lied to her husband even after she professed to being in love with him, willingly began an affair with another man as if none of it mattered." When she released his hand, she scrambled to her feet, suddenly unable to remain still. "What if that predilection is in my blood too?"

"Did you betray your husband?"

"No, but—"

"Would you willingly enter into marriage with someone knowing you intended to betray him soon after?"

"Of course not. Marriage vows are sacred, but—"

"Then I fail to understand why you believe you would follow in your mother's footsteps. Unless the inability to have your questions answered is what's driving you, since your parents died before the issue came to light." When he gained his feet, Owen tugged her into his arms and merely held her. "Is that why you aren't keen on an affair?"

Heat slapped her cheeks. How could he know her so well? "I believe I told you that depends on the man, but yes." She tucked her hands against his chest and reveled in the feel of his strong arms around her. "I want marriage again, even though I know it will entail pain eventually."

"Two people can be close without the benefit of marriage; it doesn't mean you will mourn them any less merely because the union isn't legal in the eyes of the church."

"True." Somehow that fact had escaped her. What must it have been like for her mother when news of the earl's death from a faulty heart made its way through the *ton*? Shortly before her own demise? Which had corresponded with the date of the last letter she'd written to him, the one telling him that the marquess knew about the affair and wanted a divorce. "I am not certain I could be that type of woman, for I would want the man legally, in all the ways that mattered. To not need to sneak about and keep the relationship secret."

Except, isn't that what she and Owen were doing now, hiding in the shadows at the heart of a maze because coming together as they did was the height of scandal?

"And I don't want the burden of watching something horrific happen to a wife," he said softly. "It was devastating the last time."

"Then you would leave your mistress if poor health or something else befell her?" That didn't make sense. "Even if you conducted an affair with someone then broke it off later, once you discovered she was suffering, you would still have a connection and feelings for her."

"Yes, but..." He huffed. "It is complicated, and there are the children to think about. Mary especially. I am not sure how she would welcome a new mother."

Were they dancing about a possible future relationship between her and him? "I see." That didn't bode well, but at least the knowledge was out there for them both to think about. When she attempted to pull away, he tightened his hold. "I should go back. We'll be missed."

"Stay with me, for a few more minutes," he whispered against the shell of her ear. "I didn't mean to upset you."

"You didn't." She was merely confused since things happened far too quickly.

"Ha!" He snorted. "You never did learn to lie."

Beatrice allowed herself a small smile. "I never had need to." Emotion rose in her chest. "We shouldn't have done this. It will prove problematic and I—"

"Shh. Don't borrow trouble." He fit his lips to hers in a tender kiss meant to comfort instead of arouse. "We will talk about... everything tomorrow when we're afforded a moment, hmm? There must be a reason we were brought back into each other's lives."

"All right." She burrowed into his strength, content to rest for a few minutes more even if her mind was anything but peaceful. "I hope no one suspects we are both missing together."

"I rather think we are more intelligent than to have that happen." He pressed his lips to her forehead. "You merely tore a hem and went to stitch it up in your bedchamber while I must have eaten something that didn't agree with me, which led me to casting up my accounts in the garden."

"Why do I have the feeling you've dissembled before?"

"I was rather a handful in my youth and the early part of my commission, until responsibility and duty beat it out of me." Though amusement rang in his tones, so did weariness and resignation. "All will be will, Beatrice. Please don't worry, and for what it's worth, you are *not* your mother. You have your own path to walk. It has always been your choice of where to tread."

Another wave of quick tears stung her eyes. "Thank you."

That remained to be seen.

CHAPTER ELEVEN

July 28, 1820

B ECAUSE IT WAS raining, participants of the house party were forced indoors to find their amusements. Since the young people decided that parlor games would suffice, the other attendees dispersed to the library, the parlor and study for cards and conversation, or various other rooms for different pursuits.

Not particularly wanting to sit through endless rounds of charades or watch unskillful attempts at flirting and flattery during Blind Man's Bluff, once Owen checked to make certain there were already enough companions and responsible adults in the drawing room, he slipped next door to the billiards room. Remarkably, none of the men had wished to partake of the game, so he was afforded a few moments' peace.

Immediately, the scents of leather and faint tobacco wafted to his nose. Dark-stained wooden furniture filled the space, along with two billiards tables, complete with green felt interiors. Candlelight glimmered off gilt frames on the wall as well as highlighted other bric-a-brac set about the room. In one corner, a curio cabinet hosted interesting items, definitely not of English origin. Were the Cloverfields world travelers? Budding archeologists? Or had some of those items acquired been given over as alternative forms of payment for their jewelry services?

Not knowing, he concentrated on his own life. Dinner had been served an hour past, buffet-style in the dining room, and while he hadn't eaten his fill, his appetite hadn't been that robust since he'd met Beatrice the first day of the house party. He rested his cane against one of the leatherbound chairs as his mind wandered.

At first, he'd been delighted and amused since they'd known each other in childhood. The chance to reconnect with a whole lifetime between them had been a bit of an adventure. Then, after sharing their history, he'd come to understand her, and what was more, some of her experiences had overlapped his. They'd been united in grief and the feelings associated with seeing their children ushered into adulthood. To say nothing of that attraction, the connection that blazed between them he couldn't quite figure out.

That said passion had finally culminated in a rushed, hurried coupling in the heart of the maze where they had first met still left him in the height of satisfaction, but confusion had also come calling. What the hell had possessed him to do such a thing and put them both at risk? To say nothing of being so irresponsible as to not take any sort of preventative measures. Yes, it was true the lady wasn't young any longer, but there was always the worry of a late-in-life pregnancy.

I don't want any more children.

With his hands planted on his hips, Owen drifted to one of the two billiards tables and regarded it with a fierce frown. What was he doing? He didn't fit in with the people here, and he certainly didn't know how to play this particular game. To say nothing of flirting with the possibility of having an affair—or tryst for the remainder of the house party—with Beatrice.

"You know, every time I'm in a room such as this, it reminds me of my father." The sound of her voice brought him spinning about as Beatrice entered the room. "The marquess, that is," she added in low tones with a rueful smile. "Whenever he was conflicted, he would drift into the billiard room if we were at the estate in Kent. It didn't matter if he was alone or with his contemporaries, Father used to spend hours in there." A gentle laugh escaped her. "I used to believe it was because he adored the game so much and wanted to practice his shots, but now I'm of the mind he was simply working out problems in his head."

"It's interesting how much we don't know about life when we are children or entering young adulthood." When he met her gaze, the emotions in her eyes were unreadable. "Or how we knew nothing of the thoughts adults struggled with."

"In many ways, those days were infinitely easier." She drifted around the other side of the table from where he waited. Tonight she'd chosen to wear a gown of muted blue silk, which made the blue in her eyes more intense. "When I couldn't find you in the drawing room, I came searching. One of the chaperones said she'd seen you come in here."

Ah, then that meant there was no opportunity to steal a kiss or quick caress. "I required quiet to order my thoughts." With a shrug, he rested a hand on the smooth wood lip of the table. "Filling time in useless parlor games doesn't tickle my humor just now."

For long moments, Beatrice watched him. "You are worrying about what happened last night." It wasn't a question.

"Perhaps, but let me preface that by saying it was every bit as enjoyable as I could have hoped." Careful to keep his voice low since the door to the corridor as well as the one to the drawing room remained open. Laughter and chatter from the party within the adjoining room drifted through the air. "However, there were no precautions taken."

Her laughter was a smoky affair that had awareness prickling through his shaft. "You needn't worry over that. I believe I am past the age where that matters."

"I wouldn't know, but the last thing either of us need is a complication of such a nature."

"Fear not, Major. I wouldn't demand you do anything out of obligation. I would simply retire to my brother's Kent property and live the remainder of my life there with the evidence of what was a beautiful tryst." There was a longing of sorts in her tones that gave him pause. "However, I would be lying if I said I didn't wish for the marriage."

"I see." What a coil, and what a nodcock he'd been in the heat of the moment. Needing something to occupy himself, Owen paced the length of the table, turned and then came back. "I have always been honorable in my life's pursuits since entering the military. If time reveals damning things—"

"Hush. I refuse to have this conversation now or here." The admonishment in her whispered tones cut through him with the accuracy of a knife. "It is obvious you and I want different things from the latter portions of our lives, and neither of those is wrong." But the disappointment in those cornflower blue eyes sent him into a brown study.

"I never thought I would see the age of forty, but here we are." He kept his tone quiet, for he didn't wish to be overheard but also sharing what was deepest in his heart was a tad difficult. "Now that my wife has been gone for a while and my children are grown, I find myself in an odd place."

"How so?"

Owen sighed. "I miss being needed. I suppose that's the easiest way to explain it." He rubbed a hand along the side of his face, traced the edge of the eyepatch. "Obviously I'm no longer a husband and both of my children need me less and less." When he raised his gaze, he found solace in hers, and understanding. "Now that I am older and wiser, I wish to have fun in my life, to fill my days without constant responsibility, even if I'm scarred and my looks are nothing to recommend me."

The delicate tendons of her throat worked with a hard swallow. What went through her mind? Did she take his words as a personal rejection? "There are times when I think we rush to marry, and then the whole of our identities are tied up in that other person, in the family we have created, that we lose the core thread of ourselves... the dreams we had before life happened."

"Yes." There was a certain finality in that statement that sent a chill down his spine. "I don't want to be forgotten, Beatrice," he admitted in a voice graveled with unexpected emotion. How she managed to pull out his secrets, he didn't know, but there was no way except through them. "Though I don't fear dying—the military changes a man in that way—I *am* afraid of leaving my children behind with no direction, or conversely not being able to care for myself in old age. Every choice I might make from here on out will have vastly different consequences."

It was terrifying, and he didn't know if he was mentally equipped to battle any of them.

"All of your concerns are valid, for I have had them as well." Slowly, she came around to his side of the billiards table. "With the revelations of my mother's infidelity, my father burying himself in every vice imaginable and leaving the family coffers empty, and my own identity being called into question due to false paternity, I'm feeling angry, lost, confused."

"You have every right.

She shook her head as she held up her right hand. A rectangle-shaped emerald ring winked in the candlelight. It was a jewel he'd not seen her wear before. "This was a gift from my father—or rather the man I assumed was my father—upon my marriage. I can't bring myself to give it to Eliza or anyone else, for it's a reminder to me."

"Of?" But he knew enough about her to follow her train of thought.

"That I wish to be better than my parents regarding honor and fidelity."

"Already you are, if those things bother you." The gist of the conversation caused his heart to squeeze unexpectedly, and the pain made him wonder what any of it meant. Was their time together suddenly given an expiration date? Panic climbed his throat as he looked at her. "They made their choices; yours will never be the same."

"Perhaps, and while I don't wish to lose the woman I have

grown into, I also don't want to give Eliza reason to feel what *I* feel for *my* mother." When her voice broke over the words, his chest tightened all over again. "But I also don't want to live the remainder of my life alone." Tears shimmered in her eyes, rendering them luminous and gorgeous. "I need a man by my side, committed to me and willing to meet life's challenges with me."

"Meaning?" He could hardly force out the word from his constricting throat.

"I have everything I require for a comfortable life, Owen, but what I want for me is to marry again. I desire a husband, and I won't waver from that." Moisture spiked her lashes as she looked at him. "I'm not trying to pressure you merely because of what we did last night." When a soft smile curved her kissable lips, the breath stalled in his throat. "It was quite a lovely time, and I enjoyed myself immensely."

"As did I." Truth be told, he wanted much more of that with her.

"While you wish for no responsibilities, I crave them, wish to take care of someone again, be that everything to them while pursuing the dreams I was forced to leave behind the first time."

"I see." While he understood those needs, he didn't know if he could offer up his heart to the potential of additional pain. Not again. Being a father and finding peace would have to be enough to sustain him. He forced moisture into his dry throat. "I'm certain you will make someone a wonderful wife." An ache had formed in his chest, and it spread to his heart. What the devil did that mean? Was this how his life would end, then? By his heart attacking him in the middle of a house party? "If you will excuse me? I'm not feeling up to snuff at the moment and wish to lie down."

Barely had she nodded with concern in her eyes before he'd gathered his cane and exited the room with as much dignity as he could gather. This was not how he'd assumed the day after a coupling would go.

Much later that night

THE LONGCASE CLOCK at the end of the corridor chimed the midnight hour as Owen turned a page in his book. Perhaps it was a way to torture himself, but he'd chosen Shakespeare's *Romeo and Juliet* to read before he turned to sleep.

Not that he would find solace there, for his ability to find uninterrupted slumber had been stolen from the moment he'd reconnected with Beatrice.

When a faint knocking sounded on his door, he sighed. "Come in." Perhaps it was just as well, for his eye ached from strain.

"Papa? I'd hoped you hadn't retired yet."

What the devil was Mary doing out and about? "Is all well?" He frowned as he closed the book. "Why are you not abed?"

"I couldn't sleep. Everything is exciting and frightening and new." His daughter crept forward. In her white lawn nightclothes and her dark hair in a long braid that hung over one shoulder, she resembled the little girl she'd once been when he would sit her on his knee and tell her fairy stories to her heart's content. "Might I talk with you for a bit?"

"Of course." He set his book on the nightstand beside the brass candleholder.

Mary settled on the side of the bed. "I have a few questions regarding boys."

Bloody hell.

"I will strive to answer them as best I can." Regardless, even if moving into this new phase of life was terrifying for him.

"Good." For long moments she regarded him with round eyes. "I suppose I'll jump right into it, then. How do you know when a boy is having feelings for you?"

Why do the gods hate me?

"Ah, well…" How to answer her without sounding like a

complete nodcock? "In my experience before I married your mother, I wanted to be everywhere she was. I found myself listening for the sound of her voice or living for a whiff of her perfume."

"That makes sense." She tangled her fingers in her lap. "If a boy is interested in a girl, does he often try to find her alone?"

"He can if the moment arises." The trick was to tread carefully with these answers, but that didn't stop heat from climbing the back of his neck. "There are conversations a couple can have when they are alone, but there are certain rules everyone needs to abide by." He sighed. "What you don't realize is things can grow out of hand quickly when alone, and that will lead to other problems, so I would caution you to not put yourself in those situations unless your young man comes up to scratch."

Please don't let that happen any time soon.

She nodded, and her expression was all too solemn. "What if the boy doesn't have common interests with her?"

Well, then that would present various issues. "If that happens, you must decide if what you do have in common will be enough to continue on in a relationship." Was that true, though? When it came to him and Beatrice, they had more things in common than not, but the differences were significant enough that they might as well be gulfs between them.

Did he *want* a future with her, and if he did, in what capacity? Would he be happy with a mere friendship when she didn't wish to have a mere affair?

"If a boy wants to be with a girl, wouldn't he do everything in his power to be what she needs?"

Well, damn. That was a difficult question. "While that is a romantic notion to be sure, both people in a relationship must make certain they are not swallowed up within each other." Yet that was all too difficult when sometimes being with a woman felt much like being drunk on them if one was lucky. "Each party will have dreams and goals, fears and vulnerabilities, and all of that is a good thing. No two people should have to be the same or think the same."

"Then how does love even work if two people don't mesh together perfectly?"

Another interesting query. When did his daughter grow so curious and wise? "When two people are in love, differences don't matter. Two people accept them and work with them… if they are fortunate. You see, love doesn't discriminate. It fills holes and cracks, and merely accepts another person as they are."

"Oh, I know all of that." She sighed with exasperation. "What if what a boy wants isn't what a girl wants? Even though there is love present, will those things ultimately tear them apart?"

That was the very thing he struggled with, and he didn't have the answers. "That is something only a boy and a girl involved in the relationship can answer." He frowned as he looked at his daughter. "When it comes down to brass tacks, they would need to decide what it is they want over everything else, and if they can come together in agreement, there is every possibility things will work out. If they cannot, the relationship will end before it can gain traction."

A depressing thought, that.

"I see." Mary took a deep breath and let it ease slowly out. "Once a boy kisses a girl, do emotions and feelings complicate those thoughts?"

"Has a boy kissed you?" If the question was more harsh than he'd intended, Owen couldn't help it. "You are much too young—"

"Stop, Papa." She leaned forward and touched his hand. "All is well, and no, that has not occurred except for a kiss to the hand." A chuckle escaped her. "I am merely curious and would rather not subject myself to such messiness until I'm ready."

Thank God.

"Ah, well in that case, emotions do have a tendency to manipulate a person, so you must take everything someone says or everything you feel with a grain of salt." He shook his head. "Much of what you think will be topsy turvy, and it will definitely feel confusing, but you mustn't lose sight of who you are and what you ultimately want."

"I see." For long moments, she regarded him with a mixture of speculation and doubt. "The business of love is quite confusing."

He snorted. "Yes, it is, which is why I want you to wait as long as possible before you embark upon it, because once your heart is involved, you will be changed. For good or bad, there is no going back."

"I think I understand." She hopped off the bed then closed the distance between them and slipped her arms about his neck. "Thank you for the talk. I will mull over what you said."

"You are most welcome. My job as your father is to keep you as safe as I can."

"Even when I don't agree with that?"

"Even then. It is what a father does."

She bussed his cheek. "Or a man in love?"

"I suppose that is true as well."

"Ah." Though her expression brightened, she didn't expound on the subject. "Well, goodnight. I hope you pass a pleasant night, Papa."

"You as well, poppet." Owen sighed as she closed the door behind her. He simply wasn't ready for his daughter to have romantic feelings for a boy. There hadn't been enough time for him to acclimate to such a change... or his different role in her life.

Besides, he had other more pressing issues to fret over. What exactly was the status of his relationship with Beatrice now that they'd hit an impasse?

As he blew out his candle, his mind remained conflicted. No, there would be no restorative sleep tonight.

CHAPTER TWELVE

July 29, 1820

BEATRICE WAS LARGELY out of sorts.

Not wanting to be a part of yet another walking party, she had pleaded a megrim with Eliza, and then once everyone departed for their daily pursuits, she'd dressed and went down to breakfast. Thankfully, Owen wasn't there, and she hoped he'd gone out to help chaperone the walkers. Afterward, she drifted through the library, and when nothing in particular captured her fancy, she took herself off to explore the manor, which was how she'd arrived in the portrait gallery.

From her vantage point, she could stare out a bank of floor to ceiling windows that overlooked the rear lawn. In the distance, the hedge maze could be seen, and cold chills twisted down her spine to know that anyone standing here could observe the interior of the maze—including the heart and the rose garden therein. Of course, the distance was too great to make out faces or anything else, but if one knew what a particular party had been wearing, it could be damning to see them moving about the maze or meeting someone within the heart.

Had anyone seen her and Owen the two times they'd gone inside? Well, really the first time, for the second had been after dark set in, and even then, they'd moved farther into the rear where trees and shrubberies had provided cover.

Ignoring the heat in her cheeks, she frowned as she continued to gaze outside at the lovely sunny day. It was the sort of day she would have adored being out in, and though she'd wanted to have another go at picking berries, she didn't wish to risk being come upon by the major. Yes, she'd had the best fun bedeviling him, perhaps even encouraging his advances, but ultimately, if he wasn't a man who wanted marriage to come out of an unlikely courtship, she needed to leave him be.

Even if doing so felt as if she were wrenching out her own heart with a dull spoon.

Which was ridiculous. He'd only just come back into her life a handful of days ago. What she felt was friendship, perhaps, and definitely attraction, but those two emotions shouldn't have affected her on a deep level as they had. One rushed coupling didn't amount to a future. Did it? But then, that was exactly what had happened when she'd met the man who would ultimately become her husband. Her heart had fallen before her head had caught up.

The difference between the two men? Geoffrey had wanted marriage—more than anything—while Owen simply now... didn't.

Because of that, there was no point in continuing to pursue him. It made her almost physically ill to think about.

"Somehow I knew you weren't abed and suffering with a megrim. You wouldn't allow such a thing to confine you."

Beatrice gasped at the sound of *his* voice. She turned about so quickly her skirting swirled around her ankles. "Owen." Even though she'd seen him last evening, she raked her gaze up and down his person as if they'd been separated for years. The jacket of bottle green superfine set off the breadth of his shoulders and pulled out tiny specks of gold in his brown eye, but it was the buff-colored breeches tucked into scuffed Hessians that called her notice to his lean, muscled legs. Those limbs that she'd not had time to explore that night in the maze she'd hoped to feel wrapped about hers. "I assumed you would have gone out on one of the walking parties." There had been two: one for the girls and one for the boys with plans to meet at one of the lakes to go boating.

He waved away the comment. "Since Mary is currently reading under one of the trees in the side garden and escorting the remainder of the young people didn't truly appeal to me, I had every intention of finding my own quiet place in the manor and taking that well-deserved nap."

She frowned. "So why didn't you?" Now that he'd had what he'd wanted from her, why was he still seeking her out?

"I didn't wish to leave things unsettled between us." He gripped the head of his cane so hard his knuckles turned white. "You were upset last night when you left, and I didn't have much sleep, which speaks to the worried state of my mind."

The whispered confession surprised her. "Oh." What did it matter to him? He'd made his position clear, as had she. Even if they came to an understanding, their ultimate goals were different, so it was better to part ways now before emotions were more involved. "Well, set your mind at ease, Major. Tomorrow is the fete, with the ball following. After that, the house party will break up. We will all be home before you know it. Then you can return to trying to find a place to hide from life." She didn't mean for the words to sound bitter, but there was no recalling the tone.

Hurt flickered in his eye for the space of a heartbeat, then vanished at his next blink. "I am well aware that time is limited for the house party." His own words were clipped and cold. "However, I don't wish for us to part on bad terms. Not after we were given the opportunity to reconnect after so many years apart." A muscle ticced in his cheek. "I had thought if nothing else, we could be friends."

"Friends. After… everything." Another rush of confusion came over her, and knowing she'd never learned how to hide her emotions, she turned back to the window. Did she refer to the lives they'd led between childhood and now, or to the coupling in the maze? Perhaps it didn't matter. As she watched, one of the walking parties had stalled on the back lawn, and stood clustered in a small group, no doubt distracted by talking and giggling over secrets. Oh, to be that young and unbothered again! To not have her head turned by a man and her heart mystified.

"Is that so difficult to imagine?"

"Truthfully, I don't know." Over the course of the week, she'd discovered she didn't know many of the things she'd thought she had. Beatrice continued to frown out the window. "I have always been one to value honesty above all other things."

"That is often the best way to conduct one's life." The sound of his voice was closer, so he must have moved to stand behind her.

She nodded. "I can only be who I am, and that woman is unashamedly fond of the married state. For the sake of my daughter, I am compelled to put forth a good example. It is important that you know this, even if you wish for only a friendship."

"Please look at me." When he put a hand on her shoulder and encouraged her to turn about once more, the confusion and upset etched on his face gave her pause. "It wasn't my intention to hurt you."

"You didn't—"

"—yet something happened after that night we had together to change your opinion of me." Emotion was evident in his whispered words. "I enjoyed what we had, what occurred in that maze, and I thought you did too."

"I did, but then I wasn't prepared for the feelings that followed." The weight of his hand on her shoulder was both comforting and distracting. "I thought what I wanted was a tryst... and there is enough attraction and passion between us to warrant such a thing... and the old familiar connection is lovely—"

"Hush." The major interrupted her babbling by sliding a hand to the small of her back, pulling her close, and claiming her lips in a gentle but firm kiss that told her he wasn't in the mood for disagreements.

It was highly inappropriate, but given what they'd already shared between them, it was quite tame, and though she had told herself she shouldn't continue to be involved with him for her own peace of mind, Beatrice couldn't help but melt against his chest. With a tiny sound of acceptance, she kissed him back then uttered an equally tiny protest when he pulled away.

"Why do you tease me?"

He snorted but rested his forehead briefly against hers. "I don't believe I can help it." When he chuckled, the warmth of his breath skated over her cheek. Then he pulled back in order to peer into her face. "Is it me you object to you or what we did the other night?"

"Oh, Owen, it is neither." Not knowing how to explain, she moved beyond his reach to watch the walking party on the lawn below. Her daughter was easily spotted in her jonquil-colored dress. "I was taken by surprise at how much I have enjoyed each of our meetings, but the scandal that has rocked my family remains uppermost in my mind." Her mother's infidelity colored everything that Beatrice was or might be. "I cannot help but think my actions with you will cause me to be ostracized by the same society that is tearing my mother's reputation to shreds now, and that is not something I want for my life. Or yours," she added, and her voice broke on the word. "Or even our children's futures."

"You needn't worry about me. My choices and my actions are my own." He delved a hand into the interior pocket of his jacket and withdrew a rose bud just beginning to open. The dark maroon petals were still tightly folded on each other, but the hue was gorgeous. The major presented it to her with a theatrical flourish. "For you."

"Why?" Despite her better judgment, she accepted the bloom from him, and when their fingers brushed, heat twined up her arm to her elbow.

"Why not? Every woman wishes for—and more importantly

deserves—flowers."

"I see." She brought the budding bloom to her nose. The perfume was fresh, intoxicating, and the scent of roses would always remind her of him. "Burgundy is for simplicity and beauty."

"Yes." His grin was strained. "That is exactly what you are."

"Somehow, I rather thought I was more mysterious than simple."

"Oh, there is a hefty dose of that for sure, but that simplicity is something I appreciate about you." He moved closer and then leaned his cane against the window glass, but he remained standing behind her. "One always knows where one stands with you, for you don't mince words or play games."

She snorted. "Except when flirting?"

"There is that." His grin was no less forced than before but there was a trace of amusement in his eye. "There was something freeing and vital in that." Silence brewed between them. Then he sighed as if wasn't accustomed to the quiet. "Do you remember the last time we saw each other in that wildflower meadow?"

"Yes. Why?"

"That day when I kissed you, I was a young man with more than a few dreams in my head." As he spoke, Owen slipped his arms about her waist and slowly drew her body back against his.

A tremble of need moved down her spine, for he was warm and strong, and she adored the manly feel of his arms around her. "You wanted nothing except to go into the military."

"Not true." The butterfly touch of his lips at the crook of her shoulder had her stomach muscles tightening. "I wanted a comfortable life, where I'd find love and acceptance."

"Then why didn't you stay in Kent?" Seeing him again had made her remember things she'd forgotten about those long-ago days. "I adore the man you were becoming, the boy who had stars in his eyes and a love of Shakespeare. The boy who wanted to change the world."

The sound of his low laughter rumbled in her ear, and she felt it in her chest. "Well, I'm not all that different than I was back then. However, I'm a bit more dented and battered." When he dragged his lips along her nape, she gasped. It was a daring move, and she hoped the majority of the residents of the manor were still occupied with their own devices. "I ultimately left Kent because my father died, and life was turbulent. London provided certain… entertainments for a man like me, which I took advantage of before I left for India."

"You could have had all you wanted if you hadn't left." They'd already discussed this, and it didn't matter now.

"Perhaps, but your brother took care of that. He protected you from the reckless young man I was back then, protected you from possibly having your reputation shattered and your life altered." The tips of his thumbs brushed the undersides of her breasts. "I was in no position to take a wife or have a family so early in my life. It took a year or so in the military for me to see that truth."

"And when you returned on your first leave, I was already married." It was a story that happened between two people more often than not. Childhood infatuations never lasted and neither did they end happily if they did.

"To say nothing that I'd met Lynette." Cheeky man that he was, he moved his hands upward slightly to cup her breasts, glide his thumbs over her nipples until they hardened. "I wouldn't have traded my life—those experiences—for anything else."

"Neither would I." As much as she tried to ignore his caresses, the insistent evidence of his arousal remained pressed against the curve of her bottom. She glanced out the window, saw her daughter moving across the lawn with a few other girls while the remainder of the party walked in the opposite direction. "I just hope Eliza has the same lovely, magical, wonderful time that I did when I was her age." Her voice caught and she lowered her tone even further. "And I also hope that when she is told about what her grandmother did, she chooses to focus on the love within that relationship instead of the scandal."

"She will because you will make sure of it." Slowly, Owen turned her in his arms until she rested in a loose embrace, staring up at him with the rose held gently in her hand. "You are *not* your mother, Beatrice. Her sins, her actions, her reasons, are hers alone, and worrying over them won't change the outcome."

"While this is true, I'm still left in confusion, uncertain of who I am in this new family I have been given." She rested her free hand on his chest. The major had been a constant grounding force in her life this past week, and she appreciated that quiet strength more than he would ever know. "I don't know where to go now, and I suspect even if I married, that might feel a bit like hiding, like giving myself something else to concentrate on so I won't need to face the fallout of my mother's decisions." A sigh escaped her. "Perhaps I am spending far too many moments thinking about this when it is merely a tempest in a teapot." People had affairs all the time in society, so why was she so concerned with the scandal that had happened within hers?

"There is always that. You are entitled to your feelings, though."

"Yes, I am. I think much of it stems from the fact we were raised to be entirely too proper whenever we were out in society, yet here is this huge, looming thing that is far from proper." She sniffed. "I cannot wrap my head around it at times."

"That is understandable, but for what it's worth, I will be right here, willing to listen and provide support when or if you need it." Sadness clouded his eye. "I might not be able to give you everything you want, but I am gladly offering you what I can."

"Oh." That was one of the sweetest things she'd ever heard, and her heart fluttered. Not having the words to respond to that, she laid her hand against the side of his face, lifted onto her toes, and kissed him.

A sigh shuddered from him as his arms came firmly around her, and he applied himself with enthusiasm while kissing her back. Urgency jumped between them and brought heated passion with it, just like it did every time they were together. Surely that couldn't be discounted, but neither was it a firm foundation, for eventually that heat would fade. With a groan, Owen pulled away. He offered a rueful grin. "You should probably go."

"Why?" Desire clouded her brain, which made it difficult to think. Why couldn't she pull him into one of the unused rooms on this floor and have her way with him?

"It would appear your daughter is about to enter the manor, and I wouldn't doubt that she'll come looking for you since the ball *is* tomorrow." He cupped her cheek, traced the pad of his thumb along her bottom lip, but his eye was dark with the same desire coursing through her blood. "Mothers and their daughters usually are closeted away together talking over wardrobe choices and such."

"Ah." That hadn't occurred to her, but it did seem Eliza was quite determined. "Where will you be?"

He shrugged. "Here for a bit until various portions of my anatomy settle." A mottled flush rose up his neck. "But I will see you for tea, hmm? Perhaps I'll read to you from Shakespeare. As an homage to the beginning of our friendship."

"I would enjoy that very much." And while he did so, she would let her mind run amuck and wonder what his form looked like *sans* clothing.

After all, there was nothing that said she couldn't woolgather even if she did want marriage over an affair.

CHAPTER THIRTEEN

July 29, 1820

IT WAS THE afternoon of the ball, but the only thing on Owen's mind was being with Beatrice. When he'd found her in the portrait gallery, it had been an extra boon, and though she seemed out of sorts, he hadn't wished to leave things between them on bad terms.

Yes, he still didn't wish to take another wife, and she didn't want an affair, but that didn't negate the attraction or connection between them. Above all, he didn't want to damage their friendship, so when she allowed him to join her and they talked, he couldn't help himself. He'd needed to touch her, to kiss her, to be close to her, and must have felt the same, for she'd reciprocated those affections.

Where did that leave them? And for that matter, knowing how he was acting around her and remembering the conversation he'd had with Mary a couple of days ago, where those symptoms similar to a boy being in love—infatuated—with a girl?

Well, damn.

He'd need to think more about the issue, for that would change everything.

"Papa, have you heard anything I have said?" The sound of Mary's voice yanked him from his musings, and once more he found himself walking beside his daughter on their way to the racecourse.

"I apologize, poppet. I was woolgathering." He glanced at her and gave her a grin. "What were you saying?"

A huff escaped her. "Mr. Featherington is suffering from a stomach ailment this afternoon and won't be able to ride in the derby. We'll be a rider down, which means the race will be somewhat flat."

"I'm sorry to hear that."

Suddenly, Mary halted mid-stride. She turned to him, clutched his arm, and peered earnestly up into his face. "Why don't you take his place?"

"I am only supposed to be a judge."

"Pish posh. We can have someone else do that." Her grin was wide. "You are already dressed for it, and you used to be a cavalry officer, so you know how to ride to advantage. It would add interesting drama to the race."

Owen frowned. "I haven't ridden in some time." At least a few months, for life had been busy and the ennui he'd suffered from didn't allow him the exercise. "To be quite honest, I'm not certain my muscles will allow such strain." It was embarrassing to admit, but there was nothing for it.

"Please, Papa. I would truly enjoy it, and you could show off your skill in front of the young men here." She lowered her voice. "There might be a chance Lady Beatrice will attend the race. Wouldn't it be nice she could see you astride and remember how you all rode as children?"

Well, damn. She certainly was skilled in manipulation. "How did you know that we rode back in Kent?"

She shrugged. "I'm sure you mentioned it in passing during the week."

"Perhaps." With a sigh, he tugged out his pocket watch, flipped it open, and then read the time. "Three-quarters of an hour until the race begins." At no point yesterday did Beatrice mention she would attend the unofficial derby or even that she had an interest in watching a horse race. "Had Mr. Featherington selected a horse already?"

"Not that I know of. One of the rules stated the mounts were available on a first-come basis. That way no rider would have an advantage." Mary tugged on one of his lapels. "Does this mean you'll race in his stead?" There was such hope in her eyes that his resolve immediately crumbled.

What wouldn't a man do to see his daughter in happiness? Or impress a certain widow? Weak muscles be damned. "I suppose it couldn't hurt, but we'll need a new judge."

Mary nodded. "I'll run back to the house and see if one of the chaperones wishes to do it. You should get over to the stables so you can be assured of having a good horse."

"Good idea." Though, it didn't matter, for a good horseman could urge his mount into its best paces. It was only a matter of understanding the equine. "You'll be back in time for the start?"

"Of course." She lifted onto her toes and bussed his cheek. "I wouldn't miss it for the world." Then, she set out with a wave and hiked up skirting that allowed her to run.

With a shake of his head, Owen put the watch back in his pocket. He changed his trajectory and instead of heading toward the makeshift racecourse, he moved toward the stables. Knowing Mary, there was every possibility his daughter would convince Beatrice to come out and act as the judge. If that were so, he would try to look the part of the cavalry officer he used to be in the hopes of showing himself to full advantage.

By the time he arrived at the stables, three other gentlemen were there. Two young men he'd met earlier in the week when the impromptu derby was announced, and a man a handful of years older than them, the same man he'd spoken with on the first night of the house party when they'd shared brandy. To say nothing of the fact that this man had shown a passing interest in Beatrice.

That he just couldn't let stand.

"It's a fine day for a horse race, isn't it gentlemen?" The comforting scents of sun-warmed earth, clean straw, leather, and horse excrement met his nose while various horses were led out into the stable yard. Obviously, they'd already chosen their mounts.

"Hope you'll judge fairly, Major," one of the young men said with a grin.

"Ah, about that." He walked down the aisle toward one of the remaining stalls that housed a horse. "Since Mr. Featherington is ill, I have been convinced to take his place. My daughter has run to the house to find a replacement judge."

"Is that right?" A light of interest and challenge appeared in the other man's eyes. "I look forward to putting my skill against yours when it comes to commanding horseflesh. Even if you are not a young man any longer."

Well, that was certainly a blow to the ego. "Indeed." Despite his earlier reluctance, Owen grinned. "It'll be refreshing to find myself back in the saddle." And if all went well, let some of his competition breathe in the dust from his departing hooves.

The younger man touched the brim of his top hat. "Best hurry, Major. The race will begin soon. Wouldn't want you to miss it because you're slow to find a mount." Then, with a wink, he left the stable and went toward a groom who waited with a handsome bay mare.

A chuckle escaped him. Perhaps it was time he taught this group a thing or two. Being a man his age didn't mean he was a doddering fool.

Not a quarter of an hour later, Owen sat atop a black horse with a sprinkling of gray spots on his muzzle and hind legs named Thunder, and with each shift of the animal, the tautness of his mount's muscles and the nervous energy therein transferred to him. Of course, the stallion wanted to run. So did he, if he were honest, for this might be just the thing to banish the last lingering vestiges of ennui and perhaps clear his mind of the confusion surrounding his feelings for Beatrice.

At least ten members of the house party lined the starting

point of the racecourse, along with some of the villagers who'd probably heard about the race and had been caught up in the excitement. Plus others who were in the area for the ball that would begin in little more than three hours. No doubt the spectators would move to the ending location as soon as the riders were clear of the start.

Excited chatter and the buzz of conversation filled the air along with children's laughter and the occasional barking of dogs. There were five riders in total, all waiting with the same level of anticipation and anxiety that gripped him. Beneath him, his horse fidgeted and impatiently stamped a foot.

"Easy, Thunder. We'll be underway soon." As Owen patted his mount's neck, he glanced at the rider on his right side, gave the man a friendly nod. Then he turned his head and did the same to the rider on his left. "Good luck, my friend." Not that he remembered the man's name.

"To you as well." With his chin, he indicated the arrival of Beatrice. "Mr. Cloverfield has graciously stepped in to replace you as the judge, but I'm angling for a kiss from the lady once I win."

Owen snorted. "What makes you think she'll grant you such a boon?" He glanced in the direction the man had indicated, and when his gaze connected with Beatrice's, heat went through his blood, for she wore both her excitement and worry like a garment. Eliza stood at her side with the apprehension in her expression, but Mary wasn't with them. "I believe the lady has more discriminating tastes."

"Ha!" The other man tightened the reins in his gloved hands. "Never say you're sweet on her, Major." When Owen didn't answer for fear of perhaps betraying his muddy feelings, a laugh followed the statement. "Should we wager on which one of us will cross the finish line first? Then you and I can race again tonight to see who the lady favors on the dance floor."

"I'd rather not wager anything if you intend to bandy the lady's name about." In this, he could at least keep Beatrice from the worst of the gossips. "However, I wouldn't say no to the winner buying us all a round at the village pub. That'll put us in high spirits to celebrate at the ball, hmm?"

"You have yourself a deal, Major."

The man on his other side chuckled. "I'm glad you fellows decided that, since I'll be the one you praise in that pub." He grinned at Owen. "And then I might have your permission to lead Mary out for a waltz tonight, Major?"

Knots of worry pulled in his gut, but he couldn't always be so overprotective of his daughter. Besides, he would be in the room the whole time. He gave a curt nod. "That would be acceptable."

"I look forward to the outcome."

"As do I." Owen tightened his grip on the reins as his gaze once more strayed to Beatrice. He would do whatever he could to win a waltz from her, and then perhaps they could remove to the heart of the maze and enter into a serious conversation. A real talk that might bring them closer to the middle with their current views on the future. With a grin, he nodded to her, and then shock went through him to see the maroon rose he'd given her yesterday pinned to her bonnet.

What did that mean? He didn't know, but it gave him hope, nonetheless.

"Attention! May I have your attention?" Mr. Cloverfield stepped into the country lane and clapped his hands. Immediately, the laughter and chatter stilled. The house party's host smiled at everyone, and he looked every inch like a country squire even if he was a banker by trade. His wife stood nearby with a hastily created wreath of wildflowers in her hands, which would be slipped around the neck of the winning horse. "It would seem I'm to judge this makeshift derby, and my dear wife has been pulled away from her responsibilities from tonight's ball, but what better way to wind down this weeklong house party than a horse race?"

Laughter and shouts of agreement cycled through the gathering.

Excitement danced in Mr. Cloverfield's eyes as one last rider trotted up beside Owen and the other two. A slouch-style cap was pulled low over the man's eyes, but he was slight and leaned over his horse's neck as if anticipating getting out ahead of the others.

"All right, gentlemen, here are the rules." Mr. Cloverfield took an object from his wife, and when he held up his hand, a pistol rested there with the sunlight glinting off the barrel. "When I fire this pistol, the derby officially begins. It seems the course will run through and over the acreage, around the hedge maze and will end in the orchard on the east side of the property. My daughter tells me it's just over two miles, so with any luck, it'll take five minutes or so to run the circuit." He met the gaze of each rider in turn. "No cheating by coming through the maze or cutting corners, else you'll be disqualified. Flags mark the path as well as attendants who will know if you don't stay on the course."

Murmurs went through the assembled crowd. By all accounts, the derby was the premier event of the house party, and if all went off as planned, Cloverfield could probably be implored upon to host it every year after this.

Owen glanced once more at Beatrice. When he met her cornflower blue gaze, he grinned. Confidence buzzed at the base of his spine. He would try his level best to teach these pups how an experienced rider could handle an easy ride such as this.

"Good luck," she mouthed with the lift of her free hand.

"Thank you," he mouthed back, and then touched the brim of his hat in acknowledgement.

"Everyone ready?"

Each rider tightened their grip on reins and wriggled into a more comfortable position astride their mounts.

"Well then." Cloverfield raised his arm, the nose of the pistol pointed upward. "May the best man win."

The crowd stilled at the sides of the racecourse.

Bang!

"Run, Thunder!" Owen leaned into the horse's neck, the reins grasped sure and steady in his gloved hands, and he dug his heels into his mount's side. Thunder surged forward with the other racers, and for a few seconds, the whole of Owen's world was sun-warmed horseflesh, guttural yells, and the feel of his tight muscles as he found a comfortable spot in the saddle. His pulse pounded. Anticipation flowed through his veins. Sweat pasted his shirt to his back. The strength of the horse became his as the sound of hooves echoing over the ground made an undeniable cadence in his ears.

"Out of the way, Major!" one of the riders called and attempted to edge in front of him.

"Not a chance," he responded with good-natured rivalry. "The day will belong to me." He leaned low over his steed's strong neck. The horse strained forward as much as he did.

All four riders rode abreast down the first straightaway, but when the first turn happened around the maze, one rider fell back, for his horse proved lame and couldn't keep up the pace. A low-hanging tree branch snatched at Owen's top hat, and he made a mental note to retrieve it later, but he kept onward, crooning to Thunder, encouraging him to do his best.

A second rider fell back on the second turn, for his horse had decided to go in a different direction despite the rider's intentions. With a chuckle, Owen saw that it was the man who'd wished to wager a kiss from Beatrice at the conclusion of the race.

It was now he and the unknown young man racing side by side.

As they both cleared the hedge maze and bolted down the second straightaway toward the orchard, Owen spared a glance at his last opponent, but the other man was focused, and since he was slighter, he was nearly standing in the saddle, knees bent, low over the horse's neck, and in essence, he did pull a half-length ahead.

"Well done," he whispered with begrudging admiration as the wind ruffled through his hair and set his cravat waving. Obviously, the rider had learned from someone who had experience with horses.

The scenery went by in a blur; the familiar landscape that he'd walked nearly every morning flew by. He and his opponent startled a flock of sheep that scattered to both sides of the road as they thundered past. There was only a straight stretch of road lined by villagers, all of whom shouted and waved ribbons and generally spurred them both onward.

"Almost there." Owen leaned forward in the saddle. He held the reins tight in his gloved hands even as memories from his time during the conflicts in India assailed his mind. Shoving them back in an effort to ignore them and not let them be distracted, he dug in his heels, encouraging his mount to surge forward. Thunder's muscles bunched and rippled beneath his legs. He tossed his head. Spittle foamed at the bit, and from all accounts, the equine was enjoying himself hugely. The muscles in his injured leg strained and tremored, but Owen ignored that too. He was so close to the conclusion of the race and could rest at that time.

First his opponent pulled ahead, then it was Thunder that was leading. Both of them were nearly at the orchard now. Already he could see the gathered crowd at the end of the avenue where victory would be declared. Neck and neck, they flew through the entrance to the orchard. Small green apples were beginning to populate on the trees; elsewhere there were pear and walnut trees that would bear fruit soon, but he couldn't spare a moment's glance, for both he and the other rider rode close together and were well-matched.

It would be anyone's guess who hit the ribbon first.

Calls and whoops of excitement drifted to his ears. Within such concentration, it was jarring. His horse tossed his head while the whites of his eyes showed. Obviously, the horse didn't like the distraction either.

"Focus," he warned Thunder. "Don't pay them any mind." Owen could scarcely breathe, so tight was his chest, so fast was his heartbeat, but they were almost there. "I'll make sure you get a double portion of oats tonight if you extend yourself," he told the horse.

Then a youth shouted from his perch hanging off a tree

branch that stretched out over the path. It gave Owen a start but caused Thunder to snort and miss a step. The rider to his side had similar issues as that horse spooked as well.

"Damn it. Settle, Thunder!" He tried to refocus his horse's attention, but no amount of tugging on the reins or guidance with his knees had an effect. The other rider pulled inches ahead and then Thunder followed, stole a bit of space from the competition. "That's it." The roar and cheer of the gathered crowds reached his ears, but then another boy swung down from his own branch, nearly knocked Owen from the saddle, but it was enough to thoroughly unnerve his horse.

With a great whinny, Thunder slowed then reared on his hind legs. Owen clung to the reins, clenched his legs to the saddle, and all would have been well, for he'd been familiar with such actions while in the military, but the other horse, perhaps unused to such drama, spooked further. That second equine reared and bucked.

A cry of alarm issued from its rider, and Owen's heart nearly stopped its frantic beating, for he recognized that voice.

"Mary?" Daring to turn his head and glance at the imperiled rider, the blood froze in his veins, for the cap had fallen from the head. Indeed, it was his daughter dressed in a boy's clothing and riding astride the damned horse. Of course, he'd taught her that skill, but that didn't mean she should have done it today.

There was nothing he could do, for though he could have maintained control of his own steed, she wasn't as experienced and was on an unfamiliar mount besides. As the horse bucked again, terror prolled one word from Mary's throat.

"Papa!"

As he wrestled with Thunder's reins and tried his best to keep his seat, he watched in horror as his daughter was pitched from the saddle, flung over the horse's head, and then launched into the air. A cry of pain let him know that she'd landed hard, but he couldn't see where, for the scene had discomfited Thunder to the point that all he wanted to do was see Owen off his back.

"Shit!"

When Thunder reared again, Owen finally lost control. There was a feeling of being weightless for a few seconds before he fell heavily to the hard-packed earth. The back of his head hit a decent-sized rock to one side of the path where he would often sit and catch his breath during his morning rambles around the property. Stars burst behind his eye. Pain exploded through his head. His whole body felt extremely heavy. "Mary?" But his daughter didn't answer. When he attempted to move, the pain held him immobile as his head spun. A groan left his throat and darkness crept in at the edges of his vision.

From what felt like a long way off, the cheers from seconds before had changed into shouts and cries of alarm and dismay. He had no idea where the horses had gone. "Where is my daughter?" He couldn't move, for the sucking darkness pressed deeper around him, pulling at him, wanting him greedily in the vortex.

"Owen!" So much horror and fear rose on that word from Beatrice that he fought valiantly against the darkness.

As he faded quickly from consciousness, he became aware of that lady running toward him with a group of people behind her, and the bright marigold color of her dress would always be fixed in his mind. God, he really had come to rely on her in such a short period of time, had looked forward to seeing her every day. "Beatrice." He stretched out an arm, but that proved to be too much for his body to handle.

The pain in his head increased. What had happened to Mary? But he couldn't get to her, couldn't move, couldn't see as the darkness closed in around him.

Bloody hell. I didn't figure this would happen…

With a tiny sigh, he let the inky void swallow him whole. At least then the pain, the worry, would cease.

CHAPTER FOURTEEN

*O*H, *DEAR GOD!*

Beatrice couldn't think, couldn't breathe, couldn't do anything except run down the rutted path in the middle of the orchard in an effort to reach one of the two fallen riders.

"Why was Mary in the race?" she asked of Eliza, who easily kept pace with her.

"She wanted it kept a secret," the girl responded in some breathlessness. "Wished to show her father that she was every bit as good a rider as the boys."

"Well, it was evident for as long as she kept her seat, but they're both hurt." Who to go to first? Who was injured the worst?

"You help the major. I'll check on Mary." A note of command echoed in her daughter's voice that gave her pause.

"Are you certain?" Never had Eliza wished to help with such things before.

"Mama, I have never been more sure of anything in my life." Then, with a nod, the girl veered off the path to kneel at Mary's side.

That bore further investigation, but not now. Not when Owen lay in a lifeless slump on the ground with one arm outstretched.

An ache set up around her heart. Vaguely, she was aware that a circle of onlookers had formed around them as she fell to her knees at his side. "Owen?" Gently, she took one of his gloved hands in hers while peering into his face. *Oh, he's entirely too pale.* His dark lashes lay against his cheek. When he didn't answer her or even stir, cold fear twisted down her spine. "Say something."

Please don't be dead.

The murmurs of the people around her, the concern in their eyes, the calls for help, all faded into the background as her heart beat thudded hard through her veins. "Owen?" Desperate to ascertain his level of injury, she drew her hands down his arms, his legs, over his ribcage in the quest to find broken bones. When none were apparent, she quickly examined his head, and a cry of dismay left her throat when blood stained her gloves. "Well, you have quite the lump back here," she whispered to him.

A glance about showed matching blood on a large rock nearby. He must have hit his head on that after being thrown from his horse.

Frantic and with a tight chest, Beatrice leaned over him and put her ear to his chest. There was a pulse, but it was faint. Then she listened for breathing. His chest rose and fell, but all too shallowly. "Damn you, Major, for putting yourself at risk," she whispered.

With tears in her eyes, she slipped her arms beneath his shoulders and tugged his upper body into her lap regardless of the disheveled state of her skirting and the fact the fabric rose up her legs while she did so. Let the damned gossips of the group tear her to ribbons. She was beyond caring. As best she could, she let his head rest against her breast. It didn't flop about as it would if his neck had been broken, so she breathed a small sigh of relief for that, but when she glanced down at him, a sob wrenched from her throat. A streak of red stained her bodice. It was a healthy amount, and they needed to stem it soon.

"He's hurt and bleeding quite a lot." Tears stung her eyes, and she blinked them away. There would be time enough to lose her composure in the privacy of her room. "Someone go for help.

The major remains unconscious and will need assistance back to the house."

Mr. Cloverfield was there with shock etched on his face. "Of course. I'll gather some men together and find a wagon." As he left, he took several people with him. The orders he issued rang with worry, but at least someone was sent to track down the horses.

"Thank you." She cast a frantic glance about the area. When the remaining crowd shifted, she could barely see Eliza as she helped Mary into a sitting position. "How is Miss Kenton?"

"Mary is bruised and shaken but she will recover nicely," Eliza hollered over, and the relief in her voice was evident.

"Good." When Mrs. Cloverfield came into her line of vision, Beatrice met her gaze. "Get Mary back to the house."

"We're waiting on the wagon. The ball will, of course, be postponed, and my husband has sent someone to fetch a physician. He lives not far from here, and would have attended the ball tonight in any event."

"I'm glad to hear that." During the whole exchange, Owen didn't wake. "I fear the bump on the head might have hurt his brain." After surviving the war—twice—would an ill-advised horse race be the thing that ushered him off this mortal coil?

"It's in God's hands now, dear." The woman, probably of an age with Beatrice, laid a comforting hand on her shoulder. "Try not to fret."

Beatrice snorted. "Easier said than done." She finger-combed Owen's hair, but the continual bleeding discomfited her. "Will you please reassure Miss Kenton her father lives but that's he's currently unconscious?"

"Of course." With a sad smile, Mrs. Cloverfield went across the lane with a few ladies trailing behind her.

Most of the young people had gathered about Mary and Eliza, which gave Beatrice a bit of peace. She glanced down into Owen's face, and the muscles in her belly pulled tight with concern. "Please come back to me." Then she pressed her lips to his, but not even that could make him stir.

Moments later, Mary came into her sight, supported by Eliza. Worry lay stamped across both girls' faces, but the panic in Mary's eyes tore at her heart. "Lady Beatrice, is my father...?" A half-stifled sob stole away the remainder of her words.

"He lives, but he hasn't regained consciousness." She glanced at the girl, and when Mary fell to her knees at his side, tears filled her eyes. "How are you?" The girl's face featured scratches and bruises, and she held her left arm in her right.

"I'm achy but that is nothing compared to what my father has suffered." She brushed the fingers of her right hand over his forehead. "Do you believe he will be all right?"

"That is the hope as well as the assumption, but we will need to be vigilant until he wakes, and we can assess his health." When shouts went up in the distance, she glanced over, for the wagon was on its way. "Help is arriving and soon we'll have the doctor look at him. Keep the faith, Mary. He has survived far worse than this."

"Oh, I am so frightened." Mary took his hand and held it. "I cannot lose him."

"I know exactly how you feel," Beatrice said softly with another glance into Owen's face. He seemed so peaceful and finally had the rest he'd wanted.

If only it wasn't in such a horrid way.

Ignoring the approaching wagon and the crowd of people that came with it, she tried to regulate her shallow breathing. The budding feelings she'd recently become aware of might go deeper than she first thought. Yes, a certain sense of nostalgia remained between them for the old friendship they'd had in childhood, but seeing him again this week had sparked something different entirely. And after that coupling, other emotions had sneaked in to further muddle things. Where she wanted forever, he wanted temporary and no commitments.

But what of love? Were those feelings in play? Perhaps it was too soon to tell.

Then there was no more time for ruminations, for a contingent of males descended—gentlemen, youths, and servants—and after they gently encouraged the ladies away from Owen and Mary, Mr. Cloverfield kneeled on one knee at Beatrice's side.

"We are going to take Major Kenton and place him in the wagon bed. Some of the boys have fashioned a pallet of sorts so he'll be comfortable as we take him up to the manor."

Slowly, Beatrice nodded, but her heartbeat rushed like mad, and she held Owen all the tighter against her. "I should like to come with you."

"No, it needs to be me." Mary struggled to her feet, supported by Eliza. "I'm his daughter, and if something happens to him between here and there…" The delicate tendons of her throat worked with a hard swallow.

"Agreed," Beatrice whispered with a look at Mr. Cloverfield. "Please, be careful. We don't know the extent of his head injury."

"I will look after him as if he were my own brother."

Eliza touched a hand to her shoulder. "It's all right, Mama. By the time the major arrives at the house, the doctor will be there."

"Fine." With a poorly stifled sob, she let go of Owen's form as Mr. Cloverfield and one of the young men picked him up between them. "Watch his head." Immediately, she mourned the loss of his warmth and the solid press of his body against hers. Panic climbed her throat. Anxiety knotted through her insides.

Please, Owen, wake up!

Mary followed them, but she was all too pale herself, and she was far too unconcerned about appearing in front of most of the house party clad in male's clothing. Someone would need to caution her against being a hoyden.

Just not now.

"Come on, Mama. Let's get you back as well. You look a fright." Eliza assisted Beatrice to her feet and then slipped an arm about her waist. "You need a rest and some tea. After the physician has examined the major, I'll sit with him a bit."

"I should—"

"No." Her daughter shook her head. "You have had quite the shock; we all have. You rest first, then you can relieve me after."

When had her daughter grown so mature? It was both refreshing and relieving. "Thank you. I appreciate the concern." And the girl was right. She couldn't care for Owen if she burned her own candle at both ends.

As the longcase clock at the end of the corridor chimed the seven o'clock hour, Beatrice entered Owen's bedchamber. Eliza glanced up from the book in her lap. She sat at the bedside in a straight-backed wooden chair. The beginnings of sunset shone through the window behind her, and they were both brilliant and sad in their vivid coloring. The glass had been thrown open to allow a faint breeze into the room, and already there was a vase full of cut roses resting on the bureau top.

No doubt Mrs. Cloverfield's handiwork.

"Has there been any change?" One glance at Owen on the bed and a chill twisted down her spine. Strips of cotton had been wrapped about his head to stem the bleeding, but there were faint shadows beneath his eye that seemed all the more purple for the pallor of his skin. The eyepatch served as a grim reminder that he'd already seen trauma in his life. The bedclothes had been pulled up to his chin, but it was all too obvious he'd been stripped to the waist. What she wouldn't give to have a look at his chest! The peeks of chestnut hair that stuck up from the bandages were a sad reminder of the lively man he'd been not five hours past.

"I'm afraid not." Her daughter closed the book—Shakespeare's *Romeo and Juliet*—and then laid it on the bedside table. Clearly, she'd indulged in Owen's personal collection. From the looks of it, he'd brought at least ten books with him. They lay scattered about the room as if he'd chosen to read them depending on his location or mood. "But he is resting comfortably and the bleeding from his head has stopped. His pulse is also normal."

"Good." Beatrice frowned at the man on the bed. "What did the physician say?"

"Much of what we already considered. That we won't know anything until he awakes. Speech and memory cannot be measured before then." Eliza covered a yawn with the back of her hand. She gestured to a brown bottle resting on the bedside table. "He left laudanum for the pain when the major does wake."

Beatrice glanced at the bottle and shuddered, for it was all too real. "Let us hope he will be able to make use of the drug if the pain proves too much, but I hope he suffers no serious injuries." She sighed, for waiting was never her strong suit. "How are *you* feeling?"

"I am worried, of course, but now I'm wondering about you." She moved closer, and the cloying scent of roses only made her remember the times with Owen at the heart of the maze. "Do you have an interest or even an affinity in healing the sick or injured?"

A dainty blush stained her daughter's cheeks. "More and more I feel that I might."

"There is nothing to be ashamed of." Beatrice tucked a stray lock of hair behind Eliza's ear. "You are young enough that you have the freedom to explore everything before any sort of decision needs made."

"What do you mean?"

"Just this." A sigh escaped her. "I married your father when I was around your age. Because of that, my dreams of perhaps playing pianoforte on stage or professionally were forgotten." When her daughter frowned, Beatrice smiled and patted her shoulder. "Not that I would trade motherhood or being a wife. That life was quite lovely."

"But I'm growing into adulthood and Papa is gone," Eliza finished in a soft voice. "You are wondering if perhaps you made a mistake."

"Not a mistake."

Her daughter flashed a knowing smile. "Yes, but you wish for me to pursue the healing arts if that is where my heart lies, before I enter society with the intent of catching a husband."

"You are a clever girl, I think." She nodded. "There is nothing wrong with postponing your Come Out for a year or two. Or, conversely, you may have said Come Out if only to stay current with your friends, but you needn't marry that year or the next."

"Ah, Mama, you're adorable." Eliza stood and then threw her arms about Beatrice. "Thank you. I will think over your words, for I do feel pulled to see where learning nursing skills leads."

"Then chase that." She hugged her daughter close. "Besides, any gentleman worth his salt will support your dreams, so keep that in mind as well."

"I promise." Then she glanced at Owen before meeting Beatrice's gaze once more. "You know, Mama, it's not too late for you either."

"Meaning?"

A knowing light jumped into Eliza's eyes. "Dreams aren't merely for the young. There is still plenty of time in life to do whatever you wish to pursue."

Heat slapped at her cheeks. "It seems there is much to think about for both of us." Now was not the time to discuss such things with her daughter. "Do you want me to relieve you?"

"Not right now." Despite telling herself not to, Beatrice glanced at Owen. It was slightly terrifying that he hadn't woken yet. "I'm going to check in on Mary. Keep me apprised of the major's condition?"

"Of course. Mary was in earlier, but I sent her back to her bed."

"I appreciate your caring and concern." She offered an encouraging smile she didn't quite feel. "You will make a lovely nurse or apothecary if that is the path you choose."

"It is all so exciting that I can't dare to hope." Eliza waved her off. "Make sure Mary is resting. She's been so banged up that those bruises will be setting in, and her worry will make her want to shake off the feelings of restlessness."

Beatrice paused at the door. "Where did you learn such things?"

Her daughter shrugged. "Instinct, I think, and observation. Taking an interest."

"I'll see she's tucked into bed. No doubt she'll have many visitors tomorrow." The trip to the other end of corridor took very little time. Even on this level of the manor, the feeling of subdued sadness could be felt, for instead of a ball, there was worry. At the girl's open door, she paused. "Mary?"

The young lady sitting on her bed beneath the covers glanced up with a smile. "Lady Beatrice! Come in." She waved her into the room. "How is Papa?"

"He is the same, I'm afraid, but his bleeding has stopped." Beatrice perched on a comfortable brocade chair near the bedside. "Don't give up on him; I haven't. Your father is quite a fighter."

"He has always been lucky, or so he's made it seem from his stories." The girl set aside a sketchbook where she'd been drawing a picture of a horse. "He *will* wake up, won't he?"

"Yes, I believe he will." She laid a hand on Mary's arm. "The man I know would never want to be so far away from you. He loves you and your brother very much."

Tears welled in the girl's eyes. "I love him too, and though I antagonize him because he thinks I'm still a child, if I had known this would have happened…" She shook her head. "I wouldn't have snuck into the race dressed like a boy, wouldn't have lied to Papa…"

"Oh, dearest, I know you wouldn't have." There was so much guilt and doubt in the young lady's countenance that it stirred up her own. Beatrice left the chair and resituated herself on the edge of the bed. Impulsively, she gave Mary a hug, and when the girl clung to her, she held her even tighter. "Believe it or not, we as parents don't have all the answers. We make mistakes and are still learning. Where you think we have too many rules and restrictions, it is only because we have the experience to know what you do not."

Mary sniffled. She pulled back with watery eyes. "Oh, I know that, but it chafes, because how else are we supposed to gain experience if we're not allowed?"

"It's an age-old question." Beatrice rooted around in the bed-side table drawer, drew out a handkerchief, and then handed it to the girl. "Families have been muddling through for just as long. Everything will work out."

"Thank you." Mary nodded as she mopped at the moisture on her cheeks. "I'm glad you are here, my lady."

"Please, call me Beatrice. Your father and I are old friends."

"Very well." A sigh issued from the younger woman's throat. "There are times when I miss my mother quite fiercely. You and Mrs. Cloverfield make that ache a bit… less."

"Oh." Her heart squeezed. "I am flattered, but I understand. I lost my parents a few years back. If the accident had happened when I'd been your age, I would have been lost."

Her heart skipped a beat. She sucked in a quick breath and blinked as if her vision had cleared. Suddenly, her mother's infidelity didn't matter. *Oh, dear. I have fixated on the wrong thing entirely.* Her father's indifference didn't matter. The hopelessness regarding never being able to meet her birth father didn't matter. Her thoughts went to Owen and how much she wanted him to wake. Life was so short and precious. She shouldn't fill it with worry and anger and wondering. Instead, she should hold the people who were in her life right now close, enjoy who they were for the people they were, and let the future unfold as it would. *And to think it took the children to show me the way.*

"How are you feeling?" If her voice was more graveled due to emotion, Mary didn't mention it.

"The physician who examined my arm said it might be sprained or I could have deep bruising within the muscles. He wants me to wear it in a sling for a couple of weeks." She rolled her eyes. Clearly, she hadn't taken the diagnosis to heart. "Other than that, I have bumps and bruises and a few scratches."

"No doubt you'll feel better in a few days. Perhaps I could convince Mrs. Cloverfield to have a bathtub brought into your room."

Mary's eyes rounded. "Oh, that would be lovely. Thank you."

"You are truly welcome." When Beatrice stood, the girl caught at her hand. "Did you need something else? Otherwise, I'll let you try to relax."

"Will you sit with me for a bit?" When she did, Mary sighed. "Might I ask you something in confidence? And will you answer me truthfully?"

"I shall do my best." Worry pulled knots through her belly. What now?

"You said that you and my father are friends, correct?"

"Yes. We knew each other as children when we were younger than you."

Mary nodded. "He once told me his first kiss had been with a girl from a neighboring property. Was that you?"

Heat went through Beatrice's cheeks. "It was, but that was a very long time ago indeed."

"How has it been reconnecting with Papa here? I imagine it was a bit of a surprise for you both."

"It was." The girl was becoming all too curious. She would need to guard her answers.

"But you seem to have resumed your friendship." It wasn't a question.

"We have to a certain extent." Or exceeded it, depending how one would look at it. After all, friends didn't share a heated coupling in a maze for no reason other than attraction.

Did they?

"Would there ever come a time when you might feel something for my father other than friendship?" There was nothing malicious in the girl's expression, only curiosity.

Oh, dear. Another round of heat went through Beatrice's cheeks. "Honestly, I couldn't begin to say." It was still a complicated endeavor. If she didn't utter what she was beginning to feel into words, then it wouldn't be real.

Would it?

"I see." But there was a trace of speculation in Mary's eyes. "Well, Papa is a good man if you should decide otherwise, and it would be fun having another lady in the house." With a sigh, she sank deeper into her bed pillows. "Perhaps I can match him with someone once the ball comes about. Mrs. Cloverfield said something about perhaps holding it in a few days." Her voice broke. "That is, if Papa wakes…"

"Shh." Beatrice squeezed Mary's hand. "He will. Don't give up hope." Then she leaned over and kissed the girl's forehead. "I'll let you rest." The damning ache about her heart betrayed the fact she was jealous over seeing him potentially matched with someone else.

Him not wishing for a second marriage aside, she also didn't want another woman hanging off his arm, for perhaps she wasn't quite done with him. If having an unorthodox affair was the only way to have him, would that be so bad?

Everything hinged on what happened once he regained consciousness.

CHAPTER FIFTEEN

August 1, 1820
Cloverfield Trace
A few miles east of Chippenham
Wiltshire, England

T HE LILTING, TINKLING notes of a pianoforte danced through his brain, and the song was both happy and sad by turns, but the notes continued, haunting him, nudging him, beguiling him toward a light, toward a place where sound existed, where there was sun and wildflowers and roses.

Beatrice!

Didn't she play the pianoforte? Yes, she did, but he'd not heard her with that particular instrument. Why the devil not? Everyone enjoyed it, and the sound was quite soothing on the nerves. Something prickled at the edges of his consciousness. What was it?

Damn, was he in the war again? He had felt the weirdly floating feeling before after he'd nearly been killed by the man with the saber in India. Was this death trying to snatch him from the world again?

I won't go.

There was a warmth on the left side of his face, on the eye patch. God, it felt wonderful, like life, and that constant nudging, that prodding at him to get moving continued to nag at him, but moving toward that warmth proved problematic. It was almost as if his limbs were weighed down.

He tried again, for the music continued to trip through his mind, growing stronger, as did the scent of roses, and both of them were reminders of his time with Beatrice. She made him think, look at things differently, and he was so damned glad she'd come back into his life from childhood. He'd missed her, had always wondered what had become of her.

Again, that insistent tugging pulled at him. Her face drifted into his mind, and those striking blue eyes encouraged him to come back from the darkness where he currently resided.

Beatrice, wait!

Using willpower he didn't know he possessed, Owen raised his hand to grasp at her outstretched one, but instead of being pulled upward and out of the nether world of sorts, he startled violently, and with a gasp, opened his eye to find himself in an unfamiliar bedchamber, and the first face he saw when he turned his head toward the sun's warmth wasn't Beatrice.

It was her daughter.

"Eliza?" Confusion gripped him, left his brain fuzzy. A persistent ache in his head forced him to recall what had happened. He lifted a hand to his head, explored the bandage, and then once more looked at the young lady who sat at his bedside. "Where am I?" His voice sounded like a rusty gate, and why was his throat so dry?

"Oh, good heavens! Major, you're awake." The elation in her tones managed to confuse him even more. A clink of crystal against crystal rang out and then she pressed a glass into his hand. "Here. See if you can swallow some water." She positively beamed at him.

Why?

"Thank you," he managed to squeak out before gulping down the water as if he'd been wandering the desert for a week.

"Would you like more?" Eliza grabbed a decanter from the

bedside table. When he nodded—and drat if the room didn't spin because of it—she poured another measure into his glass. "What is the last thing you remember?"

After he'd drunk the remainder of the water, he stretched, rested the glass on the bedside table, and then collapsed back against his pillows. The room settled once more. Obviously, it would take some time until he could be upright. "There were horses involved." Of that he was certain, for he stunk like them. "And trees." He frowned. "And your mother with a rose in her bonnet brim."

Where was Beatrice?

"All of that is correct," Eliza said in a soft voice. Somehow, it soothed the confusion that persisted in clinging to his brain. "You had taken a boy's place in a horse race."

Slowly, flashes of images flitted through his mind's eye. "There was an accident."

"Yes." Eliza nodded. "Both your horse and Mary's were spooked from some rather enthusiastic boys in the trees above your heads. You were both thrown."

"Ah. That explains the headache. I'm having the devil of a time whenever I move my head."

"If you are suffering, the physician left laudanum, but I would rather you not take it unless absolutely necessary since you just came awake." Concern rang in her voice and was reflected in her eyes. Gently, she took his hand, pressed two fingers to the pulse point on his wrist, and then cocked her head as she apparently counted out the beats.

He frowned. When had this young lady become a physician's assistant of sorts? "Where is Mary? How is she?" As he attempted to struggle into a sitting position, Eliza put a hand on his shoulder and eased him back against the pillows. Which was all well and good, since his head felt like exploding once more.

Truly, she was stronger than she seemed. "Hush, Major. Don't excite yourself. Your body needs time to recover." She clicked her tongue as she looked at him. "Mary is healing as expected. Initially, she had cuts and bruises. And her left arm is a bit sprained, but don't fret. I am looking after her and making certain she keeps it as still as she can by putting it in a sling when she's out and about."

The way she said that reminded him of Beatrice. Quickly, Owen tamped down the urge to grin lest she think he made jest of her. "I don't remember coming back to the manor."

"You were unconscious at the time due to hitting your head on a rather large rock."

"For how long?"

Eliza shrugged. "Nearly three days. It's approaching teatime of the third day."

When his stomach let out a loud growl, they both chuckled. "Ah. That explains why I'm feeling famished."

Immediately, concern wrinkled her brow. "We tried to keep you nourished. Cook boiled down some vegetables and then mashed them up. Then they were diluted with water so we could encourage you to swallow at least something."

That explained the horrid taste clinging to his palate. "Thank you for the diligent care."

"It wasn't only me. Mama and Mary and I took shifts. At times Mrs. Cloverfield sat at your bedside, but most of the time it was the three of us." Her smile was as modest as the Madonna's. "This happens to be my shift. Mama will come relieve me for tea."

A shiver of interest went up his spine. He desperately wished to see her. "Is she not playing the pianoforte?"

"Not that I'm aware of." Eliza frowned as she looked at him. "Are you quite well?"

Then the delicate, haunting notes he'd heard had been a figment of his imagination. "I hope so." Briefly, he closed his eye as his stomach growled again. Then he sighed. "If you will excuse me? There are certain… things I need to attend to before this conversation can advance."

"You can, of course, go behind the privacy screen, but I won't leave you in the event you suffer a collapse." She stood up from the chair, waiting patiently as he put back the bedclothes.

Then he became aware of his state of undress. Who had stripped him to his breeches? "It is hardly proper. Your mother won't be pleased." To that end, she had no doubt seen the wicked scar that ran the length of the left side of his body. Had she told her mother about it? Did they both pity him?

She huffed. "Mama knows I intend to study the art of healing and nursing. Since that is so, I will see far worse than a half-naked man."

"Well, that is very true." While the heat of embarrassment took hold, he swung his legs over the side of the bed, and with Eliza's assistance managed to stand, albeit on shaky legs and aching head, but he stood. "You certainly have my respect. Ministering to the sick and injured isn't for the faint of heart. I saw far too many horrible things during my time in the military to tell you the job will be an easy one."

"Thank you. Easy or not, it is something I feel I need to do before anything else."

God, she was so collected and sure of herself, and at that young age! "I'm glad your mother has given you her support."

"She was the one who suggested I follow my dreams before letting society have at me."

"Good advice." What had prompted that conversation? Though his muscles hosted twinges of aches, by the time he crossed the floor to disappear behind the privacy screen, it wasn't so bad. His head still hurt, but he couldn't determine if it was from the bump he'd taken or from lack of adequate food and water. Embarrassment continued as he made use of the chamber pot, for he knew Eliza could hear everything, but there was nothing for it. She was as stubborn as her mother, it seemed. By the time he moved to the wash basin to brush his teeth and scrub some of the stench from his body, he'd acclimated to her presence. "Thank you for watching over me so intently."

"As I said before, Mama and Mary helped." She once more

took hold of his arm and assisted him across the floor to the bed even though he didn't require the aid. "Mama sat vigil more than any of us. She finally sought out her bed this morning from exhaustion."

"I see." The fact she'd not left his side for the duration both flattered and concerned him. "She didn't need to do that."

Eliza snorted. She fussed with the bedclothes and tucked them around him while he propped himself against the pillows. "Oh, I know, but she insisted. Mama has been very upset about your health."

"How *is* my health?"

"Well, that largely depends on any injury to your brain." Being the efficient soul that she was, Eliza moved across the room. She opened a drawer in the bureau, brought forth a clean linen shirt, and brought it over to him. "Do you know what year it is?"

"1820. The month of July... er, rather August now, I suppose."

She nodded and handed him the garment. "What is your name?"

"Owen Michael Kenton. I am forty years of age. A widower and the father of two grown children."

"Good." While she watched, he donned the shirt and smoothed it over his torso. At least he was covered, so it wasn't quite as scandalous conversing with her. "It seems the only faulty memories are the ones of your accident and directly following. According to the physician that is normal."

"Ah. Then can I assume the bump on my head is just that?" He again explored the bandages with his fingers, hissed when he encountered the tender spot that still sported a lump.

"Yes. It will no doubt take a bit to heal completely, but the wound is no longer bleeding, so I would say you are well on your way to recovery." Eliza's smile put him in mind of Beatrice. Damn, but he missed her! "If you should need it, the laudanum is here, and someone will sit with you for another day to make certain you don't fall into a coma."

The sound of rapid footsteps in the corridor beyond interrupted the conversation. Then Mary dashed into the room with round eyes. "I heard talking and I hoped... Papa! You're awake!"

"Hello, poppet. It is good to see you." His chest tightened at the sight of her.

Tears filled her eyes, but she rushed over the floor, climbed into the bed with him, and then promptly flung her arms about him and buried her head in the crook of his neck. "I'm so sorry that I went against your wishes and dressed as a boy so I could join the race! What if your accident was my fault?"

Oh, God.

Not knowing what else to do, Owen wrapped his arms around his daughter and simply let her cry out her angst. "I understand why you did it, but you must practice at being more proper. You are no longer a little girl."

"Yet you treat me as if I am!"

Her tears wet his neck. As Eliza crossed the room and yanked on the bellpull, Owen sighed. "I promise to remind myself that you are nearly grown, but acting the hoyden won't easily help you to meet your goals."

She lifted her head and met his gaze. Despite her tears, there was a mischievous light in her eyes. "But it will be more fun."

If he weren't careful, she'd land in scandal and damage her future permanently. "Perhaps, but only you can decide what path to walk. I just want you to be happy and have as many opportunities as you can."

"I will be fine." As quickly as they'd come, her tears evaporated. "I want *you* to be happy as well." She hugged his neck. "Are you well?"

"As far as I know."

"Good." Mary eased out of his arms to sit next to him. She turned to face him with her eyes alight with curiosity. "Now that we have established you are on the way to healing, how do you feel about Lady Beatrice?"

Eliza spoke briefly to a footman who answered her summons. After she ordered tea, she drifted back to the chair at his bedside, and once she sat, she focused intently on his face. "Yes, how *do* you feel about my mother?"

This is my worst nightmare.

"I'm not certain this is appropriate conversation for ladies of your age."

Both girls snorted.

"Papa." Mary put a palm to the side of his face and turned his head toward her. "This is important. I happened upon you in the portrait gallery the other day, and *that* was an eye-opening talk."

Bloody hell.

Before he could speak, Eliza nodded. "I overheard part of your conversation with Mama while you were in the billiards room. *Something* is between you, for certain."

Perhaps he should have remained in blissful unconsciousness longer. "Uh…" With the two girls staring at him in expectation, there was nothing for it but to confront his own truths. They would probably badger him until he told them anyway. A sigh escaped him. "First off, eavesdropping on conversations where you were not invited is bad form."

Mary pointed her gaze to the ceiling. "No lectures, Papa."

"And if those conversations were meant to be private, you should have ensured you were somewhere away from where others might be near."

"Fair point." The young ladies were far too clever for their own good. "Regarding Lady Beatrice…" When they both stared at him, the heat of embarrassment pushed through his chest. "Yes, it is true. I want her but she wants marriage—deserves it, in fact—to be a good example for you, Eliza."

Mary's forehead creased in confusion. "Yet you don't wish to marry her?"

"I…" Owen sighed. "It is complicated."

"I rather think it's not, Major. People add their own feelings to love and that's what complicates it," Eliza added in a hushed voice with a knowing light in her blue eyes.

"*Why* don't you want marriage, Papa?" His daughter apparently refused to drop the subject. "And you should hurry. Once news that you are awake circulates through the house, you won't have a moment's peace."

As if I have that now?

"I know when I've been cornered." He poorly stifled a yawn. "When your mother died, losing her tore me up on the inside. It shredded my heart." How else to explain when these two had no romantic frame of reference? "I don't want to go through that again. So regardless of how I feel about the lady, friendship is the only thing we can have in our future."

"Oh, Major, such excuses." Eliza snorted. She rolled her eyes and looked just like Beatrice. "As if you wouldn't feel the same if my mother were to expire now."

Damn. That was exactly what Beatrice had said. "But I—"

"No." She shook her head. "Whether you want to believe it or not, the two of you *are* in a relationship, and I fully believe you have bonded physically and emotionally."

"I…" Heat rushed over his neck and into his cheeks. "That is—"

She interrupted him. "After your accident, my mother was beside herself with concern, and though I might not have experience in romance, I understood why."

"And?" Obviously, he wasn't thinking clearly if he couldn't puzzle out why.

"Oh, Papa." Exasperation rang in Mary's tones as she shook her head. "She fancies you."

They were good together in a physical sense, but did she truly have feelings for him?

Eliza softly cleared her throat, and the sound yanked him from his musings. "Honestly, I believe you are afraid, Major. It is obvious the two of you care for each other. We have all seen the looks you give each other."

"You have." It wasn't a question.

"Of course. Some of us have even discussed the possibilities of the two of you making a match of it." Her eyes sparkled with excitement. "But you must be honest with yourself, Major." Her expression sobered. "You would mourn and hurt and rage if Mama were to expire, so stop fooling yourself. Do the right thing and stop making you both miserable."

Well damn.

He stared at her as if he were truly seeing her for the first time. The girl had matured so much since the house party began. And what was more, Eliza was just like her mother. It was a good thing, for they were both splendid. But confusion still held him captive. He bounced his gaze between the two girls. "What *should* I do, though? I'm rubbish with courting."

Mary snorted. "I doubt that. Mama adored you."

"But it was so much easier with her," he added in a quiet voice. "Beatrice is of the *ton*, and a marquess's daughter to boot. I am well below her in status."

"Another excuse." Eliza shook her head. A trace of disappointment went through her eyes. "Love doesn't discriminate, Major. If you like Mama and she returns those feelings, where is the harm?"

A huff of frustration escaped him. "I fear I have already mucked things up with your mother though. Where I should have offered courtship, I fear I have overstepped…"

"No." She shook her head. "Sometimes things grow out of hand and don't follow a usual path. Besides, Mama tells me all the time to be true to myself. You need to do the same." Finally, she offered him a smile. "You will merely need to wrack your brain for romantic ideas that will win her over."

"Oh, yes!" Mary fairly bounced in her own enthusiasm. "That will be such fun to plan!"

"How, though?" Still, he remained baffled. "She is quite different than the woman your mother was."

The young ladies exchanged annoyed glances.

"Of course she is! No two women are the same." Mary shook

her head as if she couldn't believe he'd gained forty years without her insights. "Take what you know about Lady Beatrice and then go from there."

Eliza nodded. "Yes, and since the ball was postponed due to the accident and out of respect to your health, perhaps they will hold it in a few days. Mama enjoys dancing as well as wearing pretty gowns, and there is talk of having a lavish dinner beforehand."

Oh, God. Everything was moving so quickly. "Is that enough time to plan something to secure a great second romance?" Is that the direction he was truly moving in? While it was more respectful toward Beatrice than indulging in an affair, was his heart already engaged enough to warrant embarking on a courtship with the intent to marry? Could he willingly offer up his heart knowing it could be broken again?

Mary smiled and took up his hand as the footman returned with a tea tray. "You won't know until you try, Papa, and she is ever so lovely."

"That she is." Relief shuddered through him at Mary's apparent approval. "Go grab a notebook and pencil. This might take some time, and my head aches fiercely already."

"Oh, this is so exciting!" His daughter sprang off the bed and ran for the door, nearly upsetting the footman on her way out.

Owen looked at Eliza. "I hope you're right about your mother."

She took the tray from the footman and laid it atop the bureau. "Mama needs to be needed. She adores being in love, and I can definitely see the beginnings of that in her." As she poured out a cup of tea, she sighed. "This will be so romantic if you come up to scratch. And I will enjoy seeing Mama happy again. She's been through so much recently."

"Agreed." But damn, what lay ahead was a bit more frightening than preparing on the eve of a battle.

CHAPTER SIXTEEN

August 3, 1820
Night of the ball

I T HAD BEEN two days since Owen awakened, and in that time, Beatrice had only seen him once, in passing. Of course, he'd received many visitors, and when he was awake, he regaled the young men with stories from his time in India.

When she'd been allowed in the room—for whatever reason, both Eliza and Mary were strict about who could see him and how long they could stay—he had been visibly tired and nearly nodding off. They'd spoken politely for a few minutes, and she'd expressed how glad she was he hadn't been injured seriously, but with one or the other of the girls hovering in the background, it had been impossible to hold a conversation of any depth.

Finally, her daughter had sent her off to rest, which Beatrice had done because with Owen injured and not lurking about to catch her unawares, much of the life and interest in the house party had faded for her. Then, an hour ago, Eliza had popped into her room and bedeviled her into dressing for the ball.

"I'm only a chaperone. What does it matter how I look?" Beatrice had uttered in protest, but her daughter had been quite firm.

"It matters because this is now a celebration of gratitude.

Everyone is relieved the major is back to full health and that the injury he sustained isn't serious. Additionally, we are all excited for the ball since we have had to wait." Her daughter had rooted through the clothespress. "You should strive to look your best. It is summer and it hasn't rained, and it will do you good to socialize or dance."

Even now, as Beatrice finished with her toilette, Eliza insisted no one was to disturb the major, for he needed all his available strength since he wished to make an appearance at the ball. She would have accepted that as fact since her daughter took her role as nurse seriously, except she and Mary were often seen with their heads together, whispering and giggling over something they were equally as adamant at keeping from her.

"Oh, this is ridiculous! If I want to see Owen, I should be able to. After all, Eliza is my *daughter*, not *my* mother."

The maid slipped a final pin into Beatrice's upswept tresses and snickered. "There is something afoot there, my lady. Those girls have been closeted together for two days."

"Do you think they're plotting to somehow be alone with a boy tonight?" At this point, anything was possible. It had never been like Eliza to keep secrets from her before. Why she'd chosen to do so now was problematic.

The maid's eyes rounded. "There is talk in the servants' hall of matchmaking, but no one knows who the intended couple is."

Oh, dear. Perhaps her daughter had her head turned after the derby debacle. Or worse, still, what if it was Mary who'd gotten involved with a boy while Owen had been incapacitated? She was certainly inquisitive enough, and hadn't she flirted with scandal by entering into the horse race while wearing boy's clothes?

Owen will never forgive me if she tries to bolt to Gretna Green.

Beatrice frowned. "I'll have to double the vigilance on the young people tonight."

"You are a good sort, my lady." The maid nodded as she handed over Beatrice's gloves. "Dinner will begin soon, and I'm told Cook outdid herself. Everyone has been in such a pallor since the accident that she wants to spoil the Cloverfields with their favorites."

"I can't say I blame her. It will certainly be lovely not to worry any longer." Which meant she would watch her daughter like a hawk tonight.

"All right, then. I'll just go see if Miss Ashdowne needs assistance."

"Thank you." She then contemplated her reflection. It had been an age since she'd made appearance in public; the last time was for Graham's nuptial ceremony.

The blue gown of a satin and silk blend had been a bold choice for a chaperone, but she was also a marquess's daughter—for all intents and purposes—and she did adore dressing in such finery. A gauze overskirt of nearly sheer silk embroidered with silver vines and flowers moved almost like gossamer, and the matching satin slippers were like heaven on her feet. There was no need for other ornamentation, for the gown was striking enough, but she did make one concession to jewelry by wearing the emerald ring her father had given her.

Everything shifted, then, as she stood looking back at her reflection in the cheval glass and saw what everyone said were the Winterbourne features: blonde hair, blue eyes, aristocratic lines. *I want to meet my half-siblings and I am tired of feeling angry, and ashamed of what my mother did.* What happened had happened. The Earl of Ettesmere had fathered her and her brothers. It was time to meet that extended family and perhaps let Eliza meet those unexpected cousins, aunts, and uncles.

Life was indeed too short to spend fretting. With a smile, she turned from the mirror. Owen had taught her that, and his accident had driven home that point. To that end, as soon as she saw him tonight, she was going to take him aside and talk candidly to him.

"Mama!" Eliza came pelting into her room with her hair only half set, but the gown of pale-yellow silk was as gorgeous and fresh as she was. Tiny, embroidered daises lined the bodice and short sleeves.

"What is it?" Immediately on alert, Beatrice crossed the room and clutched her daughter's hand. "Has something happened? Are you well? Is the major?" Oh, dear God, what if he suffered a relapse?

"No, nothing like that." Her upset was clear. "I simply cannot attend the ball without it, though!"

Beatrice frowned. "Without what?"

"I think I left it in the heart of the maze. I must have dropped it there, and it's making me sick to my stomach," Eliza rushed on. She did look a bit wild around the eyes. "What am I going to do?"

"Calm yourself." Not having the slightest clue what the girl was going on about, Beatrice gave her daughter's shoulders a shake and then stared into her eyes. "What do you mean? What have you lost?"

Eliza put a hand to her throat. "The white enamel heart on the golden chain Papa gave me just before he died. I remember taking it off in order to wade in the fountain the other day with some of the girls because I didn't want it to get wet, but then I forgot to put it back on." Her eyes filled with tears. "I simply must have that necklace."

"Why? We can easily retrieve it tomorrow."

"Mama, please! I want that little piece of Papa with me to-night. For luck and courage." The pleading in her eyes went straight to Beatrice's heart.

She twisted the emerald ring around her finger. "I understand all too well."

"Then you will fetch it for me?"

"Me? Why don't you run down there?" Sunset was a couple of hours off, so there should be no issue with her losing her way.

Eliza pointed to her hair. "I need to finish getting ready, and you are already done." She clutched Beatrice's hand. "Please, Mama? The footmen are all busy with the ball preparations else I'd ask one of them. I promise I won't ask for anything else." A sigh escaped her. "I think caring for the major and looking after

Mary has overworked my nerves, which has made me a watering pot. I cannot wait to have fun tonight."

The poor girl. "Don't fret, and don't cry. Your face will be blotchy and your eyes red." She squeezed her daughter's fingers. "I'll go down and retrieve the necklace. Where is it?"

"Hanging from Aphrodite's fingers."

Of course it was. "Very well. You go finish your toilette. I'll return as soon as I can."

"Oh, thank you, Mama!" Eliza threw her arms about her and bussed her cheek. "You are such a lovely mama."

"You can thank me by acting the perfect society miss tonight, hmm? I'll see you at dinner." Then, taking up her gloves, Beatrice left the room.

The things we do for our children.

Her slippers glided over the grass of the back lawn. She'd managed to avoid most people on her way out of the manor, but she had run into a couple of the other companions who seemed surprised she was on her way outside.

"It's but a quick errand. I shall return immediately. My daughter left something in the maze, and she simply must have it before the ball."

Then she'd continued on and reached the hedge maze without incident, but that was where her luck gave out. What was it about entering the twists and turns of the dratted interior that stole away her sense of direction? Twice before she had been inside the maze, but her brain protested, for she couldn't puzzle out which turns and paths to take, so it took her seemingly forever to finally reach the heart.

As soon as she stumbled into the space, shock smacked into her and left her stumbling to a halt. "What is this?" Paper streamers and flowers had been strewn about the shrubberies and trees in the heart, and all in the same color scheme the ballroom had been decorated in. Pinks, whites, and golds winked at her in the evening sun. When the heady scent of roses rose up around her, she glanced at the gravel and shell path. "Oh goodness." Rose petals in various colors dotted the pathway that led around the rose garden, and where the petals stopped, her gaze landed on Owen as he stood near the fountain, and he was clad in his evening finery.

"Good evening, Lady Beatrice."

The rumble of his voice sent flutters through her lower belly. "What are you doing here?" *Oh, no!* What if she'd inadvertently interrupted a tryst? With a furtive glance about the area, she frowned. "Are you waiting for someone?"

"I am." He grinned and kept his hands clasped behind his back.

"Oh." A rush of disappointment came over her. "Did you decorate for them?"

"Not directly. I had loads of help."

"I see." The longer she peered at him, the more emotional she became, for it had been a trying few days. "You look well." In fact, he was one of the most handsome men she'd seen in recent months. "It's good to see you up and around."

His chestnut hair had been arranged into a latest style, or as best it could be with one bandage remaining. In the requisite black evening suit and sapphire waistcoat, his form was shown to advantage. His cane rested against one of the rose bushes, and when she met his gaze, amusement danced in his brown eye. And when that slow, devastating grin curved his sensual lips, frissons of need spiraled down her spine.

"Thank you. I feel like a new man. Thanks in large part to your daughter's excellent nursing and her strict orders I remain in bed for days."

"She does have a surprising talent for it." A nervous laugh escaped her tight throat. "Well, I will leave you alone. I'm sure the lady you are waiting for will be alone soon."

"Stay, for she has already arrived."

What did that mean? Confusion took hold. "I don't understand." Hoping he would explain, she twisted her gloves in her hands.

"It *is* rather baffling. That was how I felt when the girls tried to explain what I needed to do tonight." Finally, he relaxed his posture and slowly came toward her. In his hand, he held a deep crimson rose that was open almost all the way. "For you."

"But what about the woman you are meeting here tonight?"

"I'm waiting for *you*, Beatrice." When she didn't immediately take the rose, he closed the distance and then tucked the bloom behind her ear as he'd done before. The faint brush of his knuckles against her cheek erupted a whole ballet of butterflies within her belly. "Couldn't you guess that?"

"No." She bounced her gaze from him to the decorations and then back to his face. "Uh… why would you be waiting for me? And for that matter, why is any of this here?"

"Perhaps I should explain."

"That would be nice." Because if he didn't, she might burst into stupid, silly tears, and she was well past the age where that would be acceptable.

With a continuation of his grin, Owen took one of her hands. The gloves she'd yet to don fell ignored to the grass. "The afternoon when I awoke, your daughter was there and then Mary came. After she apologized for entering the race in disguise, the girls started asking me a multitude of questions."

"They are quite astute in that regard." Her hand shook in his. "How did decorating this space happen?"

The major chuckled, and the sound only served to height her awareness of him. "They both wished to do something special for you. Then they instructed me to wait here, for I'd told them I wanted to talk with you privately."

"Oh!" Her eyes widened. "You aren't having a tryst." It wasn't a question.

"That remains to be seen, but I *am* waiting for you. Eliza said she would invent a story believable enough to make you come here and that when you saw me, everything would fall into place."

"Fall into place? How and why?" Threads of annoyance went

through her chest. "I suppose she didn't really leave her necklace on the statue?"

"Probably not."

She frowned. Eliza had lied? "I don't understand. Her story seemed so convincing." When she took a step toward the pathway, he tightened his hold on her hand and tugged her into his arms. "I need to go. Dinner will begin shortly."

"Dinner will go off splendidly without you or me. For the moment, please dance with me." Emotion clouded his eye, but she didn't dare try to interpret it. "With the bandage and the limp, I might not be able to find the courage to do so in the ballroom later, but I know you enjoy the exercise, and I have wanted nothing more than to share a waltz with you since we arrived at this damned house party."

When he flashed another grin, it reminded her of that day so long ago when they'd walked through that wildflower meadow, the day she'd realized she'd been mildly infatuated with him, and it was the same grin he'd given her that day when they'd met in this very maze. Her resistance and confusion crumbled, and all she knew was the feel of his strong arms about her and the heat of his hand at the small of her back.

"I'm afraid I was remiss in something," he said in a whispered voice, as he set them into motion on the path about the fountain and rose garden.

"Oh?" She could hardly remember how to speak due to him overwhelming her every sense. His citrus and sage scent teased her nose; the hardness of his chest beneath her palm made her want to do wicked things to him. And with the strip of cloth about his head, he looked both vulnerable and dashing.

"Indeed. I should have told you straightaway how beautiful you look tonight in that blue gown." The major fit his lips to the shell of her ear. "It will look even better in a heap on the grass because then I will be given leave to devour you as I see fit, and I just know you will be gorgeous nude."

"Owen!" Heat rose into her cheeks, but the cheeky words

ignited tiny fires into her blood. "I thought we had suspended such nonsense between us due to having differing goals for the future." What exactly was he about?

For a few moments, he whisked her around the fountain as if they glided over the ballroom's parquet floor. "I came awake after hitting my head to the sound of the pianoforte. And it was your voice, your face, your outstretched hand that pulled me from the darkness into the world of the living."

"You dreamed of me?"

"It would seem I did, and it was the sweetest dream I have had in a long time."

"Oh." While those words were the height of romance, they didn't answer her question. "And?"

"And I very much dreaded a future that didn't have you in it. No matter the capacity, I believe we can puzzle out the issues keeping us apart." The look in his eye was quite intense. "The girls hinted to me that you might harbor feelings for me."

"I… Well, I…" She curled her hand into his lapel. "I need to think upon that a while longer, but I was *exceedingly* worried after the horse threw you." To the point that she couldn't eat, couldn't sleep, nearly made herself sick from concern.

"Quite telling, that." When they reached the fountain once more, Owen drew them to a halt and pulled her a tiny bit closer. "It is my hope—nay, my determination—that after tonight, you and I will know exactly where we stand with each other."

A tingle of anticipation went down her spine. "If given my druthers, I would rather do that while lying down," she whispered as a host of flutters danced through her lower belly.

"Ah, sweeting, you and I are going to have such fun together while we come to an understanding." Before she could form an answer, he pressed her closer, slid his other hand into her hair, and then claimed her lips with his in a kiss that set her senses spinning and completely turned her blood into molten rivers of pure desire.

She never quite knew if it had been the unexpected endearment he used, the naughty teasing, or the kiss itself, but Beatrice shoved all her doubts, her confusion, her worry, and her thoughts to the back of her mind. Then she gave herself over to the glory that was kissing the major, or learning the secrets of his mouth. While she worked the buttons of his tailcoat from their holes, she dragged her lips along the column of his strong neck. Oh, she would see him tonight—*all* of him—and she didn't care if that made her a wanton.

It was magical, emotional, almost spiritual what they shared, and she wanted so much more from him.

From herself.

With a groan, Owen deepened the kiss, and she gladly let him. For several minutes, their tongues mated and tangled, fought for dominance. First he led the kiss then she did, and all the while those kisses gave over to bold caresses that left her heated and needy.

The second he cupped her breasts, held them, worried her nipples into tight buds with the pads of his thumbs was the moment her hold on reality began to fracture, and just like that day when they'd given into passion in this same place, Beatrice shoved the tailcoat from his shoulders, and this time she wouldn't stop until she had looked, tasted, touched her fill.

"You make me feel like a whole man again," he whispered against the underside of her jaw, the side of her neck. "It's so very good for my ego."

"Mmm, I'd like to think I'm good for you in other ways as well." She slipped a hand down the proud length of his back and when she reached the curve of his arse, she squeezed a firm buttock.

"Damn, woman, you must know that you are." He nipped at the spot beneath her ear and as he did, Owen put his hands at her waist, lifted her, and then set her on the lip of the fountain. "So beautiful," he murmured then his hand went beneath her skirting.

"Oh!" All too soon he strummed his fingers along her sensitive flesh, and she couldn't help but part her legs to give him greater access. Since the first time they'd come together, she'd craved him, couldn't wait to join with him again, but with the decision to deny herself unless he wanted marriage, those feelings had been thwarted. Now he was here, and his touch felt all too wonderful. "Owen, yes…"

"I adore how responsive you are." Once more, he claimed her lips and at the same time fit his hand more firmly between her thighs, rubbing, stroking, exploring. "Every sound you make affects me and I feel rather possessive of you, hope you'll utter those noises *only* for me… *because* of me."

"Yes." She gave into a full-body shiver. Gooseflesh popped on her skin. "I want you, Owen. All of you. Good or bad. Fearless or brave. All of you."

"I have waited a long time to hear those words." Then he penetrated her body with a forefinger, and she nearly shuddered off the edge of the fountain from the sheer bliss of that moment.

Her bottom slipped into the water, which meant the gown was probably ruined, but she didn't care, not when the major leaned over her as she clung to his shoulders. He teased her body, moved his finger in and out, ever so slowly, and kissed her with all the leisure in the world. Needing to touch him and feel the heat of him, she fumbled with the knot of his cravat, but as he increased finger-thrusts and rubbed his thumb against the swelling nubbin at her center, Beatrice's concentration once more fractured. It was all she could do not to give into the urge to spend.

"Show me how much you want me, sweeting. Fall into the feelings. Don't be afraid to take what you need." He followed the whispered words with licks and nibbles down the column of her throat. Then his hand was at her bodice, wrenching it down as he continued to work the flesh between her thighs.

"Ah!" The moment he fondled her nipple, gave it a light pinch, she hurtled over the edge into the crest of a swift and powerful release that stole her breath.

"That's it." When he withdrew his hands, she whimpered a

protest, but he only chuckled. "We are not nearly done."

"Oh, I certainly hope not, for there is much I want to do." She grinned, for he'd picked her up into his arms and carried her to the patch of grass where a quilt had been spread out that she hadn't seen before, where the rose petal trail ended, and a few pieces of her heart flew into his keeping.

Perhaps there was hope for them after all.

CHAPTER SEVENTEEN

OWEN WAS ALREADY drunk on the woman in his arms. After bringing her to a rather quick release on the lip of that fountain, he wanted nothing else than to send her over again, but first, he would see her out of that spectacular gown.

As soon as he reached the quilt nestled near the rose beds at the very heart of the maze, he held her head between his palms then proceeded to claim her lips again and again, for they were as soft as the rose petals he'd caressed before selecting the perfect crimson bloom for her tonight. There was something about this woman who challenged him, supported him, set him ablaze, that made him feel vital and needed, and lord knew he hadn't experienced that since well before his wife had died.

And he couldn't have enough.

"Why did you and our daughters wish to lure me out here on false pretenses when an unused room in the manor would have sufficed just as well?" As she spoke, Beatrice helped him shed his tailcoat that already hung haphazardly from his frame.

"That would hardly have made a romantic picture, and I certainly didn't wish to give the girls the idea that indiscriminately coupling is acceptable." No, he wasn't providing a good or noble example of how a man should properly court a lady, and he would take full responsibility for that. Just now, he couldn't think straight, not when said lady's fingers worked the laces at his back.

When she removed the waistcoat from his person, he let her, for he enjoyed the feel of her hands on his body far too much.

Her fingers stilled on his chest, and the warmth of her seeped through the lawn of his shirt. "Oh, please tell me they don't suspect what we're doing." Worry clouded those gorgeous blue eyes, made more brilliant in the slanting rays of the sun that didn't quite reach into the heart of the maze.

"I hope not, but both of them are clever and intelligent." He brought her close, kissed her to hopefully banish her concern. "I only told them I wished for an opportunity alone with you to talk candidly. What else they think is anyone's guess."

"Mmm, true, and surely they can get themselves to dinner on time. That will distract them," she said in a husky whisper that went straight to his stones. Slowly, she drew her hand over his chest, traced her nail over one of his nipples and chuckled when he hissed in a sharp breath. "Ah, poor man. Are you in need of attention, then?" That teasing, sing-song quality of her tones had his thoughts skidding into an erotic direction. What would her fingers feel like on his bare skin or pumping up and down his length that was burgeoning into life the longer she teased? Their last coupling was far too rushed for either of them to fully explore.

And damn but he wanted that now.

Wanted her.

Wanted a chance at a lifetime.

"Perhaps I am." Watching her, he plucked off his collar and cuffs, letting them drop to the quilt. There was something far too scandalous undressing while being observed. Awareness of her prickled his skin and worked to further tighten his shaft. "You will surely take all the attention from admiring gentlemen tonight at the ball." His cravat followed the other pieces of his clothing he'd already shed. It landed like a dead snake on the dark green grass. "It might make me jealous."

"Ha. I'm attending as a chaperone, remember. Men don't ask such women to dance." When her gaze dropped to his mouth, and her blue eyes darkened, renewed desire pulsed through his blood.

"Poppycock and gammon. If you wish to dance, then do so. However…" He scooped up one of her hands, pressed his lips to the back of her wrist. Her heartbeat fluttered there, a sure indication she was excited as he. Then he moved up the inside of her arm, nibbling and licking the satiny soft skin fragrant with the elusive floral scent she favored, and was rewarded with a faint, shuddering sigh. "If I had my druthers, I would prefer that you dance *only* with me."

"Oh?" Interest and need mixed in her eyes. Again, she skated her fingernail over his aroused nipple. Exquisite sensation streaked through him. "How presumptuous of you."

"Indeed, but there are times when a man knows exactly what—or whom—he wants, and he will challenge anyone who wishes to prevent that." He tugged her lightly into his arm, became distracted with nuzzling the crook of her shoulder, but managed to work the few pearl buttons at the back of her gown.

"That possessive streak of yours is rather attractive." She tugged his shirttails from the waist of his trousers. "Tell me what else you might do with the woman you've set your alleged sights on."

Of course she was teasing, and this conversation was all part of the flirting dance that would end with them both naked and sated, but he frowned, for he was dead serious about courting her. "What wouldn't I do for a woman who could have an army of men do her bidding with merely a casual glance? A woman who has lived a lifetime but is still vital and gorgeous at her age?"

"Is that the best you can do? The man who has adored Shakespeare since as long as I've known him?"

That husky quality had returned to her voice, and he was in danger of losing himself in her. "How could I assume to ever be as romantic as the Bard?" With the ease of familiarity but the trepidation of entering into something new and unknown, Owen slid her gown and petticoat down her shoulders until the thin fabric hovered, hung suspended, at the slope of her breasts, the progress impeded at edge of her stays.

Damn, but that was one of the most sensual things he'd ever seen.

"Give it some stick, Major. A woman wishes to be wooed, after all, regardless of the passion between them."

At least it was a sign he was doing something right. "I shall try my best." Despite wanting nothing more than to throw her onto the quilt and mindlessly join with her, the act would be that much sweeter for them both if he finessed it, allowed emotions to be involved that weren't the last time they'd come together. Because he couldn't stop touching her, he nibbled the side of her neck, and that silky skin beckoned him onward.

"This is a good start." Beatrice's eyes shuttered closed.

He lifted her chin and dragged his lips beneath her jaw, nipping, licking, kissing. "I apologize for giving you such a scare with that accident."

"It's all right. At least it gave me clarity of thought." With the same hunger in her expression that held him captive, she shoved one of her hands beneath his shirt.

Owen hissed his encouragement even if her every touch sent him inexorably toward the edge of no return. "That is what I had upon waking. I wanted to waste no more time." Enough of the slow teasing. He wanted her naked, now. With more haste than elegance, he continued to divest her of the gown and petticoat. Once the garments pooled at her feet, he worked the laces of her stays until they, too, drifted to the ground. The outline of her hardened pink nipples was clearly visible beneath the thin lawn of her shift. "Dear God." Was there ever a more beautiful sight than a woman becoming aroused? He stifled a groan. "You are a temptress."

"Such gammon. I am too advanced in age for that." But her smile added to that persona.

"Who is speaking gammon now? I adore that you haven't hidden away or stopped living your life merely due to your age or circumstances." He licked the hollow of her throat. "Age is meaningless."

"I quite agree." A wicked gleam lit the depths of her eyes, and a shiver went down his spine, for that didn't bode well for him. "Since you insist on conversing instead of using your mouth for more interesting things, let me put out an opening salvo."

That bossy, adventurous streak left him utterly captivated. He toed off his shoes. "Do your best, my lady, but remember, turnabout is fair play."

"I should hope so. In fact, I'm counting on it." With a giggle, Beatrice dropped to her knees in front of him. Then her nimble fingers were at the buttons of his frontfalls and soon the panel was free. His hardened length sprang out, and he hoped to God she liked what she saw. "I am so glad my imaginings of how you'd look weren't wrong." Before she did anything else, the lady encouraged him out of his trousers.

"Oh?" Surprise plowed through his chest. She'd thought about his equipage? "What else have you fantasized about?"

"This."

Any other thoughts flew out of his head the second she took him in hand. Need shivered along his length, tingled through his stones. Glad once again that she wasn't an untried miss, he bit back a groan as she stroked her curled fingers up and down his shaft. If she didn't leave off, he'd explode, and that would cheat them of the pleasures to come. "Perhaps this wasn't a good idea." When he attempted to break their connection, Beatrice tightened her fingers, rendering him immobile.

And ready to break.

"Don't be a coward, Major. You were the one who started this. I merely mean to usher you to that edge in the hopes you'll do the same for me." She smiled up at him seconds before she touched the tip of her tongue to the mushroomed head of his shaft and gave him a lick as if she were savoring dropped syllabub.

"Oh, God." A shiver of pure need streaked through him. All

too soon she employed both her hand and mouth in working over his member. Owen's mind fractured into a million pieces from the wild sensation roaring up his spine and through his length. How the devil did she know what he liked, how to make him lose his grip on reality? But then, it didn't matter, for the raw act changed his blood to rivers of molten lava. "Bloody hell. You feel so good." It wasn't exactly how he'd planned the start of the evening, but then, she was so damned unique. He put a hand to her head, gently thrust into the warm cavern of her mouth, not daring to go deeper lest he lose his rapidly dwindling hold on control.

When she giggled, the vibrations about his shaft hurtled him closer to the edge. "Is there a problem, Major?" She caressed the fingers of her free hand along his left leg, tracing the saber scars there, making him feel that perhaps it didn't matter he wasn't whole.

"No," he managed to gasp out from around clenched teeth. There was something both wicked and endearing about this woman, with her blonde hair upswept and emerald in her ring flashing as she did unspeakable things to him. His hand trembled as he buried his fingers in her soft tresses, plucking out the pins as he went.

Beatrice hummed her approval while continuing to work him over. She bobbed on his erect shaft, and that wicked light of amusement in her eyes fascinated and alarmed him.

As much as he wanted to bury himself stones deep into her, he had always wondered what she looked like with her hair down. "You will be the death of me." She was better than he'd dreamed about, both during his youth and more recently. "If you don't leave off, the night will be over before it begins." And still he continued to thrust into her mouth, and the heat that closed around his shaft would drive him mad. Once her hair was free and the pins had fallen to the quilt, he shook himself from the stupor he'd fallen into. With his hands on her shoulders, he pulled her upward until she stood before him with a faint pout on her swollen lips. "When I come, I'll do so inside you, not on you or down your throat, for that is not what I want from this night."

Perhaps later, though, since she'd largely been enjoying herself.

"Spoil sport." She unlaced the placket of his shirt. "Then how *do* you wish to spend this night? I, for one, hope it's interesting." When she winked, the feeling of falling assailed him.

"I think you can guess." Seconds later, he tugged his shirt up and off his body, and when she inhaled sharply, slipped the fingers of one hand over his skin and through the sprinkling of hair there, he balanced on the edge of being lost. "Didn't you say you'd wanted to explore?"

"Oh, yes, and might I add, you haven't disappointed me yet." Lifting onto her toes, she kissed his lips, but went she added her other hand and truly caress his skin, the muscles in his abdomen went taut while his shaft tightened with painful urgency.

"I suppose I'm not bad looking for such an aged man."

"Ha. You are a year older than me. If more men appeared as you do at this age, perhaps more marriages would be much happier."

Damn how he adored her mind! As much as he wanted to preen, she had his full concentration, and he would explode soon, for her touch was electric, the heat of her intoxicating. Then she examined the scars on his side and back, murmured over them, even went so far as to press tiny feather-weighted kisses to those old injuries.

"I rather think they make you distinguished." A certain reverence echoed in that whisper. "A reminder that you survived and that you aren't quite finished in this life." Her voice broke and his heart squeezed. "That you are needed."

Truly, there was no one like her, and if he wasn't careful, too many emotions would show on his part before he was ready. "My turn to bedevil you." Then he removed her shift and lost the ability to breathe, for the sight of her nude body, coupled with her unbound hair and the desire in her cornflower blue eyes, left him in awe. "You're like that statue of Aphrodite in the roses." What had he done right in his life to warrant being here in this moment with her?

"Too many more compliments like that and I might fall tip over tail for you." Yet the pink blush that stained her cheeks and upper chest betrayed her feelings. "Please overlook the places where time hasn't been kind." When she tried to cover her breasts or the silvery marks on her belly acquired from bearing a child, he took her hands and gently eased them behind her back as he kissed her to show how much he appreciated her figure.

"Everything about you is perfect. Never think otherwise." Then her lips weren't enough; he had to taste her, explore every centimeter of that glorious body. Much like he'd done on that night when they'd come together in similar fashion, he knocked her feet out from under her, and as she tumbled downward, he came with her, cushioning her fall until she laid beneath him on the quilt.

"You have no idea how much I have wanted a return of this intimacy even if we don't agree on where the future is going."

"After tonight, I am hoping those doubts will forever be set-tled for you." A groan escaped him as he lifted off her merely to look his fill at her body in the gathering shadows made by the hedges as the sun slowly sank. A goddess indeed, and she was his for the moment. If he were fortunate, she would eventually be his for a lifetime. It was remarkable how clear his thinking and goals had become since recovering from that accident. He grinned as he skimmed a hand along the sweet curve of her hip. Then he explored the nip of her waist, cupped the slope of one breast and with a gentle kiss to her lips, he proceeded to moved down her body, blazing a heated trail along her torso.

Licking and nipping, he caressed and kissed his way down-ward, past the soft swell of her belly to linger at her mons, and further still. When she caught her breath, he chuckled, and hoped the sound added another layer of delight to what he was already doing to her. So easily he was lost as he explored every inch of her satiny skin with his tongue, lips, and teeth. He caressed her form in a quest to learn every secret she held. The soft sounds of pleasure and encouragement she made at the back of her throat became the beat of his heart as he continued to work.

The lady accommodated him with splendid instinct. She bent her knees, and he settled all too easily in the cradle of her hips while paying lavish attention to her naval. A moan from her prompted him onward, and when he strummed the fingers of one hand along a taut, pebbled nipple, she gasped and arched her back. A hand curled into the quilt.

"So damned beautiful." With a feeling of pure wickedness, Owen continued to move down her body. As he spread her thighs wider, he met her gaze and grinned at the questions in her eyes. Then with another chuckle, he licked at the folds that were slick with her arousal.

"Oh, yes." Need echoed in her voice. "I had hoped you might… My husband never…" A sigh of pure bliss was released onto the air.

And again, he was lost. How fortunate was he to do this to her where no one else had? "Enjoy, sweeting." With his fingers, he spread her flesh as if unfolding the petals of a rose. Then he encouraged her pearl out of hiding and worked at that tiny bundle of nerves with the tip of his tongue. Over the years of doing this to his wife, he knew friction was the key, and when Beatrice bucked her hips, putting her more firmly into his care, he grinned and continued to experiment in order to discover how best to pleasure her. She guided him to where she wanted him with a hand in his hair. Chuckling, for it was so damned erotic, he alternately sucked on that button, teased it until she bucked her hips with need evident on her face.

"Owen… Oh, yes. Just there!"

Was there anything as wonderful as a woman lost in carnal pleasure? "Come for me, sweeting. Catch that bliss." He went up her body, replacing his mouth with his fingers.

"Ah… Oh!" The half-stifled cry sounded overly loud in the

quiet of the maze's heart. Seconds later, she shattered in his arms, her body stiffening, her toes curling into the quilt, her fingers flexing as she threw back her head and shook with the effort of spending.

There was nothing as rewarding as that. Quick tears stung his eye. He'd made her feel that rush, sent her over that edge into pleasure. The pure bliss in her expression was something he would never forget. "Beatrice, I..." What? He couldn't put into words what he felt, so he wouldn't even try.

Not yet anyway.

Once he'd settled between her bent knees, he took his weight on his forearms, aligned his tip with her wet opening, and then penetrated her fully with a commanding thrust that saw him fully seated in her honeyed heat. "Ah, Beatrice," he whispered with a kiss to her lips. The last time he'd joined with her, he hadn't the wherewithal to merely pause and enjoy the act of coupling.

And it was one of the most wonderful things he'd ever experienced.

"My favorite moment." She looped her arms about his shoulders, pulling him closer, as she lifted her legs and wrapped them about his waist. "Send me flying."

"Gladly." Only then did he pull out, but when he joined with her again, they both moaned in approval.

From that moment on, words were superfluous. Owen communed with her, worshipped her body as he sought to bring her pleasure through slow, leisurely strokes. Not to be outdone, the lady easily matched his rhythm, canting her hips in such a way that he went deeper, every thrust making him see stars and fly all too close to that tempting edge.

During that dance as old as time, he peered into her eyes and tumbled into those cool, inviting pools. There was something about this woman he craved, that he admired. She was exactly the type of woman he needed by his side, to spend the remainder of his life with, so why had he ever hesitated to want a second marriage?

Damn, Kenton, you've been an idiot.

Over and over and *over* he moved, and the physical coupling became something else entirely while they were lost in that world of their own making. Urgency raced through his shaft and tingled in his stones. He'd crossed that point of no return. "I won't last. Say you're ready."

"Give me all that you are, Owen. It's all I have ever wanted." The desperate whisper rasped in his ears. She slid her hands down to his hips, holding tight, when she pressed her lips to the side of his neck, he was gone.

She had never altered in her request of him. It both humbled him and gave her a renewed shot of courage.

With a grunt, he did as she asked. Increasing his rhythm, he went deep, changing to short, fast strokes, giving her all that he was and rocking them both on the quilt. Delving a hand between their bodies, he found that slippery nubbin at her center and played it for all he was worth. Too soon, a cry wrenched from his throat; he was done. His shaft jerked as he hurtled over the edge into bliss. Seconds later, as Beatrice pressed his hand to her center, a scream left her throat. Her body stiffened. She clutched at him, held him closer, bucked against his hips as her passage fluttered around his length. Those wonderous sensations overwhelmed him, left him pinwheeling tip over tail into bliss, secure in the knowledge he would win her.

"Well, damn." Owen collapsed on top of her. He wrapped his arms around her, and she did the same to him. The ragged sounds of their breathing blended with the awakening dusk world around them. Sweat gave a sheen to her skin, the salty taste came away on his lips as he kissed her throat, beneath her jaw, her cheek, her forehead. As he struggled to regulate his breathing, his heartbeat thundered through his chest and still he lay with her, loath to let her go.

"We shouldn't keep making this a habit," he whispered into the crook of her neck.

A giggle escaped her. "I rather think coupling in a maze adds an interesting layer to this relationship."

"Perhaps." It was certainly unique to them.

Moments later, he rolled off her, but tucked her firmly against his chest with their legs twined together. "You are amazing."

"In fact, *we* are amazing." She rested her head on his shoulder, and a piece of his heart—nay, his soul—flew into her keeping.

Yes, he was well on his way to being lost, only this time, he didn't want to find his way back. "We do seem to have an affinity for each other." Had that foundation been laid long ago in their childhood? It was difficult to say.

Content enough to hold her, Owen buried his nose into her floral-fragrant hair. Nothing would be the same after this night, but then, that was the glory of living. There were always surprises around every corner, and if a man was fortunate enough, he would have the best of all companions at his side.

He didn't know how long they laid on the quilt as the sun set and night's midnight fell around them, but he had nearly dropped into a delicious doze when the sound of a gasp shot through his consciousness.

"Lady Beatrice!" Horror and shock clung to the surprised utterance.

Owen jerked awake at the same time that Beatrice gasped. Two women he recognized as companions stood at the entrance to the heart of the maze, both staring at them with round eyes and gaping mouths. "Shit." Quickly, he pulled the folds of the quilt over his body and Beatrice's to shield her from the worst of their scrutiny.

"We came to fetch you for the ball," one of them said.

The other one—the same woman who'd wanted to dance with him at the rout, nodded. "When you didn't return from your errand, we began to worry…" Her gaze roved over them, and he hated the intrusion into those stolen moments.

"Oh, dear lord," Beatrice said with mounting dread in her tones. "I cannot believe this is happening. Eliza is going to hate me."

CHAPTER EIGHTEEN

BEATRICE STARED IN horror at the women, and she wished they would just go, even if that meant the gossip would soon take hold of the house party and brand her as a desperate widow.

Burying her face in the crook of Owen's shoulder, she whispered, "Tell them to go away. This situation is already embarrassing enough. I don't want to dress in front of them."

The rumbling of his laughter tickled through her chest. "If you don't mind, could you allow us privacy?"

"Haven't you had enough of that, Major Kenton?" There was no doubting the outraged dignity in the first woman's tones. Her gaze swept the previously romantic area, took in the clothing strewn about, the rose petals, the decorations before it landed once again on them. "And Lady Beatrice! Out of all of us, you should know the penalties for creating scandal. You have a daughter to think of!"

"As if *you* bear no responsibility in this," she whispered into his ear. "What of *your* children's sensibilities? What of *your* daughter's future prospects?"

"Do hush," he whispered back with a pinch to her bottom under cover of the quilt. "Be that as it may, Miss Cooper, you'll be much more offended if I stand up in the nude, but it's your prerogative if you wish to remain." As he made to set the quilt aside, the woman fled with equally offended squeaks. "At least they're gone."

"Yes, off to shred my reputation." The urge to cry climbed her throat as she peeked around to make certain they were once more alone. "Eliza will never forgive me if her future chances are ruined because of me."

"Nothing like that will happen."

Tears welled in her eyes. "How can you know that?" When she trained her gaze on his face, an unexpected wave of feeling moved over her. No, she wasn't ashamed of what she'd done with the major, but if this interlude destroyed her daughter's life, she would never forgive herself. "Oh, Owen, I have made an utter mess of everything."

"You haven't." As he wrapped his arms around her, his body tensed. Seconds later, he flipped them both over so that she was sprawled with unladylike delicacy over him. "Don't let miserable people steal the joy you have found in your life."

Despite the bit of misfortune that had befallen them, tingles of awareness rippled over her skin. What she wouldn't give to ride this man until all of her fears and worries dissolved like they had not an hour past. As the quilt slipped down her back and revealed her nakedness to his darkening gaze, she shivered. "It's not about the joy." Need renewed itself and started tiny fires in her blood when he slid his palms up her hips to rest at her waist. "I should have conducted myself better, adhered to the same stringent rules of the *ton* that I expect my daughter to abide by." She shook her head. "Perhaps I take after my mother after all." No matter that she'd recently made peace with that particular issue, it came roaring back, glaring, now that her own indiscretion had been brought to light.

What is wrong with me?

"There is something to be said for being a consenting adult." He continued his caresses and as his fingers brushed the sides of her breasts, an involuntary whimper escaped her.

"Eliza is old enough to consent. So is Mary, and that is what I'm worried about." Her voice caught and tears crowded her throat. "What if they think my behavior is what a lady should do? Such actions might force them into marriages they don't welcome or want."

"Don't borrow trouble." With a sigh, Owen tugged her down over his chest. He tangled a hand in her hair, claimed her lips, and kissed her with a tenderness that soothed the worst of the turbulence in her chest. Once the embrace concluded, he cupped her cheek. "We'll go face everyone in that ballroom together."

"Oh." A tiny piece of heart flew into his keeping and put her in mind of what they'd just done, when bits of their souls had been exchanged during love making. She hadn't felt that content since her husband had been alive. "Thank you, but I can fight my own battles." As she tried to pull out of his arms, he tightened his hold.

"Beatrice, look at me." He encouraged her head downward until their gazes connected. Along with a fair measure of earnestness, *something* else glimmered in that brown pool, something she feared putting a name on. "I know you are strong enough to do that, but you don't need to. I'm here with you and I'm not going anywhere."

Suddenly, all of this was too frightening. It had happened too fast, hadn't allowed her to catch her breath or think it through. "We should never have done this." Quickly, before she could change her mind, Beatrice squirmed out of his embrace and scrambled to her feet. "I'm taking Eliza home at first light."

"Ah, sweeting." A trace of frustration was evident in his tone as he sat up. Goodness but he was all too enticing with the edge of the quilt rumpled about his legs and just barely covering his half-erect member. "Hiding and keeping your daughter away from everything in life won't solve anything."

"Perhaps, but I can try, because I don't want her to follow in my footsteps." She heard the tears in her own voice and hated herself for that show of weakness. "Everything I have done at this house party has caused scandal. If Eliza is destined to walk that same path, I'd rather she not do it in London. I'll take her to my brother's property in Kent."

"Then I will follow you there, since my own property borders that one."

How had she forgotten that? "Please just leave me in peace. I cannot think when you are near." Tears made finding her clothing and then subsequently dressing more difficult. Well, she could but all of those thoughts centered on him and how he'd brought fun and excitement back to her days. "Perhaps it was a mistake to embark on…" In some confusion, she fluttered a hand to indicate what they'd done that night, "… this with you. I should have left you to fond memories."

"Don't you think that some romances shouldn't be relegated to the past?" When he gained his feet and came near, she shook her head.

"Stay back. My brain is mush when you touch me." Though she struggled with her stays, she refused to ask him for assistance. "And put on some clothes. You are just too, too…"

"Yes?" His eyebrow cocked, but it was that grin that curved his lips that made her think of wicked things.

"Too *much*," she finished and ignored the heat in her cheeks. In haste she donned the petticoat, and when she struggled with the gown, his chuckle warned her he'd come near. Seconds later, his hands were on her person, helping her with the fabric, assisting her in putting the garment on.

In silence, he gently turned her about and did up the few buttons at the back. Then he gathered her hair and put it over one shoulder. "I'm sorry everything went wrong tonight. This wasn't how I wanted our time together to end."

"Uh…" She cleared her throat. "How, ah, exactly did you want it to end?" Despite her anguish and embarrassment, curiosity got the better of her.

"That is privileged information, my lady." He moved away to retrieve his trousers. "If you wish to know, you will need to linger with me a bit longer."

As if spellbound, she peered at him while he donned the

article of clothing and then tucked in his half-aroused equipage. Then she shook herself out of it. "I'm sorry. I must go." Already, she'd made a mess of things. Knowing it was hopeless to root around for the discarded hairpins, Beatrice retrieved her slippers, and seconds later fled into the maze.

What am I going to do now?

By the time she arrived at the manor house, the ball had already begun. Nearly every window in the two lower stories of the building were awash with golden candlelight, and the French-paned doors had been thrown open to encourage the sweet, night air into what was probably an overheated room.

As best she could, Beatrice twisted her hair into some semblance of a knot and secured it with a strand of hair. With nothing for it, she entered the ballroom from the empty terrace hoping not very many people would notice her, but luck wasn't with her.

A set had just ended, which meant everyone's attention landed on her. For one horrible moment, all sound in the room ceased, and far too many pairs of eyes were on her. Embarrassed heat encompassed her form. She put a hand to her throat when it became evident she might cast up her accounts, and though she wanted to flee, her feet felt rooted to the floor. Off to one side, Eliza and Mary stood in a knot of their friends, and both girls looked at her with expressions of disappointment and curiosity.

Why?

It only made her want to cry all the more. She raised her chin, and squaring her shoulders, Beatrice walked the perimeter of the ballroom. "I dare anyone who has tumbled into scandal themselves to cast a stone my way," she demanded in a jumbled paraphrase of the Bible verse. Ignoring the stares and whispers, she continued on her way with the intent to collect Eliza, but both girls broke away from their group and intercepted her.

"Where is Major Kenton?" Eliza demanded as she glanced about.

"Why?" Was he the only one they were concerned with?

"I assumed you and he were together."

Well, that only prompted more questions. "I couldn't say. Come with me upstairs."

"Not now, Mama." Her expression was painful as others from her set turned to stare.

Mary frowned. "Where is my father? He told us that you and he would be talking at the heart of the maze." She sipped Eliza a speaking look. "But you're here." As if *that* were the crime.

"And looking more than disheveled," Eliza was quick to add. Then she frowned. "Why is the skirting at the back of your gown wet?"

Oh, my goodness. Why couldn't the floor open up and swallow her?

Before she could answer, another wave of gasps and titters behind fans moved through the room.

"What now?" The urge to retch grew stronger. Thank the heavens she hadn't eaten dinner. Her heart gave a leap when Owen came into view, looking for all the world as if he'd just come from his valet's care. How dreadfully unfair that men could appear dashing even after being thoroughly pleasured while the women in such a pairing seemed... well, like they'd been tumbled?

Mary was the first one to find her voice. "Papa, what are you doing here? I thought you had *other things* to attend?" Her eyes widened as if he was supposed to know what meant.

Perhaps he did. Everything had a very surreal feel to it.

"What makes you believe I am not attending to them *still?*" He slowly approached Beatrice, the whole of his attention on her. "You left before we'd concluded our conversation."

"Oh, Major, there is truly nothing more to say." She was in no mood to argue with him or try to figure how their futures might align.

"On the contrary, there is plenty left to say. Perhaps a life-time's worth."

Another round of gasps and murmurs erupted throughout the room. Everyone moved toward their location and formed a messy ring about them, as well as Mary and Eliza.

"What are you about?" she hissed, conscious of the audience but genuinely confused.

"As I alluded to earlier tonight, my plans for the evening didn't go according to how I'd hoped, and I certainly didn't wish to have this talk in front of witnesses."

"Yet here you are having it anyway," she countered with heat in her cheeks.

"Because you ran from me."

There was that. She looked at her daughter. "Are you a part of this somehow?" The candlelight winked off a golden chain around her neck where an enamel heart rested between her collarbones. "And the request to find the very necklace you're wearing was a lie?"

"Yes." Her daughter's cheeks turned red. "Please don't be cross with me or him. It was a charming way to ensure you and the major were alone."

Mary nodded. "Papa has had something on his mind that he only just realized he needed to say to you." She glanced at him with alarm in her eyes. "Don't get to that part yet. I need to retrieve something from upstairs."

He waved her off but kept his focus on Beatrice. "Will you hear me out?"

"Do I have a choice?" She crossed her arms beneath her breasts and tried to ignore the curious stares from the people around them.

"Not at the moment." Flutters went through her lower belly from his charming grin. With a sigh, he encompassed the nearest onlookers with his gaze. "As I'm sure you already heard, the lady and I were caught in a compromising situation." The buzz of conversation circled through the room. "That is not acceptable when we are both here in the role of chaperones, and it is certainly not behavior I encourage anyone to emulate."

From one side of the circle, Mrs. Cloverfield nodded. "I should say not, Major. The whole of my house party is in jeopardy. How will anyone trust me or my husband after this?"

Oh, dear God. Heat stung Beatrice's cheeks. When she glowered at Owen, he winked back. "How the devil do you plan to fix any of this?"

"If you give me the opportunity, I will show you." His eyebrow rose in challenge. "Do I have your permission to continue?"

"Yes." She heaved a sigh and wished she were anywhere but here. What would her brothers say once word of her exploits got back to London? There would be no living it down. Edmund would tease her unmercifully while Graham would express his disappointment in her, especially since they were already combatting gossip and talk due to her mother's infidelity and their questionable paternity.

"Good." When he handed his cane to Eliza with another wink, he took Beatrice's hand. "Do you remember that I told you I'd harbored a secret crush for you in our childhood?"

"Of course."

"It was nothing but the truth. All those years ago in Kent, I thought you the most fascinating creature I'd ever met, and when I kissed you in that wildflower field, it was the highlight of my youth."

A few titters sounded, but they both ignored them.

Her hand shook in his, and she realized she'd forgotten to bring her gloves from the maze. "It was my first kiss, and I rather had a tendre for you too."

"But then life got in the way." His expression sobered. "My father died. I went into the military. Married the love of my life. Fought for England. Started a family. Outsmarted death twice." A faint grin curved his lips when impressed murmurs went through the crowd. "However, at my lowest points, there was always that sweet memory of you and me in that wildflower field when things were simpler, and a chaste kiss had the power to change my life."

Though his tale was rather lovely, it only confused her more. "What does any of that have to do with the scandalbroth we've currently landed in tonight?"

He held her hand a slight bit tighter. "After my wife died, I'll admit I was lost. Raising two children by myself taxed my patience. All I wished to do was have time to myself to read and perhaps nap without worrying, without having responsibility weighing on me."

"You told me, and I can empathize." But they'd already discussed that.

"I thought I knew exactly where my life was heading, but then I came to this house party and unexpectedly met you again." The warmth in his eye was so inviting she wished she could dive in and hide there forever. "The old secret crush I had? Well, I welcomed a return of that, especially once we'd established that certain connection between us."

"Hush." The heat in her cheeks renewed itself. "That first meeting was quite… interesting."

"Indeed." He raised her hand to his lips and kissed her middle knuckle, much to the delight of some of the ladies standing close. "Over the course of this week, we have grown closer. Though we have a lifetime separating us, there was still that connection."

"Yes, but we want different things."

"We *did*."

Beatrice frowned. "What does that mean?" Why was everything so difficult?

"While it's true I wanted the direct opposite of you, after the horse race, after my accident, when I came back to consciousness, my first thought was of you."

For the first time, her daughter interrupted. "It's true, Mama. He asked about you as soon as he could."

"You brought me out of that darkness, Beatrice. That has to count for something."

"Or it's only wishful thinking." The longer they stood there talking, the more aware of him she grew. "We haven't come to any sort of an agreement."

"No, but that is what I'd wanted to discuss with you tonight."

Before he could continue, Mary returned to the ballroom. Her cheeks were red, but her expression was triumphant. He and his daughter exchanged a glance, and she nodded. Then he rested the whole of his attention on Beatrice. "And I still intend to, for I won't leave this party—nay, this ball—before I have secured your promise."

"What?" Mild shock rolled through her chest. "What do you mean?"

"Just this." Owen went down on one knee while still holding her hand. Gasps broke out around the room. Eliza looked on with a smile. "When I awoke after my accident, I discussed the possibility of a courtship with our daughters."

Ah, now everything made sense: his change of attitude, the hints he'd made, the decorations at the heart of the maze. She forced moisture into her suddenly dry throat. "You want to court me." It wasn't a question.

"I rather do, and I hope this time your brother will approve."

Belatedly, she remembered him telling her that Graham had dissuaded him as a young man, and the heat in her cheeks came roaring back. "Nothing has changed in that regard."

"You are wrong. *We* have changed. No longer are we the youths we were all those years ago. Your father and mine are dead. Graham is now the marquess and he is married."

"And?" She could hardly force the word from her tight throat as anticipation buzzed at the base of her spine. Everyone in the vicinity stared at them, including their daughters.

"Yes, I wanted a courtship, but I have recently changed my mind."

"Oh?" Cold disappointment twisted through her gut. The wild swing of emotions would soon make her sick.

He nodded, and then the grin was back, and wicked promise twinkled in his eye. "You make me feel whole again, alive again. In you, there is no censure, but you have the knack for pushing me, for challenging me."

"I can only be who I am," she said softly in a mimic what he'd said to her in the portrait gallery earlier in the week.

"Yes." A huff left his throat. "I am rambling and on the verge of mucking this up, but what I'm trying to say, or rather ask, is will you marry me?"

"What?" A tremble moved down her spine. Slowly, she shook her head. "You are doing this out of a false sense of obligation when there is no need."

"There is *every* need!" The fierceness of his whisper surprised her. "It has nothing to do with what happened between us tonight." Titters and murmurs cycled through the crowd. "However, feelings were exchanged between us in that maze, unspoken promises given, and if you can tell me to my face that you didn't experience it too, I'll walk away right now."

"Oh, Mama, *please* tell the major you fancy him," Eliza said in the world's worst stage whisper as she clasped her hands around the head of his cane.

"I..." Did what she felt for Owen equate to love, to wanting to spend the remainder of her life with him?

"Oh, it is quite the romance." Mary nodded. She had stars in her eyes. "We have seen how you act around each other."

Owen groaned. "Trust me, they have. In the billiards room and the portrait gallery," he said in an aside. A tiny tug on her hand sent her attention back to him. "I *do* require an answer, sweeting."

"Are you quite certain you wish to marry me outside of what happened an hour ago?" She refused to be anyone's obligation.

With the last vestiges of the bandage around his head and the eye patch, he was every bit the roguish, handsome suitor. "Darling, would I be on one knee before you with aching muscles due to my age and war injury if I didn't?" The grin was back, and it was glorious and reflected in his eye.

"I..."

"We can enjoy a long engagement if you wish, but I am coming to love you, and well, you already know how we are together in a physical sense." He sighed in annoyance when the crowd reacted with shock. "We began our lives as friends. Don't you think it makes sense and we owe it to ourselves to finish those lives as lovers, as man and wife?"

More than a few titters sounded throughout their audience.

Such a Drury Lane production, but so utterly dear. The man had given her everything she'd asked for, and he'd come up to scratch beautifully. Instead of having to compromise and meet him in the middle, he'd asked for her hand, and it thrilled her heart. "Yes."

Both Mary and Eliza gasped.

"Sorry, my lady, but I do need a bit more after all of this." He winked. "So there are no misunderstandings later."

Oh, was there anyone more delightful in every sense of the word? She blinked at the tears filling her eyes. "Yes, I will marry you. Not to make right a scandal. Not because I'm afraid to be alone, but because you are an amazing, wonderful person, and I am coming to love you as well. By the time we set a wedding day, I fully expect to be tip over tail for you."

He laid his free hand over his heart. "Lovely as always," he managed to whisper. When he struggled into a standing position, Mary handed him a ring. It was his turn to gasp. "Where did you get this?"

"In the small wooden box in your top bureau drawer." She gave him an encouraging nod.

"It was your mother's ring."

"I know, but you can give Beatrice her own at a later date. This is merely symbolic." The girl rolled her eyes. "You *do* know what that means, don't you Papa?"

"Of course. I'm not quite the doddering old fool you believe I am." He glanced at Beatrice. "Would you mind too much?"

Beatrice trembled. "I think it's fitting."

"I should have known I'd forgotten something in the haste of planning." But he slipped the circlet of tiny pearls onto the fourth finger of her left hand. "I shall make a special trip to London in the coming days for a different ring."

"Don't be surprised if you have to talk to my brothers."

"They don't intimate me, for at the end, I shall have you." Then he tugged her into his arms and despite their audience, he fit his lips to hers.

Cheers and clapping broke out among the crowd.

Would she ever tire of kissing this man? He made her feel needed, wanted, and dare she say loved again at a time in her life when she'd assumed all of that was over. When Beatrice pulled away from him, she was immediately engulfed in a hug from Mary.

"Oh, I cannot wait for you to marry my father! I have so missed having a mother about."

Her heart trembled anew. "I suppose my family is growing."

"And I'll have a sister!" Again, Mary hugged her.

Then it was Eliza's turn to embrace her. Both girls were crying, which made Beatrice tear up yet again. "I'm so happy for you, Mama. The major is the best of all men, I think, and now you will have someone to keep you company when I go away to study nursing with the nuns and then after that, possibly embark in apothecary practices."

"Life is certainly changing fast." She bussed her daughter's cheek. "I suppose that's a good thing."

"Of course it is." Then she gave Owen his cane and hugged him.

Mr. Cloverfield clapped his hands and demanded attention. "Let us all celebrate this new engagement with more dancing!" He gestured to the string quartet. "A waltz, if you please."

Immediately, the crowds dispersed, Owen slipped an arm about her waist.

"Do you wish to dance?"

She urged him toward the side of the ballroom. "I would rather watch this one and merely stand by your side and simply enjoy all that has happened today." Daring much while in public, she laid her head on his shoulder. "Thank you. For everything."

"Truly, I can't wait to marry you, but thank you for revealing the reason I was spared in the military—for you."

A lump of emotion rose in her throat. Yes, she would certainly grow to adore this man.

It just went to show that a person should never assume there were no more surprises or excitement in one's life after a certain age, for fate would laugh every time.

And, after all, wasn't stumbling onto renewed joy one of the best things there was?

EPILOGUE

December 21, 1820
Delacourte House
London, England

"OH, MAMA, YOU look stunning!"

Beatrice smiled. She turned from contemplating herself in the cheval glass to greet Eliza as the girl floated into the bedchamber with Mary close on her heels. Both of the young ladies had decided to wear matching gowns of white muslin. Her daughter's featured a green satin ribbon around the waist with a sweet bow in the back, while Mary's had a red one. Each gown had tiny red roses and green leaves embroidered around the hem, and squared bodices.

"So do you ladies." Her heart squeezed at seeing their faces and the gay gowns they'd insisted upon to wear to the nuptial ceremony. Seized with a sudden bout of nerves, she drew a hand down the front of her red silk gown. "Do you think the color too bold? The style too much?" With a frown, she turned to the cheval glass.

Yes, the bodice was lower than she usually favored, but then this was a second marriage, and it was nearly Christmastide. A thin width of white rabbit fur lined the bodice as well as the short, puffed sleeves and the bottom hem. Tucked within her upswept hair was a white ostrich feather that gave her a rather jaunty air.

"It's a wonderful gown," Eliza assured her as she took Beatrice's hand and led her toward the door. "The major will lose the ability to speak once he sees you."

Due to Eliza wanting to be launched into society and then preparing to go away in February to begin training in nursing studies with a group of nuns in the Lake District, Beatrice and Owen had decided to enjoy a fairly long engagement. Somehow, due to busy schedules, they had only managed to find time to be intimate twice a month since the summertime house party, but that made this day all the sweeter. Throughout the months, they had come to know each other better, which only deepened their already existing friendship.

Besides, Mary was now nearly done with finishing school while his son Percy had finished at university and would soon go on a short tour of the Continent, generously sponsored by her brother Graham. His commission in the military would be met a few days after he returned.

Additionally, they'd wished to be married before Christmastide in order to spend the holiday season as a married couple. During the interim, she had made inroads into creating relationships with her Winterbourne half-siblings. Because of that, Lady Sophia and her ambassador husband had offered to take Eliza and Mary to France along with Sophia's daughter for a winter trip, so that Beatrice could enjoy a couple of months alone with her new husband.

Everything was an unexpected boon, and each day that went by had provided a new and exciting opportunity or revelation. She would remain grateful for all of it.

Mary nodded and slipped her arm through Beatrice's as they gained the corridor. "The red is lovely and suits you well." A giggle escaped her. "Does Papa know you'd chosen that color?"

"No. I wished to keep the gown a secret." And it matched the necklace he'd gifted her with last month for her birthday. Seven square-shaped rubies set in silver winked like mad around her neck. "Why?"

Eliza slipped her arm through Beatrice's other one, which made a rather tight fit as they walked toward the stairs. "You'll see."

"How mysterious." Knots of worry pulled in her belly. "Is it a happy surprise?"

"Oh, yes." Mary nodded. "Percy was even impressed. Then he made jest of Papa's romantic side. Said he read too many of Shakespeare's romances and was touched in his upper stories."

"I adore your father's love of romances and romantic comedies." They had passed many a pleasant afternoon in either her drawing room in London or his in Kent by Owen reading to her from the Bard's plays. Sometimes, as a treat, she and Eliza would act out a few scenes for his entertainment. At other times, she played the pianoforte for him in order to practice, for she would perform in a musical evening during the Christmastide season.

Thanks to his support. It was one step into following a dream, and would never have come about without his gentle prodding.

"That's what I said," Eliza was quick to say.

Then the girls were forced to unlink arms as they all descended the stairs to the second floor.

Mary sighed. "When I marry, I hope the courtship is as romantic as yours was with Papa."

"If you choose a man as noble and darling, I'm sure it will be." With Mary underfoot, along with Percy, she had expanded her maternal capacity by half. Having additional young people about the house meant there was no shortage of excited chatter full of hopes and dreams and optimism.

It kept her feeling young.

"I am not in a rush," Mary promptly added. "I rather admire Eliza's desire to go off and follow her passion. I would like to study under a drawing master."

"Then you should talk to your father, and perhaps we can arrange that for you." It delighted her heart that the two girls were willing to pursue other things first before marriage.

"I will. I promise."

Then the three of them entered the drawing room, and Beatrice stopped with a gasp. Throughout the room, arrangements of red and pink roses gave color and life to the space. The jaunty hothouse blooms added pops of joy to the room done in shades of blue, and their perfume filled the air. She waved to Graham, who waved back with a startled expression. Surprisingly, the Earl of Ettesmere was there as well. He nodded to her in acknowledgment before resuming his conversation with Graham. The two had become fast friends over the course of the year. Also in attendance were Lady Sophia and her daughter, Hannah. Both of whom beamed at her and waved.

The Winterbourne clan had taken their siblings in and made them a true family. The only one missing was Edmund, for he had stolen some of the happiness from this day by eclipsing her nuptial ceremony with his own hastily arranged wedding.

But that was a story for another day, and she wouldn't allow his troubles to mar the perfect joy of this occasion, though she did silently wish him well.

"Oh, my goodness." Then her gaze landed on Owen, who stood near the fireplace where cheerful flames danced behind a decorative metal grate. Clad in black evening attire even if it was nearly ten o'clock in the morning, he was just as dashing and handsome as he'd been when she collided with him that day in the Cloverfield maze. His waistcoat of crimson silk embroidered with silver swirls was his only concession to color in the outfit. With the eyepatch, he was beyond rakish and handsome. Percy stood next to his father with a red rose bud pinned to the lapel of his black suit. Perhaps fifteen guests milled about the room, talking in low voices, her brothers included. "It's lovely. He's... incredible."

Both girls giggled and prodded her forward.

Mary beamed. "I told you."

Slowly, Beatrice walked through the room to join Owen, and when he rested his gaze on her, desire darkened the depth of his eye. "You remembered the roses," she said to him in a soft voice.

With a nod and reddened cheeks, Percy left to join his sister and Eliza.

"How could I forget? It was a large part of how we met." So saying, he took up a crimson rose from the mantel and then tucked it behind her ear as was his wont. "They will forever remind me of you."

Her heartbeat accelerated. "I feel the same way." Unable to not touch him, Beatrice brushed a shock of hair from his forehead. She let her fingers trace against the side of his eyepatch and cheek, and when he briefly closed his eye in apparent bliss, she smiled. "You are quite handsome today."

"And you are stunning. You should always be in red." He took her hand and pressed a kiss to the back of it. The ruby in the ring on the fourth finger of her left hand sparkled in the morning sunlight. It matched the necklace she wore and had replaced the ring he'd given her on the day of their engagement. The pearl ring had been put into Mary's safekeeping.

"I rather like it too. Somehow, it's both a freeing and empowering hue."

Owen fit his lips to the shell of her ear. "As soon as the wedding breakfast is over, I plan to waste no time in removing that fantastic gown from your body. It has been far too long since I have seen you naked."

"Oh!" Tingles shivered down her spine. He was quite an attentive and intense lover. "I could say the same of your clothing."

A low growl proceeded his response as the longcase clock at the opposite side of the room chimed the ten o'clock hour. "Shall we begin, then? I'd say we have waited long enough for this day."

"Absolutely." Excitement circled through her insides, and she couldn't stop smiling. Never did she think she could fall in love a second time, but Owen had proved her wrong.

"Good." He beckoned to an older man in a dark suit she assumed was a vicar. "I love you, sweeting. Never think otherwise."

It always gave her a thrill to hear those words. Beatrice clutched his hand, threaded their fingers together. "I love you too. Perhaps deep down I always have." In mere moments, he would be hers forever.

And she couldn't wait to discover where else her future would lead.

The End

About the Author

Sandra Sookoo is a *USA Today* bestselling author who firmly believes every person deserves acceptance and a happy ending. Most days you can find her creating scandal and mischief in the Regency-era, serendipity and happenstance in Victorian America or snarky, sweet humor in the contemporary world. Most recently she's moved into infusing her books with mystery and intrigue. Reading is a lot like eating fine chocolates—you can't just have one. Good thing books don't have calories!

When she's not wearing out computer keyboards, Sandra spends time with her real-life Prince Charming in central Indiana where she's been known to goof off and make moments count because the key to life is laughter. A Disney fan since the age of ten, when her soul gets bogged down and her imagination flags, a trip to Walt Disney World is in order. Nothing fuels her dreams more than the land of eternal happy endings, hope and love stories.

Stay in Touch

Sign up for Sandra's bi-monthly newsletter and you'll be given exclusive excerpts, cover reveals before the general public as well as opportunities to enter contests you won't find anywhere else.

Just send an email to sandrasookoo@yahoo.com with SUB-SCRIBE in the subject line.

Or follow/friend her on social media:
Facebook: facebook.com/sandra.sookoo
Facebook Author Page: facebook.com/sandrasookooauthor
Pinterest: pinterest.com/sandrasookoo
Instagram: instagram.com/sandrasookoo
BookBub Page: bookbub.com/authors/sandra-sookoo